Graham Greene

Lord Rochester's Monkey

being the Life of John Wilmot,
Second Earl of Rochester

A Studio Book
The Viking Press · New York

Copyright © 1974 by Graham Greene

All rights reserved

This book was designed and produced
by George Rainbird Limited
Marble Arch House
44 Edgware Road, London W2

Published in 1974
by The Viking Press, Inc.
625 Madison Avenue
New York, NY 10022

SBN: 670–44055–8

Library of Congress catalog
card number: 73–17955

House Editor: Erica Hunningher
Assistant House Editor: Felicity Luard
Designer: Judith Allan
Indexer: Myra Clark

Printed and bound by
Jarrold & Sons Limited, Norwich

Color plates printed by
Westerham Press Limited, Westerham

Printed and bound in Great Britain

(reverse of frontispiece) Allegory of the Restoration

(frontispiece) John Wilmot, Second Earl of Rochester

'*Most human affairs are carried on at the same nonsensical rate, which makes me (who am now grown superstitious) think it a fault to laugh at the monkey we have here, when I compare his condition with mankind.*'

Lord Rochester in a letter to Henry Savile

'*Were I, who to my cost, already am*
One of those strange, prodigious creatures, Man,
A spirit free, to choose for my own share
What sort of flesh and blood I pleas'd to wear,
I'd be a dog, a monkey or a bear,
Or any thing but that vain animal,
Who is so proud of being rational.'

Rochester, 'In Imitation of the Eighth Satire of Boileau'

Contents

Color Plates

Preface

At the time when this book was written, around 1931 to 1934, the only modern life of Rochester in existence was that of Herr Johannes Prinz published in Leipzig in 1927.

It is difficult to think back now to the almost Victorian atmosphere of the early thirties when I wrote this book. *Lady Chatterley's Lover* and *Ulysses* were still banned, and John Hayward's rather unreliable collection of Rochester's poems, which appeared in 1926, escaped prosecution only because the edition was limited to 1,050 copies. Hayward warned me in 1931 when I was beginning to work on this book: 'The Nonesuch edition could not have been published except as a limited edition, and would indeed have been issued "to subscribers only" if the whole issue had not been taken up by the booksellers before publication. Even so the American copies were "destroyed" by the New York customs.' With all its errors it was an important publication, the first modern tribute to Rochester as a major poet. Hitherto he had been represented in anthologies of Restoration poetry in the same way as Lovelace and Suckling by a few beautiful songs. He was still regarded as a pornographic writer whose works were on the reserved shelves of the British Museum and of the Bodleian (denoted there with donnish whimsicality by the Greek letter phi – they are probably still so reserved). It was a blow to me when my biography was turned down by my publisher, Heinemann, and I hadn't the heart to offer it elsewhere. I can only hope it was the subject and not the treatment which displeased them – they may even have feared a prosecution for obscenity, as Hayward himself feared it: 'I must ask you to bear in mind that a charge of obscenity brought against you might possibly be extended to include me and my publishers!'

A few years later Professor Pinto was able under the safer cloak of university scholarship to publish his biography – I noted with some pride that he had missed a number of my discoveries, but most of the *lacunae* seem to have been filled in his revised edition called *Enthusiast in Wit* published in 1962. The interpretation of the facts is another matter: he is far more sure than I am of Rochester's innocence of the attack on Dryden in Rose Alley, and perhaps my interpretation of Rochester's character differs somewhat from his.

9

So complex a character can be 'dramatized' (in James's sense) in more ways than one. The longer I worked on his life the more living he became to me.

No one doubts now the importance of Rochester's poetry. Rochester had inherited from Donne a poetry of passionate colloquialism. Donne's studied roughness of metre has the hesitancy and the thoughtfulness of speech; even at its most musical his poetry is that of a man speaking. Rochester's individual characteristic was to pour the passionate colloquialism of Donne, extended to include the rough language of the stews, into the mould of the Restoration lyric without shattering the form. His experience of love was unhappy, and he shared Donne's bitterness. The spirit was always at war with the flesh; his unbelief was quite as religious as the Dean of St Paul's faith. He hated the thing he loved with something of the same dark concentration, the confusion of love and lust and death and hate.

> Let the porter and the groom,
> 　Things design'd for dirty slaves,
> Drudge in fair Aurelia's womb,
> 　To get supplies for age and graves.

Both poets were driven by the circumstances of their lives and the time to be satirists. Andrew Marvell, according to Aubrey, said of Rochester: 'that he was the best English satirist and had the right vein'. Pope made the mistake of classing Rochester with Buckhurst as a 'holiday' writer. But Rochester took as much pains as Donne to perfect the colloquialism of his lines. He had the arrogance of the artist, and these lines taken from the 'Epistle to O.B.' could well have been applied to himself.

> Born to my self, I like my self alone,
> And must conclude my judgment good or none . . .
> Thus I resolve of my own poetry,
> That 'tis the best, and there's a fame for me.
> If then I'm happy, what does it advance
> Whether to merit due, or arrogance?
> Oh, but the world will take offence hereby!
> Why then the world shall suffer for't, not I.

I have tried to show the life and character of Rochester always in relation to his poetry, but I have tried hard to avoid any unacknowledged use of the imagination. Wherever convenient I have quoted the authority in the text, and other references will be found at the end of the volume. Footnotes have been avoided as far as possible, for this biography is not intended primarily for students. For the sake of the general reader, my publisher and I have agreed with some reluctance to modernize spelling and punctuation. The dashes used in place of certain words are not an example of twentieth-century prudery: they were so used in the earliest printed versions of the poems.

Lastly my acknowledgments. For the appearance of the book, so belatedly, I owe my thanks to Mr John Hadfield and his colleague Mr George Speaight, who noticed my reference to it in *A Sort of Life* and to the Librarian of Texas University who allowed us to make a copy of the original typescript in his possession. Alas, after this long interval many who originally helped me are dead. First I would mention John Hayward, editor of the Nonesuch Rochester, who aided me with suggestions and references and even assisted me to avoid many of his own mistakes. (Rochester brought us together in a long friendship which ended only with his death.) My gratitude is due also to the late Lord Sandwich for allowing me to inspect the Hinchingbrooke MSS and to print two unpublished letters referring to Elizabeth Mallet; to Lord Dillon for letting me see the typescript copy of Lady Rochester's letters preserved at Ditchley Park; to Lord Sackville for permission to examine the Sackville Papers at the Record Office; to the Deputy Keeper of MSS at the British Museum for giving me access to reserved manuscripts; to the Librarian of the Shakespeare Birthplace for allowing me to examine the Fane Commonplace Book; to the Earl of Lisburne for allowing us to reproduce paintings from his collection; and for help and suggestions to the Reverend Montagu Summers, H. D. Ziman, Honorary Secretary of the Friends of the National Libraries, Colonel Wilmot Vaughan, a descendant of the poet, and Miss Elsie Corbett, compiler of *A History of Spelsbury*. Any biographer of Rochester owes a debt of gratitude to Johannes Prinz, his first biographer. His biography is not easily accessible to English readers, and his neglect of the reports of the Historical Manuscripts Commission led him to some omissions and inaccuracies.

I have not used any of the new material discovered by Professor Pinto, except that I have preferred his manuscript version of Alexander Bendo's broadside where it differs in very small particulars from the Nonesuch version. For one period of Rochester's life – his grand tour of Europe with Sir Andrew Balfour – he found a wealth of material which I missed. I have not included it here, because Balfour's account may possibly not refer to his journey with Rochester who is nowhere mentioned in it and because I have no wish to rewrite my biography at Professor Pinto's expense – only to revise it and rearrange it in such minor ways as I would probably have done in proof if I had found a publisher forty years ago.

1 Landscape

One approach to Spelsbury village in Oxfordshire is by the western road along which, during the Civil War, Essex's Parliamentary army marched and counter-marched with Henry Wilmot's cavalry hanging on its flank, over the final ridge of the Cotswolds, to Chipping Norton. Then the pedestrian, with the bare heights behind, makes his way across a level wash of fields, laid out for pasture and divided by grey walls, lapping round the small church and rising to the height of the gravestones in a foam of nettles before dwindling out against the black rise of Wychwood. A row of almshouses built by John Cary, old Lady Rochester's agent, an ancient stone shaped like a hawk in the middle of a field, innumerable heads of dandelions sparkling like points of dew in the sun – these are all that are likely to catch a traveller's attention. In the church vault the Rochester family is obscurely buried: the first Earl, Henry Wilmot, the Cavalier, whose body had been buried before at Bruges; his wife, the headstrong, impulsive, prejudiced woman, who outlived husband, son and grandson; John Wilmot, the poet and second Earl, his wife and son. No tablet in the church records their presence, no long scroll of virtues in the manner of the century.

On the north-east the shadow of Wychwood thins and gives place to the more formal trees of Ditchley Park, and it was here that the poet was born on either 1 April or 10 April 1647, in what Evelyn described as 'a low timber house, with a pretty bowling green'.

His mother, Anne, daughter of Sir John St John, was the widow of Sir Francis Henry Lee, to whom Ditchley had belonged, and whose death, two years after the marriage in 1637, left her with two sons to rear. In 1644 she married Lord Wilmot.

This was more than a remarriage; it was a change of political allegiance. Her first husband, the stepson of Lord Warwick, belonged to a Parliamentary family; her second was one of the most successful of the Royalist leaders, who the year before had defeated Sir William Waller at Roundway Down. One cannot help admiring the skill with which she kept the balance, preserving Ditchley through the period of the Commonwealth on the strength

Henry Wilmot, First Earl of Rochester, and Anne St John, Countess of Rochester

13

Charles II, disguised as a
servant, escapes from the
battle of Worcester with
Jane Lane and Henry
Wilmot

of her first husband's sympathies, retaining at the Restoration the
friendship of Charles, whose flight from Worcester her second
husband had shared. Of Wilmot she can have seen little. The
Lieutenant-General of Horse spent as much time in intrigue as in
the field. Prince Rupert disliked him, Charles I was a lukewarm
supporter, and much of the energy which should have been spent
against the enemy was exhausted against his rivals in the same
camp. In the year of his son's birth he was discovered to be corre-
sponding with Essex in the hope of forcing terms of peace upon the
King; he was degraded before the Army and only his popularity
with the men saved him from a severer punishment. He was allowed
to retire to Paris, where he fought an ignoble duel with his chief
enemy, Lord Digby, and faded for the time out of the history of his
country and his family.

At some time between his second defeat of Waller at Cropredy
Bridge and his fall, in the middle of alarums and cabals, Henry
Wilmot had found the occasion to beget a son. The crowded employments of those years may have prompted the scandal recorded
by Anthony Wood, the crabbed Oxford antiquary: 'I have been
credibly informed by knowing men that this John, Earl of Rochester,

was begotten by Sir Allen Apsley, Knt', but it is difficult to believe. Nowhere else is the virtue of Lady Wilmot questioned, unless another of Wood's anecdotes refers to her:

> The lady Wilmot of Berks, a light huswife, and one notorious for her salaciousness, being among other ladies at the music school on Act Saturday, 1656, and there hearing Mr Henry Thurman of Christ Church declaiming eagerly against women and their vanities, she thereupon openly and with a loud voice cried: 'Sir, you are out; you are wrong; you are to begin again' etcetera, thinking thereby to abash him. But he being a very bold fellow, answered thus with a loud voice: 'Madam, if I am wrong, I am sure you are right.' Upon which all the auditory laughing, she sat down and plucked her hood over her face.

It is a good story and not entirely foreign to the character of a woman who never hesitated to speak out and thought little in her old age of accusing her grand-daughter's husband of infidelity, forgery and worse; but 'light huswife' rings false. Lady Wilmot would have never shown flippancy, even in adultery. She blows like a tempest through the lives of her husband, her son, and her son's wife, disapproving always, railing always; even when she breaks down at the bed of her dying son, she retains enough spirit to hate and express her hatred of the unfortunate Will Fanshawe, one of his companions.

But there are more than negative reasons to suppose that John was the son of Henry Wilmot. The portraits of the two men, the father's formerly at Hinchingbrooke and the son's at Warwick Castle, show the same heavy lids, the same narrow face, and the

Ditchley House, Oxfordshire: 'a low timber house with a pretty bowling green'. (John Evelyn)

character of the son shines unmistakably through that of the father as he was described by Lord Clarendon. 'Wilmot', Clarendon wrote, 'was a man of a haughty and ambitious nature, of a pleasant wit and an ill-understanding, as never considering above one thing at once. . . . He was positive in all his advices in council and bore contradiction very impatiently . . .' and comparing Wilmot with Lord Goring, who succeeded him as Lieutenant-General of Horse: 'He was a man proud and ambitious, and incapable of being contented. . . . He drank hard, and had a great power over all who did so, which was a great people. He had a more companionable wit even than his rival Goring, and swayed more among the good fellows.'

Here surely is the father of the man who told Gilbert Burnet, the historian, that for five years he was continually drunk, whose wit so glowed in his cups that his companions would never allow him to be sober. Nor was the son to prove more capable of content than the father. It was a restless and dissatisfied spirit which his mother's chaplain described in a funeral sermon with reluctant and unclerical admiration:

> He seemed to affect something singular and paradoxical in his impieties, as well as in his writings, above the reach and thought of other men; taking as much pain to draw others in, and to prevent the right ways of virtue, as the apostles and primitive saints did to save their own souls and them that heard them. . . . Nay, so confirmed was he in sin, that he oftentimes almost died a martyr for it.

Again one reads of the father in Clarendon's history:

> Wilmot loved debauchery, but shut it out from his business; never neglected that, and rarely miscarried in it. Goring had a much better understanding, and a sharper wit (except in the very exercise of debauchery, and then the other was inspired), a much keener courage, and presentness of mind in danger; Wilmot discerned it farther off, and because he could not behave himself so well in it, commonly prevented it, or warily declined it. . . . Neither of them valued their promises, professions or friendships, according to any rules of honour or integrity; but Wilmot violated them the less willingly, and never but for some great benefit or convenience to himself. . . . The ambition of both was unlimited, and so equally incapable of being contented; and both unrestrained, by any respect to good nature or justice from pursuing the satisfaction thereof: yet Wilmot had more scruples from religion to startle him, and would not have attained his end by any gross or foul act of wickedness.

That passage, which reflects on the father's courage, seems to anticipate the later reflections, however undeserved, on the son's: the story of the stopped duel with Mulgrave and of the dark, confused affray at Epsom. Literary intrigues which may have culminated with the cudgelling of Dryden in Rose Alley ('unrestrained by any respect to good nature or justice') take the place of political intrigues; and one may see in Henry Wilmot's religious scruples the same mental conflict, which was the source of Rochester's best poetry. His friend Etherege described the poet in the character of Dorimant: 'I know he is a Devil, but he has something of the Angel yet undefac'd in him.'

The astrologer Gadbury published a horoscope eighteen years after his subject's death, and stars and planets seem to have been apt in their conjunctions. 'He was born', wrote Gadbury, 'anno 1647, on April the 1st day, 11h. 7m. a.m., and endued with a noble and fertile muse. The sun governed the horoscope, and the moon ruled the birth hours. The conjunction of Venus and Mercury in M. Coeli, in sextile of Luna, aptly denotes his inclination to poetry. The great reception of Sol with Mars and Jupiter posited so near the latter, bestowed a large stock of generous and active spirits, which constantly attended on this native's mind, insomuch that no subject came amiss to him.'

There was every reason to hope well of the child; the father was safely in Paris, where his drink and his quarrels could have no influence on the son, and those Civil War years in England held a certain nobility, a quality of old Rome that was lost in the succeeding reign. Great men lived and died; Strafford had given an example of heroism to the King who betrayed him. Lord Falkland, divided in his loyalties, in despair threw away his life at the battle of Newbury. Lord Fairfax, the Victor of Naseby, was the subject of an epitaph from the Duke of Buckingham, which comes curiously from the pen of Pope's 'lord of useless thousands':

> Fairfax the valiant; and the only he
> Who e'er, for that alone a conqueror would be.
>   Both sexes' virtues were in him combin'd:
> He had the fierceness of the manliest mind,
> And yet the meekness too of woman-kind.
>   He never knew what envy was or hate.
> His soul was fill'd with worth and honesty;
>   And with another thing quite out of date,
>   Call'd modesty.

The younger, raffish school of Suckling were possessed, even in their cups, with an ideal of honour, which was not to survive the long years, the poverty, the inglorious inaction and the hopes deferred of the Protectorate. Heroism was to become heroics, couplets declaimed by periwigged Caesars, Indian Emperors, Montezumas, to the black vizors in the pit and the King's mistresses in the boxes.

Lady Wilmot belonged to the earlier age; she had some of the quality of a Roman mother, and, while a kingdom fell and a husband was disgraced, she seems to have devoted herself to the upbringing of her son and the preservation of the estate which would one day be his. The latter duty became more difficult with the execution of Charles I, for her husband, who had always been the friend of the Prince of Wales, ceased to be merely a disgraced Royalist. He was now one of the leading malcontents in exile. His influence was immediately apparent in his appointment as a Gentleman of the Bedchamber to the young King; he was one of the committee of four whom Charles II consulted always in his exile; he belonged to the faction which urged Charles to action, on whatever lines, in whatever place. The sour Scotsmen came over to The Hague, offering Charles the Presbyterian Covenant to sign in return for their aid, watching with jealous shrewdness his pretence of piety, and Wilmot was one of those responsible for the useless, lying signature. It was a treacherous and ignoble business, a not unfitting opening for the new reign, and we know that one of the delegation, more sensitive than his companions, felt his conscience troubled. Alexander Jaffray, writing in his diary, recorded:

> Being again sent there [to Holland] by the Parliament, in the year 1650, for that same business, we did sinfully both entangle and engage the nation and ourselves, and that poor young prince to whom we were sent; making him sign and swear a covenant, which we knew, from clear and demonstrable reasons, that he hated in his heart. Yet, finding that upon these terms only, he could be admitted to rule over us (all other means having then failed him), *he* sinfully complied with what *we* most sinfully pressed upon him:– where, I must confess, to my apprehensions, *our* sin was more than his.

Wilmot was forward in the whole Scottish affair. He was one of the chosen few who accompanied the young King to England and one of those who scandalized the Presbyterians with their conduct. He was with the King at the Battle of Worcester and accompanied and aided him in his flight. Travelling under the name of 'Mr Barlow', not the last alias he used, he came with the King to Brighton, lodging at an inn in West Street. From there they rode to Shoreham and embarked on a fishing boat for France.

Perhaps Wilmot's conspicuous role in the King's escape forced Lady Wilmot to leave England, for she was in Paris with her children in 1653 and 1654. Hyde, the future Lord Clarendon, writing from Paris on 15 August 1653 to her husband, now created Earl of Rochester, who was in Germany trying to raise money for the King, mentions that Rochester's son is always anxious for letters from him; he adds that John, a child of six years, is an excellent youth and Rochester cannot be too fond of him. Again in May of the following year Hyde writes that Lady Rochester will not go into England until she has seen her husband; but in consultation with himself she has determined that she had better

A row of almshouses in the village of Spelsbury, Oxfordshire, built by John Cary, old Lady Rochester's agent, in 1688

remain at Paris until the King's removal is fixed; she and the children have been so indisposed, Frank (her husband's stepson) being but newly recovered of a fever, that she could not hitherto undertake a journey.

A fortnight later her patience is becoming strained. 'Your lady', Hyde writes, 'is heartily weary of Paris, and poor Henry more; and they are even ready to be engaged in that notorious heresy as to believe that Paris stands in the worst air in the world.' Lady Rochester was never a woman to find pleasure in the life of a Court, and Charles's Court at this time gave pleasure to neither the moralist nor the luxurious. On the one side it was recorded that Charles had had his seventeenth mistress abroad, that at night he would dance and play 'as if we had taken the Plate fleet'; on the other lay the shadow of increasing poverty, his servants imprisoned for debt, the pawning of plate, the undignified pleas for credit.

Ditchley Park, even under the threat of deprivation by the Protector, was more to Lady Rochester's taste than this dancing and foolery on an empty stomach, the laughter of empty hopes. She was a countrywoman; we have no record of her again in the life of courts or cities. Apart from her children her greatest affection was shown to John Cary, the agent who helped her through a long life in looking after the Ditchley and Adderbury estates for husbands, for sons, and finally for grandchildren. In her old age she wrote of him to her grandson, the Earl of Lichfield, with a tenderness unusual to her:

> Poor Cary is so strangely afflicted by the death of his wife that I am very apprehensive of our losing him too. He takes excessively on for her; 'tis very true he has lost a very good woman and an excellent wife upon all accounts to him, and an admirable huswife she was, but has been declining a long time and lived too a miracle so long as she did. I am sure I have lost a good friend too. I hear his intention is to retire from his house which he says he cannot stay in now she is gone. If he retire from business he will quickly die, for business keeps him alive. You must do what you can to persuade him for your sake not to retire himself too melancholy and where nobody can look after him, to take care of him in his old age.

One of the four silver pint pots which Rochester presented to Wadham College in 1661 'Cupid and Bacchus my saints are; May drink and love still reign: With wine I wash away my cares, And then to love again.'

How long Lady Rochester waited in Paris with her children, whether she ever saw her husband again, one cannot tell. She was back at Ditchley in 1656, for in that year she was defending the estate from Cromwell. Her husband had been ordered to send in particulars in order that it might be decimated, and Lady Rochester objected to her jointure lands, which had come to her from her first Puritan husband, being included in the particulars of her second husband's estate. She petitioned the Protector therefore 'in regard her said husband hath no interest in her said jointure lands' to stay 'all further proceedings touching or concerning the same

Charles II dancing at a ball during his exile 'as if we had taken the Plate fleet'

and to discharge your petitioner from further trouble or attendance'. The outcome we do not know, but Burnet states that Lord Rochester left his son 'little other inheritance but the honour and title derived to him'. In 1657 too Lady Rochester was at Ditchley, where she was visited by Sir Ralph Verney, that man of incorruptible and complacent virtue, who on her husband's death became guardian of her son. In 1658 Henry Wilmot died at Sluys and was buried temporarily at Bruges.

Between her departure from Paris and his death there had been one opportunity for husband and wife to meet, though whether it was taken is more than doubtful.

In 1655 Rochester came to England on the last Royalist adventure before the Protectorate ended. In spite of the advice of the secret organization, the Sealed Knot, the exiles had decided on an insurrection, and Rochester, at his own request, was sent to England to organize it. He landed secretly at Margate and reached London about 23 February, where he secured lodgings in the house of a tailor in Aldersgate Street.

It was a perilous enterprise. Cromwell's agents and correspondents were in every capital and in every port, and it is probable the Protector knew the general lines of the planned insurrection and the names of the conspirators. In the month when Rochester landed, a letter of restraint was sent to Rye and Margate, among other ports, empowering the detention and examination of all persons landing from the Continent. Twice Rochester was examined before he reached London, and it is difficult to understand how he escaped capture. He was not a man of tact or cunning; a bottle of wine would always endanger him.

In a letter from London dated 8 March addressed by Daniel O'Neill, another of the conspirators, to the King ('Mr Bryan to Mr Jackson') we gain some insight into the life of these secret men, the uncertainty, the jealousies, the deceits, the constant danger of discovery:

Sir, – After I had received your orders to compound for your debts, I made all the haste conveniently I could hither, where I found all your accounts and business in such disorder by the absence of some of your friends, and the restraint of others who are bound for you, and the despair of those you addressed me to, whom I found strong in the same persuasion they writ to you, that Mr Ambrose [Nicholas Armorer] and I began to think there was no good to be done, and that it was fitter to return to our homes, than spend money when we could do you no service. Mr Arvile [Sir Thomas Armstrong] dissuaded me from this resolution, and told me there was great position in your creditors to compound, and at an easy rate, if I would take upon me to have your authority. . . . That very day I spoke unto half a score, who with great cheerfulness offered to take two shillings in the pound rather than you should continue a banished man. . . . [Then] as God would have it Mr Rothall [Lord Rochester] came to town with your authority, which gave such life to the business, that in five days, which was the whole time of his stay here, we brought all your conditions to such a composition as we hope will not displease you. Mr Willings [the West], Mr Newet [the North], Mr Catting [Cheshire], and Mr St Owin [Shrewsbury] promised to receive satisfaction on this day, and the rest soon after. I had almost forgot to tell you that your most faithful servant Knoply [Kent] is not able to serve you for the present; so that the money which he should furnish must be supplied some other where. The reason Knoply is so disabled is because most of Mr Axford's family [the Army] lives with him. Mr Catz [Cromwell] sent them thither hearing that Mr Kinsford [the King] pretended to be his heir. . . . Mr Rothall [Rochester] is gone to Yates [Yorkshire], his own house. He was in such haste to go home, that he could not write to you, which he prays you to pardon him for. . . . I must confess Mr Rothall was the next best you could authorize to deal with your creditors, but there were many that did not like him, which I prevailed with to make no unreasonable exception; there were others that wondered Mr Ofield [Lord Ormond] had not the charge the other had to treat, for he would have been more authentic, and said, too, if he had been here when he was expected which was two months ago, in all likelihood you might have been at home with your wife and children now peaceably.

But on the night of the day when this letter was written 'Mr Rothall' met the Yorkshire Cavaliers at Marston Moor and found one hundred horsemen where he had expected four thousand. The rising was cancelled, the loyalists dispersed, and Rochester rode for the south. In other parts of the country the insurrection was equally unsuccessful; except in the west it ended without fighting.

Again, as after Worcester, extraordinary luck favoured Rochester. Disguised as a Frenchman with a yellow periwig he made his way by unfrequented roads to London. At Aylesbury he and Nicholas Armorer were examined by a county justice who ordered the keeper of the inn where they lodged to detain them, but the man was bribed by the gift of a gold chain and Rochester and his companion fled in the night, leaving their baggage behind them. Always his love of drink endangered him. Under its influence he would linger, talking with any strangers that the chance of board or bench brought next to him. In London his favourite taverns in Drury Lane became known to the spy Manning, and search was made there. Lord Byron and other Cavaliers were seized, but Rochester had vanished. After a hazardous stay in England of a little more than three months, he appeared again at The Hague early in June. There is reason to suppose that his escape had been assisted by Colonel Hutchinson, the former Parliamentary Governor of Nottingham, whose wife was related to Lady Rochester. At the Restoration, when an attempt was made to erase Colonel Hutchinson's name from the Act of Indemnity and Oblivion, Lady Rochester incurred Clarendon's anger in his defence. It was stated that: 'He gave the Earl of Rochester notice and opportunity to escape when Cromwell's ministers had discovered him the last time he was employed in his Majesty's service here in England.'

Meanwhile at Ditchley the country was establishing a hold on John Wilmot's affections that the city was never completely to eradicate. The city was to mean the clouded merriment of drink, the intrigues of the theatre, the half-hearted friendships with professional poets, affairs of love and lust, quarrels at Court, the friendship of the King whom he despised, the brothels of Whetstone Park, disease and its remedy, Mrs Fourcard's baths. The country was to be peace, even a kind of purity, finally the place to die in. Aubrey recorded of the poet that he would say 'when he came to Brentford the devil entered into him and never left him till he came into the country again to Adderbury or Woodstock'. Perhaps the Ditchley orchards were remembered in this precise metaphor:

> If the fresh trunk have sap enough to give,
> That each insertive branch may live,
> The gard'ner grafts not only apples there,
> But adds the warden and the pear,

The peach and apricot together grow,
    The cherry and the damson too,
Till he hath made by skilful husbandry
    An entire orchard of one tree . . .

The small boy is walking through the long grass at the gardener's
heels, watching the glint of the pruning knife, the slim olive stems
fall, listening to the Oxfordshire speech. The father is drinking at

Paris, in Germany plying cup for cup with the heavy princes, finally worn out and in debt dying at Bruges. The small ten-year-old boy in the orchard is now 'Earl Rochester, Baron Wilmot of Adderbury in England, and Viscount Wilmot of Athlone in Ireland'.

[2] At Burford Grammar School, 'under a noted master called John Martin', the new Earl was a model pupil. There are references to his docility and his progress in learning. His tutor at home, Mr Gifford, chaplain to Lady Rochester, told the antiquary Hearne many years later that he was then 'a very hopeful youth, very virtuous and good natur'd (as he was always) and willing and ready to follow good advice'. And on another occasion Mr Gifford told how 'the said mad Earl was then very hopeful and ready to do anything that he proposed to him, and very well inclined to laudable undertakings'.

The ghost of a pompous cleric speaks from the page. It is obvious that the chaplain thought himself the only man who could control the boy. He had hoped to accompany him to Oxford, 'but was supplanted', and the fact rankled. How different, he clearly thought, the Earl's life would have been if he, and not the egregious Mr Phineas Bury, had watched his steps at Wadham. While he was with him at Ditchley, there were no 'ill-accidents' such as undoubtedly occurred with the thirteen-year-old undergraduate, the fourteen-year-old Master of Arts. He even grudged him the learning which the Earl had already acquired at Burford Grammar School.

Anthony Wood described him as 'thoroughly acquainted with the classic authors, both Greek and Latin; a thing very rare (if not peculiar to him) among those of his quality'; the Reverend Robert Parsons, who succeeded Mr Gifford as his mother's chaplain, praised his knowledge of Greek and Latin; Dr Burnet, referring to his schooldays, wrote that 'he acquired Latin to such perfection that to his dying day he retained a great relish of the fineness and beauty of the tongue'; we have the witness of his own poems, the numerous adaptations from Horace, the translations from Lucretius and Ovid, the majestic version of a chorus of Seneca. But Mr Gifford, who had been supplanted, thought otherwise: 'he understood very little or no Greek, and he had but little Latin'. The grudge against his pupil's guardians soon became a grudge against his pupil. We have only Mr Gifford's word for their later relations, so it is only from the chaplain we learn that 'he could say anything' to the Earl. Like a dismissed nurse, who comforts herself with a day-dream of her mistress's submission ('and if she were to go down on her knees, I wouldn't return'), Mr Gifford recounts an amazing conversation, in which Rochester is purported to say: 'Mr Gifford,

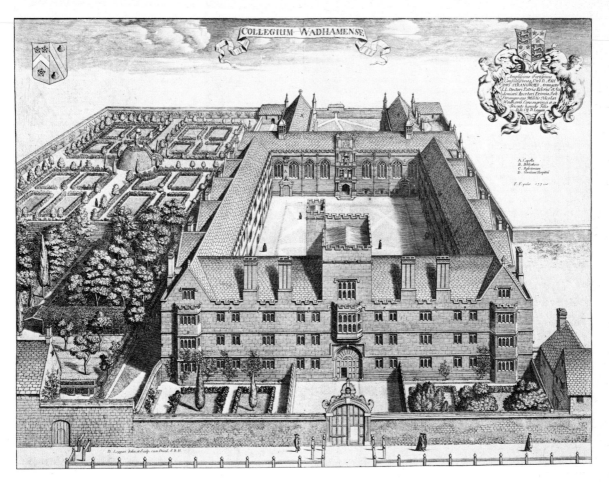

I wonder you will not come and visit me oftener. I have a great respect for you, and I should be extremely glad of your frequent conversation.' To which Mr Gifford replies: 'My lord, I am a clergyman. Your lordship has a very ill-character of being a de-bauched man and an atheist, and 'twill not look well in me to keep company with your lordship as long as this character lasts, and as long as you continue this course of life.'

So, without Mr Gifford, Rochester on 23 January 1660 was admitted a commoner of Wadham College, Oxford. He was not yet thirteen years old, perhaps another example of his mother's impetuosity. She never thought her children and grandchildren too young to bear the part she had chosen for them. In 1686 she wrote to Lord Lichfield on behalf of a great-grandson, Lord Norreys, whom she wished to see in the House of Commons at the age of thirteen: 'The reason we all desire my grandson Norreys may be chose a parliament man is because it is a good school for youth to be improved in.'

The Warden of Wadham was Dr Blandford, later Bishop of Oxford, who had succeeded Dr Wilkins a few months before, and

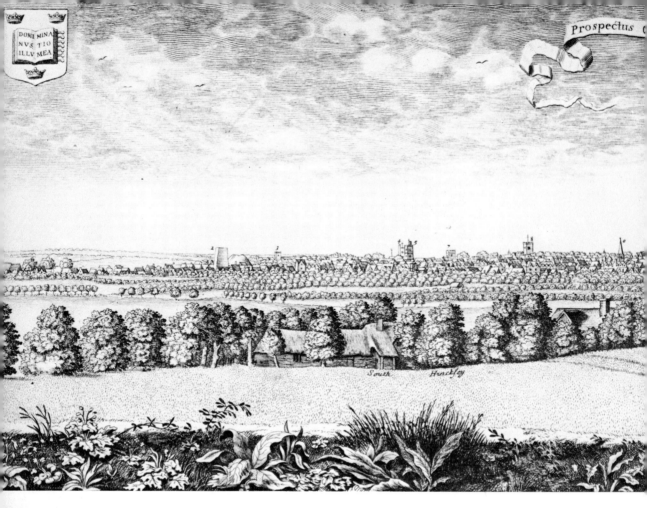

South   Hinckfey

Rochester's tutor was a young man of twenty-five, Phineas Bury, 'a gentleman of good parts who helped Dr Bernard to some emendations of his own conjections upon Josephus'. Sir Charles Sedley, later to be his fellow poet and his fellow 'rake-hell', had preceded him by a few years at Wadham, when the college, under the mastership of Wilkins, Cromwell's brother-in-law, had become a centre of scientific rationalism. Some of the first meetings of the club which was to become the Royal Society were held at the Master's lodge. It was not a school to produce the greatest scientists, but it laid the foundation on which they might build. Experiment for members of the Royal Society must precede and never follow intuition. A curious college, it may be thought, to have produced so many of the Restoration wits, but as Professor Pinto wrote in his life of Sedley, 'the excesses of these young men in the reign of Charles II may be regarded as a sort of distorted application of the experimental view of life taught by such men as Wilkins'.

This was the serious side of Oxford life. There has always been another side: of petty scandals, of malicious scholars, of tragi-comic quarrels. It is so now and it was so then, in a rather heightened form. Oxford changes slowly, a dozen years mark less change in the

life of a scholar than in that of a soldier, courtier, dramatist, and the Oxford of William Prideaux of Christ Church was no doubt in essence the Oxford of Rochester. We read in Prideaux's letters of a don hanging himself in his college room after a scholastic humiliation, of an unexpected visit one evening by the Dean of Christ Church (Dr Fell) to the newly founded Clarendon Press and the discovery that it was secretly being employed by 'the gentlemen of All Souls' in printing an edition of Aretine's postures: 'the plates and prints he hath seized, and threatens the owners of them with expulsion, and I think they would deserve it if they were of any other college than All Souls, but there I will allow them to be virtuous that are bawdy only in pictures'; of Bodley's librarian, who had been so badly beaten by his wife ('an old whore') on suspicion of an intrigue between him and her maid, that 'he hath kept his chamber these two months, and is now in danger of losing his hand, which he made use of only to defend the blows and beg mercy'.

If the men change little, the inns change less. A college would often have its own particular resort, and Prideaux tells an agreeable story of an inn over against Balliol College, 'a dingy, horrid,

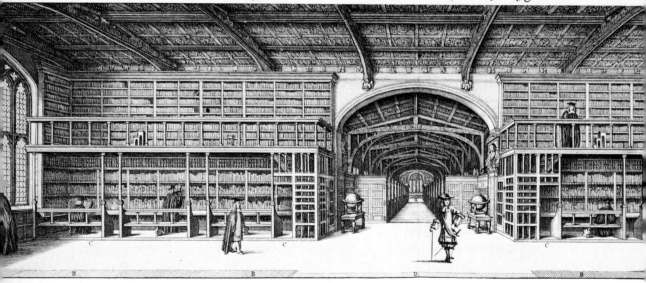

scandalous alehouse, fit for none but draymen and tinkers. . . . Here the Balliol men continually lie and by perpetual bubbing add art to their natural stupidity to make themselves perfect sots. The head, being informed of this, called them together, and in a grave speech informed them of the mischiefs of that hellish liquor called ale.' One of them, however, replied that 'the Vice-Chancellor's men drank ale at the Split Crow, and why should not they?' The Master then went to the Vice-Chancellor, but he, 'being an old lover of ale himself', was unsympathetic; and the Master, returning to his college, 'called his fellows again and told them that he had been with the Vice-Chancellor and that he told him there was no hurt in ale; truly he thought there was, but now, being informed of the contrary, since the Vice-Chancellor gave his men leave to drink ale, he would give them leave to; so that now they may be sots by authority.' If we are to believe M. Misson, who made a tour of England after the Restoration, beer-drinking did not entail any lack of variety. 'There are a hundred and a hundred sorts of beer made in England, and some not bad. Art has well supply'd nature in this particular. Be that as 'twill, beer is art, and wine is nature; I'm for nature against the world.'

It was into this kind of society that Rochester came at the age of thirteen, after a life in the country under the strict discipline of his mother. Not even Mr Gifford was with him. It is true that he had probably little money, and that his age may have preserved him from one form of debauchery, though it is hard to say with certainty of so precocious a child,[1] but his title at Royalist Oxford must have carried him far in the society of 'good fellows', who remembered how a Wilmot had twice defeated the Parliamentary armies. Some would be anxious to curry favour, for 'Mr Catz' was dead, the

Protectorate was visibly breaking up, and the son of Wilmot might expect preferment if the King returned. Mr Robert Whitehall, a physician of Merton College, 'who pretended to instruct the count . . . in the art of poetry, and on whom he absolutely doted' may have been one of these. A peculiarly colourless man Whitehall seems, from Anthony Wood's description. He 'died on the 8th day of July, in 1685, and was buried the next day in the south part of the isle of Merton College church, having for several years before hang'd on that house as an useless member'. The only book which he ever produced, and which certainly did not entitle him to be an instructor in poetry, was called *The Epigrammatical Explanation* and only twelve copies were bound up and issued at Oxford in 1677.

> It must be noted that the author had brought from Holland as many cuts of the Old and New Testament that cost him £14. Each cut he caused to be neatly pasted in the middle of a large quarto paper, on which, before, was printed a running title at the top, and six English verses at the bottom to explain the cut or picture. Which being done, in 12 copies only, he caused each to be richly bound, and afterwards presented a very fair copy to the King, and the rest mostly to persons of quality. Of which number was Charles, son and heir of John Wilmot, Earl of Rochester, for whom he pretended 'twas chiefly composed.

Four days before Rochester was entered as a commoner at Wadham Pepys in London recorded: 'All the world is now at a loss to think what Monck will do: the City saying that he will be for them, and the Parliament saying he will be for them.' It was

'Just as naturally as a cuttle fish ejects poisonous ink so did Mr Wood eject spite . . .' (Llewelyn Powys)

[1] Restif de la Bretonne claimed to have become a father at ten years old.

31

George Monck, Duke of
Albermarle: the Kingmaker

soon decided. The rule of the Puritan, of the Major-Generals, with their swords and their Bibles, was over. On 25 May, when Charles landed at Dover, Pepys sharing a boat with an incontinent dog that the King loved, civilization, in the sense of the arts, poetry, painting, drama, and dissimulation, returned to England. The King kissed the very rich Bible that the Mayor of Dover presented to him, and said it was the thing that he loved above all things in the world. It was a polite and more graceful acceptance of religion than the signature to the Scottish Covenant. No one then, any more than eleven years ago, pretended to believe that the gesture was more than a gesture, but instead of the sour faces, the uncouth accents, the compelling fingers, 'Infinite the crowd of people and the gallantry of the horsemen.' There was shouting and joy all the way to Canterbury.

At Oxford there was to be no more studying for Rochester. 'The humour of that time', Burnet wrote, 'wrought so much on him that he broke off the course of his studies, to which no means could ever effectually recall him', though it is difficult to believe that the 'pursuit of joys' in which his application, according to the pseudo-

St Evremond,[1] was lost could have been more, at the age of thirteen, than noise, drink and buffoonery. The verses with which he celebrated the Restoration had a pomposity more in keeping with what we know of Robert Whitehall, and indeed Anthony Wood states that this poem and another published the next year on the death of the Princess of Orange, were really written by him. One can well imagine the pleasure its conceits gave to the author of *The Epigrammatical Explanation*. 'Fencing her ways with moving groves of men', 'sedentary feet'. His pupil was to write very differently. His poems, which lacked Whitehall's loyalty, seldom contained conceits. They were nearly always the result of direct emotions, whether of scorn, love, intellectual doubt, lust or malice.

His terms at Oxford were soon spent. He had entered on 23 January 1660 and on 9 September 1661, at the age of fourteen, he was created a Master of Arts, being admitted 'very affectionately into the fraternity by a kiss on the left cheek from the Chancellor of the University, who then sate in the supreme chair to honour that assembly'. It is not without a certain pathos that the Chancellor who honoured him was Lord Clarendon, the same man who eight years before had praised him to his father as an 'excellent youth', and who a few years later was to do his best to arrange the young man's marriage to a fortune of the west. Clarendon had never approved of the father, and the mother had incurred his animosity by her defence of Colonel Hutchinson. It must have been the youth's own merits which won his affection. Even at that early age there was wit, good looks and a basis of learning. Six years later, as a peer, Rochester was to sign a protest of certain Lords in favour of the Commons' impeachment of the Chancellor, and the poet was to find epithets:

> Pride, lust, ambition, and the people's hate,
> The kingdom's broker, ruin of the state,

and others more scurrilous – 'This shrub of gentry', 'the Wiltshire hog, son of the spittle' – for the old statesman who had so signally honoured the juvenile Master of Arts.

On 21 November a pass was granted for the Earl of Rochester to go beyond sea, and in the company of Sir Andrew Balfour, a distinguished botanist and a safe guide, the Earl left for the customary grand tour of France and Italy. Possibly it was then he met for the first time Henry Savile, who was also travelling on the Continent and who was to prove his most constant friend. He presented to his college (even at the age of fourteen, if Burnet and 'St Evremond' are to be trusted, there was point in the gift) four silver pint pots which are still preserved. Burford Grammar School had taught him to read Horace and love poetry. Oxford had taught him to drink deep and honour his father by emulation.

[1] One of the earliest sources for Rochester's life is a 'letter written by M. St Evremont to the Duchess of Mazarine', published first in the 1707 edition of Rochester's poems. John Hayward, Evremond's editor, has decided against its authenticity. The author is therefore referred to here as the pseudo-St Evremond or simply as 'St Evremond'.

BRITANNIA
VOL. I.
OR AN
Illustration
of the Kingdom of
ENGLAND
and Dominion of WALES
By a
Geographical & Historical
Description
of the Principal
ROADS.

II The Heiress of the West

An heiress was on offer for sale in Somerset by her two guardians, her stepfather, Sir John Warre and her grandfather, Lord Hawley, and Sir John Warre replied to a proposal by the Earl of Sandwich on behalf of his son Hinchingbrooke. The letter was dated 17 December 1664.

> I had the honour by Mr Moore to receive a letter from your Lordship, by whom my Lord Hawley receiv'd another, and as to the proposals inclosed in them we are at present able to make no return without disobliging my Lord Duke of Ormond, for my Lord being in our county this summer, made some proposals himself on the behalf of his son my Lord John, which have been ever since, and are still in treaty, and what conclusion they will have will be speedily known, but until then we are not in a capacity of giving your Lordship any answer; but believe me, my Lord, you shall ever find that the honour and respects I have for your Lordship and your family are very great, when your Lordship commands any thing in the power of,
>
> Your lordship's most obedient servant,
> J. O. Warre.

With this letter is preserved a letter from Lord Hawley, tremulous with age and, from what one knows of the man, with suppressed cupidity:

> By Mr More I had your Lordship letter, and proposals in a paper from your Lordship, which myself and Sir John Warre read, but the reasons why we have not returned our opinions of them, Sir John Warre has given your Lordship an account of, therefore I shall not trouble your Lordship with the repetition of it. I shall be in Oxford if the weather be fit to ride by Christmas, and shall wait of your Lordship to receive the honour of your Lordship's commands and to assure your Lordship that no man is more devoted to your Lordship's service than, my Lord, your Lordship's most obedient humble servant.

'Absent from thee I languish still, Then ask me not when I return?'

There is no mention in either letter of the girl concerned, Elizabeth Mallet, of Enmore, in Somerset, referred to by Anthony Hamilton as 'la triste heritière'. She had beauty according to the fashion of the time (her hands would have been counted beautiful

35

in any age), wealth (more than £2,000 a year), numerous suitors, of whom Lord Sandwich's son, Viscount Hinchingbrooke, was one, and the Duke of Ormond's son, Lord John Butler, another; freedom and wit, and as the future years were to prove, no little patience and no little charity. But neither Lord Hinchingbrooke nor Lord John Butler were to win her. In the last days of 1664 a new contestant appeared in the field from his grand tour, and Henry Bennett, later Earl of Arlington, wrote to Lord Sandwich:

> My Lord John Butler was first named for her, but his father gave way to my Lord of Desmond's son's pretention to her which is supported by all the recommendations of Somerset House. Notwithstanding which my Lady Castlemaine hath rigged the King, who is also seconded in it by my Lord Chancellor, to recommend my Lord of Rochester. Now these personages being with so much advantage and preference upon the stage, I fear now no other can with any probability of succeeding enter; what I further hear of the Lady is that she declares she will choose for herself. If she hold to it, the game is upon equal terms at least.

The event was to confirm her freedom of choice, but the terms were not so equal as Henry Bennett represented. 'St Evremond' described Rochester as he appeared at Court at the age of seventeen:

> His person was graceful, tho' tall and slender, his mien and shape having something extremely engaging; and for his mind, it discover'd charms not to be withstood. His wit was strong, subtle, sublime, and sprightly; he was perfectly well-bred, and adorned with a natural modesty which extremely became him. He was master both of the ancient and modern authors, as well as of all those in the modern French and Italian, to say nothing of the English, which were worthy of the perusal of a man of fine sense. From all which he drew a conversation so engaging, that none could enjoy without admiration and delight, and few without love.

His tastes in literature we know from other sources. In French his favourite was Boileau, and in English Cowley. The verses of Waller were frequently on his tongue as they were on those of Etherege's character Dorimant. In a letter we find him quoting Shakespeare, and John Dennis in a preface refers to his love for *The Merry Wives of Windsor*. It is the portrait of a paragon that 'St Evremond' draws, but Dr Burnet, the future Bishop of Salisbury, is hardly more moderate in his praise.

Rochester had been drawn back from wine to literature during his travels with Sir Andrew Balfour, a paragon of prudence, learning and virtue. He was welcomed at Court not only by the King, to whom wit was a sufficient recommendation, but by Lady Castlemaine, the King's mistress and Rochester's distant relative, to whom a handsome face and form were of more importance, and by the Chancellor, Lord Clarendon, who alone of the three cared

Two portraits of the young Lord Rochester: 'His person was graceful tho' tall and slender, his mien and shape have something extremely engaging...' ('St Evremond')

most for virtue. The date of his appearance at Court is known, for in a letter from Whitehall, dated 26 December 1664, the King wrote to his beloved sister, the Duchess of Orleans: 'I have received yours by my Lord Rochester but yesterday.'

At the moment of his return eyes were chiefly focused on the Dutch and the strange comet. 'Mighty talk there is of this comet that is seen a'nights; and the King and Queen did sit up last night to see it, and did, it seems.' On Christmas Eve, after an early morning visit to Tower Hill, where the bellman had told Pepys that the star was to be seen, fruitless in spite of a 'most fine bright moonshine night and a great frost', he caught sight of it in the evening, 'which now, whether worn away or no I know not, but appears not with a tail, but only is larger and duller than any other star, and is come to rise betimes, and to make a great arch, and is gone quite to a new place in the heavens than it was before'. As for the Dutch, stories were reaching London of 'our defeat at Guinny wherein our men are guilty of the most horrid cowardice and perfidiousness'. War had not been declared, but Lord Sandwich had been at sea and held the Channel route in spite of winter storms,

37

and the defeat at Guinea was equalized by the capture of the Dutch Smyrna fleet. Preparations were being hurriedly made for official warfare, which began on 15 March 1665.

At Court the effect of war was exhilarating. Charles found himself for once in harmony with the country and could look forward with confidence to a large grant from Parliament. A few men were absent with the fleet. Lord Sandwich was more sailor than courtier and was not missed, and Lord Buckhurst's absence had as compensation the charming verses to the 'ladies now at land'. War entailed no long absence from 'The joys of Hyde Park, and the Mall's dear delight', and Buckhurst was already back in town for Christmas by the time the ladies had been made gracefully aware of the enforced celibacy of their lover.

> In justice, you cannot refuse
>   To think of our distress,
> Since we in hope of honour lose
>   Our certain happiness;
> All our designs are but to prove
> Ourselves more worthy of your love.
>
> Alas! our tears tempestuous grow
>   And cast our hopes away;
> While you unmindful of our woe
>   Sit careless at a play:
> And now permit some happier man
> To kiss your busk and wag your fan.

fine Oranges
fine Lemons

The theatre had woken from its long sleep during the Protectorate. Two companies were licensed, the Theatre Royal and the Duke's Theatre. At a playhouse it was often possible to see as many as four plays during the course of a week. The plays appealed almost exclusively to the courtier. The alderman or the country squire, if he went, was likely to find himself and his family the licensed butt of the comic dramatist. Generally he would be depicted as an impotent old man with a young wife, taking every care to keep her immune from the eyes of the world, but the world in the person of a young wit disguised as a parson or lawyer would always break in. Only the courtier was allowed to be gallant in love. These tales of deception, of young wives starving for love, of old men deceived, of young men disguised, were to become the realities of Rochester's life. Nature was once again to copy Art— Art represented by such titles as *The City Lady or Folly Reclaim'd*, *The Sham Lawyer or The Lucky Extravagant*, *An Evening's Love or The Mock Astrologer*, *The Husband his Own Cuckold*, *Squire Oldsapp or The Night-Adventurers*, *The Wild Gallant*, *The City Bride or The Merry Cuckold*.

The presence in the pit of black-vizored prostitutes seeking custom repelled the more virtuous citizens, as much as it secretly attracted Pepys, who at a performance of *Heraclius* in 1667 'had sitting next to me a woman, the likest my Lady Castlemaine that ever I saw anybody like another; but she is a whore, I believe, for she is acquainted with every fine fellow and called them by their name, Jack and Tom, and before the end of the play frisked to another place'. Among these vizors and the courtiers in the pit the orange women went calling their wares. Nell Gwyn at one time was one of these, and another famous character was Orange Moll. 'The house full of Parliament-men, it being holy day with them: and it was observable how a gentleman of good habit, sitting just before us, eating of some fruit in the midst of the play, did drop

Mary (Moll) Davis: her singing of the ballad 'My lodging is on the Cold Ground' 'raised the fair songstress from her bed on the cold ground to the bed royal'. (John Downes)

down as dead, being choked; but with much ado Orange Moll did thrust her finger down his throat, and brought him to life again.'

The boxes above were attended by the King and his mistresses. From Pepys again one learns how

> The King and the Duke of York minded me, and smiled upon me, at the handsome woman near me: but it vexed me to see Moll Davis, in the box over the King's and my Lady Castlemaine's, look down upon the King, and he up to her; and so did my Lady Castlemaine once, to see who it was; but when she saw Moll Davis, she looked like fire; which troubled me.

Moll Davis at the time of Rochester's coming to Court was still upon the stage. She had not yet charmed the King by her singing in *The Rival Ladies* of 'My Lodging is on the Cold Ground', a ballad on which John Downes's comment was that it 'raised the fair songstress from her bed on the cold ground to the bed royal'.

Wilder amusements of the Court were represented by the robbery and assassination in 1662 near Waltham Cross of a tanner named Hoppy by Lord Buckhurst, his brother Edward Sackville, Sir Henry Belasyse and others, and the 'frolic' the next year at Oxford Kate's tavern in Covent Garden, when Sir Charles Sedley and Lord Buckhurst appeared naked upon the balcony and preached to the crowd which gathered below. The King himself indulged in the debaucheries of the Court only up to a point, but it was a point almost invisible to his contemporaries, so that Pepys was able to write in 1663 how Sir Thomas Crew told him

> that the King doth mind nothing but pleasures and hates the very sight or thoughts of business; that my Lady Castlemaine rules him; who he says hath all the tricks of Aretine that are to be practised to give pleasure in which he is too able having a large — .... If any of the sober counsellors give him good advice and move him in anything that is to his good and honour, the other part, which are his counsellors of pleasure take him when he is with my Lady Castlemaine and in a humour of delight and then persuade him that he ought not to hear or listen to the advice of those old dotards or counsellors that were heretofore his enemies.

Yet Pepys himself was sometimes fairer than this and recognized how much more smoothly the work of the Naval Board proceeded when the King was present. What his contemporaries did not appreciate, because so much was hidden from them, was the skill of a monarch who successfully for more than twenty years played off against each other France, Parliament and Holland, filled his own pockets, strove less successfully for religious toleration and passed on the throne to an avowed Catholic.

It was a hard dry winter, that of Rochester's return from Europe, people broke their limbs in the frosty streets, and it was followed in 1665 by a dry spring and a torrid, thunderous summer. Man's

Frances Stewart as Minerva, pursued unsuccessfully by the King and the Duke of York

memory did not go back to a worse drought. Meadowlands were burnt like the highways, and fields which usually bore forty loads of hay carried a bare four. Men remembered the comet with uneasiness.

It was during this brooding spring that Rochester thrust himself first into public notice. His action is the first mystery in a complex and contradictory life. For his courtship of Elizabeth Mallet everything seemed to be in his favour except his poverty: Lady Castlemaine had 'rigged' the King, and Henry Savile wrote to his brother that Charles was encouraging Rochester to make his addresses. It was true Elizabeth had stated she would please herself, but there

was the less reason to suppose that she would yield to force. Failure would leave the game in his rivals' hands. Perhaps his age and the season and the girl's character are sufficient answer. He was just eighteen, it was late spring, Elizabeth, as she was to show with Lord Hinchingbrooke, cherished moods.

On the evening of 26 May she supped in her grandfather's company with one of the Maids of Honour, Frances Stewart, at Whitehall, who was engaged in the almost unique occupation of warding off the King. After supper Elizabeth left Whitehall with old Lord Hawley. At Charing Cross the horses were stopped by armed men under the direction of Rochester, and she was transferred by force to another coach with six horses, which was driven out of London. Two women were waiting in it to receive her. One knows nothing of what Lord Hawley did, if he did anything at all, on seeing the goose whom he had intended to lay many golden eggs raped away. The hue and cry was raised, Lord Rochester was followed and captured at Uxbridge without Elizabeth; and the King, who, according to Pepys, 'had spoke to the lady often, but with no success' on his behalf, was 'mighty angry'. On 27 May a warrant was sent to Sir John Robinson, the Governor of the Tower, to receive the Earl prisoner.

On the same day a warrant was issued requiring assistance in the search for the armed men who had aided the Earl, and aid for Sir John Warre in searching for Elizabeth and restoring her to her friends. How that restoration was affected is unknown. Presumably, with the Earl captured and in the Tower, his men found it the wisest course to surrender her. There must have been an interval of anxiety for her guardians, for she had not been found on the 28th, a Sunday, when Pepys visited Lady Sandwich.

> Hereupon, my Lady did confess to me, as a great secret, her being concerned in this story for if this match breaks between my Lord Rochester and her, then, by the consent of all her friends, my Lord Hinchingbrooke stands fair, and is invited for her. She is worth, and will be at her mother's death (who keeps but a little from her), £2500 per annum. Pray God give a good success to it. But my poor Lady, who is afeared of the sickness, and resolved to be gone into the country, is forced to stay in town a day or two, or three about it, to see the event of it.

Samuel Pepys

On 6 June Lady Sandwich's hopes were still high. 'She tells me my Lord Rochester is now declaredly out of hopes of Mrs Mallet, and now she is to receive notice in a day or two how the King stands inclined to the giving leave for my Lord Hinchingbrooke to look after her; and that being done to bring it to an end shortly.'

That mention of the sickness in Pepys's diary on 28 May is his first reference to the plague. The first week of June in London saw 112 deaths, which were to increase rapidly to a climax of 6,544 in the third week of September. On 7 June Pepys was faced with the signs of the sickness.

> This day, much against my will, I did in Drury Lane see two or three houses marked with a red cross upon the doors, and 'Lord have mercy upon us!' writ there which was a sad sight to me, being the first of that kind that to my remembrance I ever saw. It put me into an ill conception of myself and my smell, so that I was forced to buy some roll-tobacco to smell to and chew which took away the apprehension.

That was one of the worst fears the plague brought, the fear of smells, of human smells, of garbage smells, of animal smells. And they increased, as the drought continued and the heat grew. That same day Pepys went by water home, 'where, weary with walking and with the mighty heat of the weather, and for my wife's not coming home I stayed walking in the garden till 12 at night, when it began to lighten exceedingly, through the greatness of the heat'.

While Londoners fled into the country from the plague, Rochester was confined to the Tower

All night the lightning went on, but there was only one great shower of rain.

The next day the plague was for a little forgotten in the news of a great victory over the Dutch on 3 June, but on the 10th the plague took its first victims in the city. In the second week there were 168 deaths, and panic was beginning. 'It struck me very deep this afternoon, going with a hackney-coach from Lord Treasurer's down Holborn the coachman I found to drive easily and easily; at last stood still, and came down hardly able to stand; and told me that he was suddenly stroke very sick and almost blind, he could not see. So I light and went into another coach, with a sad heart for the poor man and trouble for myself, lest he should have been struck with the plague.' On the 21st 'I find all the town almost going out of town, the coaches and wagons being all full of people going into the country.'

For three of those June weeks Rochester lay in the Tower. That, in ordinary circumstances, might have been no great hardship, but to be tied to one spot in the company of the Lieutenant of the Tower gave him little opportunity to forget the spread of the plague and the sense of failure, even though the Lieutenant entertained him with his singing, having 'a very good ear and strong voice, but no manner of skill'. Rochester was to grow accustomed to disgrace; this was the first and most bitter taste of it. Pepys described Robinson as 'a talking, bragging bufflehead . . . as very a coxcomb as I would have thought had been in the city, nor hath he brains to outwit any tradesman'. Colonel Hutchinson, who had viewed him from the same close quarters as Rochester, had harsher epithets for a man who took every opportunity to rob his prisoners and the Government. The plague was eventually to enter the Tower and strike down soldiers of the garrison, but not before Rochester had left it.

Some time in June he petitioned the King for restoration to favour. Inadvertence, ignorance of the law and passion, he wrote, were the occasions of his offence. He would rather have chosen ten thousand deaths than incurred His Majesty's displeasure. It was the customary language in which to address a sovereign, but at the age of eighteen Rochester was likely enough to have felt both admiration and affection for the witty and easy King. He was to become the King's worst critic, after he had taken to sharing the same vices, but the brutality of his later satire perhaps sprang from a love disappointed and a generous mind disillusioned. On 19 June his petition was answered, and Lord Arlington sent a warrant to the Lieutenant to discharge the Earl on sufficient security to surrender to a Secretary of State, the first day of Michaelmas Term. Before that date Rochester passed through many dangers and returned, his escapade forgotten, with a reputation for courage and resource.

III *Seascape*

The Dutch East Indies Fleet was on the way home, and it was the duty of Lord Sandwich to prevent it reaching port. The Battle of Lowestoft had temporarily crippled the Dutch home fleet and enabled the Admiral to keep a close blockade of the Dutch coast. The Channel was closed, and the only route left for the East India Fleet was by the north of Scotland. Thence they might be expected to creep down the Norwegian and Danish coast, sheltering in neutral ports. It was expected and it was desired. Sir Gilbert Talbot, the English Envoy at Copenhagen, had come to an unofficial understanding with Frederick III, the King of Norway and Denmark. In return for a share of the spoils, the King was to send orders to the Governor of Bergen that, if the Dutch took shelter in the port, the English were to be allowed to follow and capture the fleet without interference. The arrangement was approved by Charles. A whole month elapsed, allowing Frederick ample time to reconsider the plot, but there was no indication that he had changed his mind. 'The King', wrote Talbot, 'has ordered his governor to shoot only powder', and again 'the King . . . sends orders to his governor to storm and seem to be highly offended, but not to shoot at the English or at least not to touch them'.

This was the position when Rochester volunteered for service with the fleet. On 6 July the King wrote to Sandwich:

> I have little to say to [you] in order to the business of the fleet, my brother having sent you all the directions necessary, and I am sure I need not be in pain for the good conduct of the fleet now 'tis in your hands; the chief business of this letter is to recommend the bearer my Lord Rochester to your care, who desires to go a volunteer with you, so I have nothing more to say to you at this time, only to wish you good success, and to assure you of my constant friendship and kindness.
>
> C.R.

Sandwich had by that time reached Flamborough Head with the greater part of the fleet. In his journal on 15 July he noted, 'My Lord Rochester came in the Success to remain on my ship for the voyage, where I accommodated him with a cabin', and two days later he replied to the King's letter: 'In obedience to your Majesty's

The Sea Triumph of
Charles II, a premature
celebration

47

The Battle of Lowestoft and (inset) the commander of the English fleet, the Earl of Sandwich

commands by the Earl of Rochester I have accommodated him the best I can and shall serve him in all things that I can.'

It was an ironical juxtaposition, that of Rochester with the father of his chief rival for the hand of Elizabeth Mallet. It may have been the prospect of Lord Hinchingbrooke's return from the Continent which had induced Rochester to use force with Elizabeth. Now that he was at sea with Sandwich he had to imagine from a distance the return of his rival (Hinchingbrooke landed at Dover on 4 August) and Lady Sandwich's efforts on her son's behalf.

Sandwich's letter continues with a description of his plans and movements. Sir Thomas Allen had joined them, and by advice of the Council of War the fleet had sailed for the Naze in Norway. On the same day he sent John Werden to Copenhagen to warn the King of Norway of his plans. The trap was laid and the fleet waited the mouse. On Sunday 30 July the trap appeared to have closed. Sandwich entered in his journal that:

> a ship was brought in that came out of Bergen on Thursday last and assures us of 10 India ships that are come in there, which was a great satisfaction to us in our former resolution; and this afternoon I sent away Sir Thomas Teddeman and the fleet (from my ship went along

with him for the voyage the Earl of Rochester, Sir Thomas Clifford, my son Sidney, Mr Steward, Captain Harbord). It blew a hard gale of wind at S. and S.E. all night and next day. . . .

There had been a rush to volunteer by the young aristocratic adventurers. Bergen meant for them in prospect, not death, wounds, or an inglorious failure, but booty, the rich lading of the East India merchants, and already in mind they shared the prize. Rochester was one of the poorest peers in the land and he courted one of the richest heiresses. Bergen might turn failure into success. The ships in which they sailed for Bergen through the storm seemed built for victory and not for defeat, with their carved and painted figureheads, their silken flags, their wrought-iron lamps hanging from great gilded galleries, the scarlet waistcloths which before battle would blow along the bows to hide the men. But as Bergen approached, the thought of possible death could not be kept out. It became a more immediate possibility than wealth. In the *Revenge* with Rochester were Edward Montague and 'another gentleman of quality' named Wyndham. Both had premonitions of death, Montague the more certain. With Wyndham Rochester entered into 'a formal engagement, not without ceremonies of religion, that if either of them died, he should appear, and give the other notice of the future state, if there was any. But Mr Montague would not enter into the bond.'

Then followed disaster. Talbot had not properly completed his mission, the Governor was unready to betray the Dutch. Arlington declared that he was 'distracted betwixt his avarice and the saving his master's point of honour'. Edward Montague was sent on shore with, it was rumoured, authority to offer the Governor the Garter. All through the night of 1 August messages went to and fro, while

An English fourth rate

49

Sir Thomas Teddeman,
Vice-Admiral, cheated by
the 'false Dane' at Bergen

the Dutch prepared for resistance. The convoy drew across the merchantmen to shelter them, and it was discovered that Dutch guns with their teams had been landed and placed with the Governor's consent in the forts. At dawn of 2 August Teddeman delayed no longer and opened fire. There was no room to manoeuvre his unwieldy fleet (one third-rate, eight fourth-rate, four fifth-rate men of war, and nine merchantmen); the roadstead was so narrow that the yardarms stuck in the rocks; the wind was from the land and prevented the use of fire-ships, blowing the smoke of the guns back into the English faces, and finally the treachery of man was added to the treachery of nature and the forts opened fire upon the fleet. In these circumstances Teddeman did well in escaping without the loss of a ship. Four hundred men were lost, four being killed and seven wounded in the *Revenge*. Among the dead were Montague and Wyndham.

> Mr Montague, though he had such a strong presage in his mind of his approaching death, yet he generously stayed all the while in the place of greatest danger. The other gentleman signalized his courage in a most undaunted manner, till near the end of the action, when he fell on a sudden into such a trembling that he could scarce stand, and Mr Montague going to him to hold him up, as they were in each other's arms, a cannon ball killed him outright and carried away Mr Montague's belly, so that he died within an hour after.

Dr Burnet, from whom this account is taken, continues:

> The Earl of Rochester told me that these presages they had in their minds made some impression on him, that there were separated beings and that the soul either by a natural sagacity, or some secret notice communicated to it, had a sort of divination. But that gentleman's never appearing was a great snare to him, during the rest of his life.

Rochester himself had behaved throughout the action with great courage. 'A person of honour' told Burnet that 'he heard the Lord Clifford, who was in the same ship, often magnify his courage at that time very highly'.

It is the first event in Rochester's life of which we have an account in his own hand and the first which has left a mark on his poetry, and this in conjunction with Burnet's story of the divination and the disappointment is significant. The religious background, the doubt of his own atheism, may well have been the origin of his mental conflict, and it was the conflict which produced the poet. Up till now he had probably written nothing but formal exercises. With Bergen his career as a poet began. He wrote to his mother a letter dated 3 August 'From the Coast of Norway amongst the rocks aboard the Revenge', with a rather careful respect for her and for the God she believed in.

Madam,

    I hope it will not be hard for your Ladyship to believe that it hath been want of opportunity and no neglect in me the not writing to your Ladyship all the while. I know nobody hath more reason to express their duty to you than I have. . . . There have been many things past since I writ last to your Ladyship. We had many reports of De Ruyter and East India Fleet but none true till towards the 2nd of the last month we had certain intelligence then of 30 sail in Bergen in Norway, a haven belonging to the King of Denmark. But the port was found to be so little that it was impossible for the great ships to get in, so that my Lord Sandwich ordered 20 sail of fourth and fifth rate frigates to go in and take them. They were commanded by Sir Thomas Teddeman one of the Vice Admirals.

It was not fit for me to see any occasion of service to the King without offering myself, so I desired and obtained leave of my Lord Sandwich to go with them and accordingly the thirtieth of this month we set sail at six o'clock at night and the next day we made the haven Cruchfort (on this side of the town 15 leagues) not without much hazard of shipwreck, for (beside the danger of rock which according to the seamen's judgment was greater than ever was seen by any of them) we found the harbour where twenty ships were to anchor not big enough for seven, so that in a moment we were all together one upon another and ready to dash in pieces having nothing but some rocks to save ourselves, in case we had been lost; but it was God's great mercy we got clear and only that for we had no human probability of safety; there we lay all night and by twelve o'clock next day got off and sailed to Bergen full of hopes and expectation, having already shared amongst us the rich lading of the East India merchants, some for diamonds some for spices others for rich silks and I for shirts and gold which I had most need of; but reckoning without our host we were fain to reckon twice. However we had immediately a message from the Governor full of civility and offers of service, which was returned by us, Mr Montague being the messenger; that night we had seven or ten more which signified nothing, but were empty delays. It grew dark and we were fain to lie still until morning. All the night the Dutch carried above 200 pieces of cannon into the Danish castles and forts, and we were by morn drawn into a very fair half moon ready for both town and ships. We received several messages from breaks of day until four of clock much like those of the over night, intending nothing but delay that they might fortify themselves the more; which being perceived we delayed no more but just upon the stroke of five we let fly our fighting colours and immediately fired upon ships, who answered us immediately and were seconded by the castles and forts of the town, upon which we shot at all and in a short time beat from one of their greatest forts some three or four thousand men that were placed with small shot upon us; but the castles were not to be [taken] for besides the strength of their walls they had so many of the Dutch guns (with their own) which played in the hulls and decks of our ships, that in 3 hours time we lost some 200 men and six captains, our cables were cut, and we were driven out by the wind, which was so directly against us that we could not use our fireships which otherwise had infallibly done our business; so we came off having beat the town all to pieces without losing one ship. We now lie off a little still expecting a wind that we may send in fireships to make an end of the rest. Mr Montague and Thomas Wyndham's brother were both killed with one shot just by me, but God Almighty was pleased to preserve me from any kind of hurt. Madam, I have been tedious but beg your Ladyship's pardon who am

Your most obedient son
Rochester.

I have been as good a husband as I could, but in spite of my wish have been fain to borrow money.

To read his letter it might be imagined that Bergen had been a victory for the English fleet. Clifford knew better and summed up the action to Sandwich in a few words: 'The issue was the place was too hot for us.' Rochester himself came to a clearer, though still inaccurate, view when ten years later he recalled the action in 'The History of Insipids'.

> The Bergen business was well laid,
>   Though we paid dear for that design:
> Had we not three days parling staid,
>   The Dutch Fleet there, C—— had been thine.
> Though the false Dane agreed to sell 'um
> He cheated us, and saved Skellum.

One wonders what Rochester, who had seen his two friends killed beside him, thought of Dryden's elegant account of the battle in *Annus Mirabilis*:

> Some preciously by shatter'd porcelain fall,
>   And some by aromatic splinters die.

The Four Days' Battle; Admiral De Ruyter

On 18 August, according to Sandwich's journal, they rejoined the main fleet now back at Flamborough Head. 'About 11 o'clock Sir Thomas Teddeman's fleet came to us, and himself, Sir Thomas Clifford, Lord Rochester etc. came on board me. I entreated Sir Thomas Clifford to go to the King and Duke, to give them more full satisfaction of passages in the fleet.'

It was a tale of complete failure that they had to tell. Not only had the 'Bergen business' ended disastrously, but De Ruyter, whom it had been Sandwich's intention to intercept on his way back from the East, had eluded him and brought his ships safely into port. The arrival of the great Admiral had raised Dutch hearts like a victory. The news reached Pepys on the 19th, and possibly Sir Thomas Clifford brought back with him to the fleet letters, which whatever anxiety they caused the Admiral, must have encouraged Rochester's hopes of the rich heiress. Lord Hinchingbrooke had been home only four days when he fell ill of the smallpox. 'Poor gentleman!' Pepys wrote, 'that should be come from France so soon to fall sick, and of that disease too, when he should be gone to see a fine lady, his mistress.'

It was necessary now for Sandwich to meet with some success to counter-balance the melancholy series of his failures. His only hope was to intercept the East India Fleet after it left Bergen. De Ruyter had sailed to meet it, but for the first time nature favoured the English. Storms broke up the fleet and sent it scurrying in small sections towards the Dutch coast. On 5 September Sandwich was able to write to the King of a small success; on the 12th he announced a victory large enough to outweigh the Bergen failure. Writing from Sole Bay he reported that he had met with eighteen sail of Hollanders and took most of them; four men of war, some

53

merchantmen and some ships of victuals and munition for their fleet. Two vessels set themselves on fire. One thousand prisoners were taken, and the only casualty he reported was that of Captain Lambert. He added that he had just met forty sail starting for the Texel, but feared to attack, being but eight or nine leagues off the Dutch coast, the weather thick and a storm rising. He had come to anchor with eighty ships, including the two East India prizes and several other prizes. Finally he referred for particulars to Lord Rochester, who was present and showed himself brave, industrious and of useful parts.

(opposite) James, Duke of York

[2] Rochester returned to England at the height of the plague. The third week of September saw in London nearly seven thousand dead of the sickness. The city held few save those who were too poor to

The Diseases and Casualties this Week.

Disease	Count	Disease	Count
Abortive	23	Grief	1
Aged	57	Griping in the Guts	45
Bedridden	1	Head-mould-shot	2
Bleeding	1	Jaundies	3
Cancer	1	Imposthume	6
Childbed	39	Infants	10
Chrisomes	20	Kingsevil	1
Collick	1	Lethargy	1
Consumption	129	Meagrome	1
Convulsion	71	Plague	6544
Dropsie	31	Plannet	1
Drowned 3. one at Stepney, one at St. Katharine near the Tower, and one at St. Margaret VVestminster	3	Quinsie	3
		Rickets	20
		Rising of the Lights	15
		Rupture	4
		Scowring	3
		Scurvy	1
		Spotted Feaver	97
		Stone	1
		Stopping of the stomach	5
		Strangury	2
		Surfeit	45
Feaver	332	Teeth	128
Flox and Small-pox	8	Thrush	6
Found dead in the street at St. Olave Southwark	1	Timpany	1
French-pox	0	Tissick	4
Frighted	1	Ulcer	1
Gangrene	1	Vomiting	2
		Wormes	15

Christned	Males	90	Buried	Males	3783	Plague	6544
	Females	78		Females	3907		
	In all	168		In all	7690		

Decreased in the Burials this Week — 562
Parishes clear of the Plague — 11   Parishes Infected — 119

The Assize of Bread set forth by Order of the Lord Major and Court of Aldermen. A penny Wheaten Loaf to contain Nine Ounces and a half, and three half-penny White Loaves the like weight.

London 39	Bur.	Plag.	From the 1
St Alban Woodstreet	23	19	St George
Alhallows Barking	41	32	St Gregory
Alhallows Breadstreet	4	3	St Hellen
Alhallows Great	59	53	St James
Alhallows Honylane			St James
Alhallows Lesse	29	26	St John Ba
Alhallows Lumbardstreet	8	7	St John Ev
Alhallows Staining	16	10	St John
Alhallows the Wall	41	39	St Kathari
St Alphage	25	13	St Kachari
St Andrew Hubbard	6	5	St Lawren
St Andrew Undershaft	25	22	St Lawren
St Andrew Wardrobe	63	54	St Leonar
St Ann Aldersgate	33	28	St Leonar
St Ann Blackfryers	79	65	St Magnu
St Antholins Parish	6	5	St Margar
St Austins Parish	2	2	St Margar
St Bartholomew Exchange	3	3	St Margar
St Bennet Fynck	1		St Margar
St Bennet Gracechurch	5	4	St Mary A
St Bennet Paulswharf	3	15	St Mary A
St Bennet Sherehog			St Mary
St Botolph Billingsgate	4	4	St Mary le
Christs Church	55	48	St Mary
St Christophers	6	5	St Mary C
St Clement Eastcheap	3	3	St Mary H
St Dionis Backchurch	10	3	St Mary
St Dunstan East	20	10	St Mary S
St Edmund Lumbardstr.	4	4	St Mary S
St Ethelborough	16	6	St Mary
St Faith	7	6	St Mary
St Foster	10	9	St Martin
St Gabriel Fenchurch	6	3	

Christned in the 97 Parishes within the Walls

	Bur.	Plag.	
St Andrew Holborn	271	247	St Botolp
St Bartholomew Great	21	17	St Botolp
St Bartholomew Lesle	14	12	St Dunstan
St Bridget	236	180	St George
Bridewel Precinct	32	31	St Giles C
St Botolph Aldersgate	68	62	St Olave

Christned in the 16 Parishes without the Walls

	Bur.	Plag.	
St Giles in the fields	140	125	Lambeth P
Hackney Parish	22	18	St Leonar
St James Clerkenwel	77	67	St Magdal
St Kath. near the Tower	93	66	St Mary S

Christned in the 12 out Parishes in Middlesex

	Bur.	Plag.	
St Clement Danes	168	140	St Martin
St Paul Covent Garden	39	29	St Mary S

Christned in the 5 Parishes in the City and Libe

fly, some conscientious officials like Pepys, the imperturbable, tobacco-chewing soldier Monck, now Duke of Albemarle, and the sick. Everyone's discourse was of death, the streets were almost empty. On 27 July the Court had removed from Hampton Court to Salisbury, but the sickness followed, and the Court went first to Wilton and then to Oxford. It was from St Giles's at Oxford that the King on 16 September answered Sandwich's letter: 'I could not give my thanks for the first good news of the fifth because I knew not whither to send them to you; now my Lord Rochester hath also brought me yours of the 12th with a second success upon the Dutch. . . .' With the Court at Oxford, it is probable that Rochester saw something, during the last months of the year, of his mother at Ditchley and of his own inheritance of Adderbury. His courage had atoned for his disgrace and merited reward. On 31 October he received £750 from the King, perhaps to enable him to pay debts incurred in the royal service. That the gift was in recognition of his courage at Bergen is probable, for at the same time a knighthood was conferred on Charles Harbord, who had served with him in the *Revenge*.

At Oxford the Court was busy forgetting the plague. In November Pepys was told how 'the factions are high between the King and the Duke, and all the Court are in an uproar with their loose amours, the Duke of York being in love desperately with Mrs Stewart. Nay, that the Duchess herself is fallen in love with her new Master of the Horse, one Henry Sidney, and another, Harry Savile, so that God knows what will be the end of it.' In London, where business was at a standstill with the Court away, boys were singing openly in the streets, 'The King cannot go away till my Lady Castlemaine be ready to come along with him'; 'she being lately put to bed'. It was a striking contrast with the storms in the North Sea, the perils of Bergen, the awareness of God's providence.

The Court returned to London in February 1666, the plague having diminished, and in March Rochester was sworn a Gentleman of the King's Bedchamber. The duties of the office are described by Delaune.

> The gentlemen of the bedchamber, whereof the first is called the groom of the stole, as it were servant of the robe, or vestment, he having the office and honour to present and put on his Majesty's first garment or shirt every morning, and to order the things of the bedchamber. The gentlemen are usually of the prime nobility of England. Their office is each one in his turn to wait a week in every quarter in the King's bedchamber, there to lie by the King in a pallet-bed all night, and in the absence of the groom of the stole, to supply his place. They wait on the King when he eats in private, for then the cup-bearers, carvers and servers do not wait. The yearly fee to each is £1000.

r to the 19.		1665	
Plag.		Bur.	Plag.
3	St Martin Ludgate	21	11
23	St Martin Orgars	9	7
3	St Martin Outwich	8	3
26	St Martin Vintrey	64	61
11	St Matthew Fridaystreet	1	1
5	St Maudlin Milkstreet	5	3
	St Maudlin Oldfishstreet	16	11
36	St Michael Bassishaw	17	12
	St Michael Cornhil	14	11
31	St Michael Crookedlane	10	10
6	St Michael Queenhithe	11	6
17	St Michael Quern	4	3
4	St Michael Royal	20	17
32	St Michael Woodstreet	6	2
6	St Mildred Breadstreet	6	3
8	St Mildred Poultrey	4	2
5	St Nicholas Acons	8	7
13	St Nicholas Coleabby	14	13
3	St Nicholas Olaves	12	9
9	St Olave Hartstreet	20	18
16	St Olave Jewry	7	5
10	St Olave Silverstreet	23	17
2	St Pancras Soperlane	2	2
8	St Peter Cheap	4	3
8	St Peter Cornhil	10	6
9	St Peter Paulswharf	12	12
9	St Peter Poor	6	6
34	St Steven Colemanstreet	47	40
	St Steven Walbrook	5	5
2	St Swithin	11	9
6	St Thomas Apostle	19	17
1	Trinity Parish	13	13

ed ——1493 Plague——1189

589	Saviours Southwark	427	403
256	S. Sepulchres Parish	301	214
79	St Thomas Southwark	57	52
176	Trinity Minories	12	10
373	At the Pesthouse	6	6
363			

at the Pesthouse——3631 Plague——3070

43	St Mary Islington	60	66
173	St Mary Whitechappel	532	502
180	Rothorith Parish	17	13
152	Stepney Parish	716	686

Buried——2258 Plague——2091

228	St Margaret Westminster	411	399
19	Whereof at the Pesthouse		7

29 Buried 915 Plague—815

The office, during the reign of Charles, was not the purely honorary one that it became under later sovereigns. The King was careful to appoint personal friends, members of what the poet Marvell called 'the merry gang', for the office entailed intimate knowledge of the King's movements. The appointment of Rochester shows that he had already progressed far in his friendship with the King. But he was still young enough to prefer adventure to debauchery, and during the summer of 1666, without warning his nearest relations of his intention, he was again at sea, this time in the Channel under Sir Edward Spragge, 'a merry man that sung a pleasant song pleasantly', but, in spite of his reputation for courage, the unsuccessful suitor of a neighbour of Pepys, 'a widow, Mrs Hollworthy, who is a woman of estate, and wit and spirit, and do contemn him the most, and sent him away with the greatest scorn in the world'.

Rochester as a suitor seemed then as unsuccessful as his commander. He had to commend him only personal qualities, and Elizabeth Mallet's guardians demanded hard cash, as claimant after claimant discovered. The two elderly men had a valuable girl to sell, and they were determined to get a good price. They chaffered and they delayed. They held Lord Sandwich at arm's length, while they bargained with the Duke of Ormond. Ormond's agent Nicholls, after the failure of Rochester's rape, made a strenuous effort to bring matters to a head. While Lord Hawley was away, he went down to the west to interview Elizabeth herself. He showed Sir John Warre a letter from Ormond's son, Lord John Butler, and then offered to show it to Elizabeth.

> Sir John Warre, when he saw the young lady so concerned to see my Lord's letter, begun to be very angry and told me he would not be circumvented by anyone, which I resented with as much anger and told him these expressions of his [were] not deserved from him for my plain and fair dealings. The young lady stood by all the while, and I believe she would have been concerned for me if she durst.

She presently after drunk my Lord Duke of Ormond's health, and my Lord John's, in a pretty big glass half full of claret, which I believe was more than ever she did in her life. Sir John and I became very good friends and he told me that they would all be for my Lord John, but if he had said they would be for themselves I would sooner have believed them.

That big glass of claret was not the only indication that Elizabeth was unsatisfied at being thus put to market by her guardians.

The young lady this morning came undressed into the parlour to take her leave of me: her mother would have her begone presently, but she would not, but stayed with me an hour at least, which time I improved to the utmost that I could, assuring her of his [Lord John's] great affection and good disposition. . . . I told the young lady this morning that however the business were managed at Salisbury Lord John would come to see her. It was before her mother, for she watched me so close that I had not an opportunity otherwise. The mother said she would not see him. I asked her, Madam, I hope you will see him. She blushed and made no reply. Why, Betty, says her mother, you have promised your grandfather; at which she answered that without her grandfather's leave she would not, but spoke it in the manner of trouble and disconsolancy which I never saw. . . . They have cunningly inveigled her to promise her grandfather that she will not marry without his advice.

Nicholls added that 'she has a great deal of wit, and affection for my Lord John'.

The latter seems true enough. In spite of her wit and her youth and her money she found herself in the power of her mother and her two guardians. She was ready to feel affection for anyone who tried to break through the malevolent circle and court her in person. Lord John Butler wished to make the attempt, Rochester had unsuccessfully done so, she was herself to appeal to Lord Hinchingbrooke to marry her out of hand.

The interview with Nicholls had taken place three days before Bergen, and by the time that Rochester went to sea for the second time one rival had left the field. Lord Hawley's demands had proved too much for the Duke of Ormond and were like to prove too much for Lord Sandwich. On 30 May 1666 Sir George Carteret wrote to Sandwich, who had gone on an embassy to Spain:

My Lord Lieutenant having quitted all his pretentions to the lady of the west Mr Moore and I had divers meetings with her grandfather, who we found more addicted to his own interest than to any thing else, and so unreasonable in all his demands that we gave him over. The father-in-law was at all our meetings who agreed in everything with the grandfather.

The girl before this had tried to break away from her guardians, sending a servant to Lord Hinchingbrooke to suggest that the marriage should be arranged without the consent of friends, but that young nobleman, 'a mighty sober gentleman' as Pepys described him, refused to listen to the proposal 'but in a way of honour'. In August 1666 the affair came to an end with an interview between Lord Hinchingbrooke and Elizabeth at Tonbridge, where she was staying with her mother. This interview, probably qualified by the maternal presence, was as far as Lord Hinchingbrooke was prepared to go towards a personal arrangement, and he was not pleased, according to Pepys, with 'the vanity and liberty of her carriage'. She declared that she had an affection for another; negotiations were at last at an end, and Mr Moore was able to rejoice, in a letter to Sandwich, that the match was off. Strangely enough indignation against the guardians' demands seemed to turn, in the final months, against the girl who had so boldly tried to ignore the customs of the day, and there is a touch of vindictiveness in Carteret's letter on 10 September to Sandwich: 'The lady of the West is at Court without any suitors, nor is like to have any.'

[3] It would be natural but probably incorrect to believe that the person for whom Elizabeth Mallet declared her affection at Tonbridge was Rochester. His behaviour as a lover had been as bold as she could desire and contrasted well with the scruples of Lord Hinchingbrooke. His courage at Bergen was well known and now, with the fleet in the Channel, he had proved his valour again.

> He went aboard the ship commanded by Sir Edward Spragge the day before the great sea fight of that year: almost all the volunteers that were on the same ship were killed. Mr Middleton (brother to Sir Hugh Middleton) was shot in his arms. During the action, Sir Edward Spragge, not being satisfied with the behaviour of one of the captains, could not easily find a person that would cheerfully venture through so much danger, to carry his commands to the captain. This Lord offered himself to the service, and went in a little boat through all the shot, and delivered his message, and returned back to Sir Edward, which was much commended by all that saw it.

The battle was the disastrous one that raged for four days in the first week of June, with a loss to England of five thousand men killed, three thousand prisoners taken, eight ships of the line sunk. Pepys could hear the guns 'most plainly' from Greenwich Park. There were many men, not so lucky as Rochester, who came out of the battle with their reputations blown upon—Albemarle himself, Prince Rupert, Teddeman. Spragge was not alone in his dissatisfaction with a captain's behaviour. Albemarle wrote home that he had never fought with worse officers in his life, not above twenty of them behaving themselves like men. Many were slain, Captains Bacon, Tearne, Wood, Mortham, Whitty and Coppin. Sir William Clerk and Sir Christopher Mings, the commander in the fleet most beloved of his men, died of their wounds, and Sir William Berkeley's body lay in a sugar chest at The Hague for all to see with his flag standing up by him. The defeat was to be avenged in August, but it seemed at the time an end to the hopes with which the campaign had started, hopes so high that Sir Thomas Clifford had written to Arlington from the *Royal Charles*: 'There is a new air and vigour in every man's countenance, and even the common men cry out, if we do not beat them now, we never shall do it.'

The disastrous battle that raged for four days in the first week of June

59

Out of the carnage of De Ruyter's four days of victory Rochester emerged with his reputation for courage enhanced. If a Gadbury in those days had been called on to foretell his future, one doubts if the stars would have predicted the narrow round of Court vice and the charges of cowardice. His marriage with the heiress of the west could have been more easily foreseen. Surely he was bound to appeal to a romantic and inexperienced girl, but it may be that his light heart found its match in hers, for it seems not to have been Rochester on whom, as she told Lord Hinchingbrooke in August, her affections were settled. It was more likely to have been a certain Popham referred to by Pepys on 25 November: 'Mr Ashburnham today at dinner told how the rich fortune Mrs Mallet reports of her servants: that my Lord Herbert would have had her my Lord Hinchingbrooke was indifferent to have her my Lord John Butler might not have her my Lord of Rochester would have forced her; and Sir – Popham (who nevertheless is like to have her) would kiss her breech to have her.'

Both were young, both were handsome, high spirited, both, perhaps, had the light-hearted philosophy of love, expressed once perfectly by Rochester:

> All my past life is mine no more,
>   The flying hours are gone:
> Like transitory dreams giv'n o'er,
> Whose images are kept in store,
>   By memory alone.
>
> The time that is to come is not;
>   How can it then be mine?
> The present moment's all my lot;
> And that, as fast as it is got,
>   Phyllis, is only thine.
>
> Then talk not of inconstancy,
>   False hearts and broken vows;
> If I, by miracle, can be
> This live-long minute true to thee,
>   'Tis all that Heav'n allows.

The live-long minute was to be seized in some sort of second elopement without 'consent of friends' and was to extend, in a fashion, to the end of life. They were never to part. She in the country would wait his coming when the bouts of vice were over, sometimes with impatience, sometimes with anger, but always with forgiveness; he in the town, whether in the arms of a whore from the stews round Drury Lane or in those of the loved mistress, Elizabeth Barry, was always aware of her constancy. It vexed his conscience, so that he would write in a mood of blind anger or sullen confession, but it tied him to her, and through the rifts of

The heiress of the west, Elizabeth Mallet, Countess of Rochester

(overleaf) The raid on the Dutch at Bergen

the Countess of
ROCHESTER

lust and drink, love broke, in a clear, beautiful, but no longer carefree, expression:

> Absent from thee I languish still,
>   Then ask me not, when I return?
> The straying fool 'twill plainly kill
>   To wish all day, all night to mourn.
>
> Dear, from thine arms then let me fly,
>   That my fantastic mind may prove
> The torments it deserves to try,
>   That tears my fixt heart from my love.
>
> When wearied with a world of woe,
>   To thy safe bosom I retire,
> Where love and peace and truth does flow,
>   May I contented there expire.
>
> Lest once more wandring from that Heav'n,
>   I fall on some base heart unblest;
> Faithless to thee, false, unforgiven,
>   And lose my everlasting rest.

Elizabeth Mallet was at Court 'without any suitors' in September. Rochester may still at that date have been with the fleet, but by the time she was summing up her servants so indifferently in November, he had returned. He was present on 15 November at a ball on the Queen's birthday, described by Pepys, a striking contrast with the four days' slaughter in the Downs from which he had emerged.

Anon the house grew full, and the candles light, and the King and Queen and all the ladies set. And it was indeed a glorious sight to see Mrs Stewart in black and white lace and her head and shoulders dressed with diamonds. And the like a great many ladies more (only the Queen, none); and the King in his rich vest of some rich silk and silver trimming, as the Duke of York and all the dancers were, some of cloth of silver, and others of other sorts, exceeding rich. Presently after the King was come in, he took the Queen, and about fourteen more couple there was, and begun the Bransles. As many of the men as I can remember presently, were: the King, Duke of York, Prince Rupert, Duke of Monmouth, Duke of Buckingham, Lord Douglas, Mr Hamilton, Colonel Russell, Mr Griffith, Lord Ossory, Lord Rochester. And of the ladies the Queen – Duchess of York, Mrs Stewart, Duchess of Monmouth, Lady Essex Howard, Mrs Temple, Swedish Ambassadress – Lady Arlington, Lord George Berkeley's daughter. And many others I remember not. But all most excellently dressed, in rich petticoats and gowns and diamonds – and pearls.

After the Bransles, then to a Corant, and now and then a French dance; but that so rare that the Corants grew tiresome, that I wished it done. Only, Mrs Stewart danced mighty finely, and many French

(above) The Palace of Whitehall seen across St James's Park

(below) Louis XIV and his Court attending a performance of the ballet *Psyche* at the Louvre

(overleaf) A banquet of Charles II

65

dances, especially one the King called the New Dance, which was very pretty. But upon the whole matter, the business of the dancing of itself was not extraordinary pleasing. But the clothes and sight of the persons was indeed very pleasing, and worth my coming, being never likely to see more gallantry while I live if I should come 20 times.

About 12 at night it broke up, and I to hire a coach with much difficulty. . . . So away home with my wife between displeased at the dull dancing, and satisfied at the clothes and persons (my Lady Castlemaine (without whom all is nothing) being there, very rich, though not dancing); and so, after supper, it being very cold, to bed.

It was a repetition of those dances in Paris 'as if we had taken the Plate Fleet'; there was no victory to rejoice over, for though the defeat in June had been avenged in August, the great fire broke out in September and the Dutch held the seas again. But it was the merchants who chiefly felt the pinch of ill-fortune, and though Tom Killigrew, in the hearing of the poet Carew, told the King frankly that there was an honest, able man at Court, at present out of employment, who could mend all things, and his name was Charles Stuart, few at Whitehall cared about the state of the country.

Of those few Rochester seems to have been one. He had seen war in the form of defeat, a more enduring experience than of victory. He had left the fleet, but he had not yet left active service. From commissions to a cornet and a quartermaster, recorded in the State Papers for 1666, it is known that he had command of a troop of horse.

But for the son of Henry Wilmot, there were other contrasts than those of battle and ball. There was the contrast between the hopes of the old Cavaliers at the Restoration and their fulfilment. Two petitions to the King in August and November of this year must have had a particular interest for Rochester. On 10 August James Halsall, the Royal Cupbearer, wrote to George Porter, Stone Gallery, Whitehall, that Mrs Carter, the poor woman they had met the day before, formerly lived with Mrs Abbott and preserved in her house Tom Blayne, Robin Killigrew, Sir Robert Shirley, Mr O'Neill (one remembers him as Mr Bryan writing to Mr Jackson), Nic Armorer (the companion of Henry Wilmot in the flight from Aylesbury), Lord Rochester himself, and many others of the King's servants. She was their confidante and very faithful and was now ready to starve. It would be a charity to get her into a hospital or find her some means to live. And with equal pathos, in the month of the Queen's birthday ball, an old man, George Middleton, of Hampshire, petitioned for an even smaller benefit. He desired only permission to remain peaceably in the Kingdom, without persecution for Nonconformity, being seventy-two years old. He found a place of shelter, he claimed, for His Majesty after the Battle of

Worcester and preserved the Earl of Rochester at the hazard of his own life, after the miscarriage of the intended business at Salisbury (a reference to the conspiracy of 1655).

It may well have been these cases, which referred to his father, that Rochester had in mind when he wrote 'The History of Insipids':

> His father's foes he doth reward,
>   Preserving those that cut off's head;
> Old Cavaliers the Crown's best guard,
>   He lets them starve for want of bread.
> Never was any King endow'd
> With so much grace and gratitude.

This was the most creditable period of Rochester's life, when he was able to watch the follies of the Court without sharing them, a period which may be said to have ended with his marriage. In September 1666 Elizabeth Mallet had, according to Sir George Carteret, no suitors. On 29 January 1667 she married Rochester; it was presumably that sudden marriage without consent of friends which she had desired, for it is difficult to believe that old Lord Hawley, or his echo Sir John Warre, would have consented to her marriage with an impoverished Earl, who had hoped in vain to find gold and silk shirts in the harbour of Bergen. That the King was a party to the elopement is known from a letter addressed by Rochester's mother on 15 February to his former guardian, Sir Ralph Verney, summoning him to her aid on the occasion of

> my son Rochester's sudden marriage with Miss Mallet contrary to all her friends' expectation. The King I thank God is very well satisfied with it, and they had his consent when they did it – but now we are in some care how to get the estate. They are come to desire two parties with friends, but I want a knowing friend in business, such a man as Sir Ralph Verney – Master Coole the lawyer and Cary I have here, but I want one more of quality to help me.

In February Pepys saw them at the theatre, six days after the wedding. It was at a performance of *Heraclius*, a translation from Corneille, at the Duke's Theatre:

> the house being very full and great company; among others Mrs Stewart, very fine, with her locks done up with puffs, as my wife calls them: and several other great ladies had their hair so, though I do not like it; but my wife do mightily – but it is only because she sees it is the fashion. Here I saw my Lord Rochester and his lady, Mrs Mallet, who hath after all this ado married him; and, as I hear some say in the pit, it is a great act of charity, for he hath no estate. But it was pleasant to see how every body rose up when my Lord John Butler, the Duke of Ormond's son, came into the pit towards the end of the play, who was a servant to Mrs Mallet, – and now smiled upon her, and she on him.

Je ne vois point que le Graueur   Car s'il est tout chargé de maux,   Tout ce qu'il a de vicieux
Ait pour raison que son caprice,   D'où procedent ils que de testes   Ne vient donc pas de sa nature,
Quand il appelle ce Resueur.   De ces dangereux Animaux,   Ou bien s'il est malicieux,
Vn homme fourré de malice   Qui trompent les plus fines bestes?   Il s'en faut prendre a sa fourrure.

IV The Age of Spleen

At the time of his marriage Rochester was nearly twenty; only thirteen years of life were left him, years which are very difficult for the biographer to chronicle. They are full of fantastic stories and impersonations – some, like that of Alexander Bendo, the quack doctor, well authenticated, others, like the mock-tinker of Barford, purely legendary. They contain his love affairs with the actress Elizabeth Barry, with Mrs Boutel and with Mrs Roberts, the King's mistress; his literary friendships and his literary quarrels, which may have culminated with a hired bravo's attack on Dryden in Rose Alley; his duels and attempted duels; his quarrels with the King. These years cannot be followed chronologically, dates are too often the subject of speculation; it is as if all those years were clouded by the fumes of drink.

The sea, with its accompaniment of heroism and disaster, was behind him, so was the adventure of marriage, and the begetting of children was the result of intermittent visits to the country, to his house at Adderbury or to his wife's estate at Enmore in Somerset, the two places where she was prepared, if not at times content, to pass most of her life. The dates of his children's baptisms stand out as islands of certainty in the misty sea of the thirteen unlucky years. On 30 August 1669 Anne was baptized; on 2 January 1671 his only son, Charles; on 13 July 1674 Elizabeth; and on 6 January 1675 his last child Mallet, or rather his last legitimate child, for in 1677 Mrs Barry bore Rochester a daughter.

The mists of drink did not close at once. 'St Evremond' wrote, 'Since his travels he had contracted a temperance, which being in itself extraordinary in an age so dissolute, was soon, tho' by insensible degrees, laid aside.' It was his misfortune to share his father's characteristic: that his wit shone brightest when he was in his cups. 'The natural heat of his fancy', Burnet wrote, 'being inflamed by wine, made him so extravagantly pleasant, that many, to be more diverted by that humour, studied to engage him deeper and deeper in intemperance: which at length did so entirely subdue him, that . . . for five years together he was continually drunk: not all the while under the visible effect of it, but his blood was so inflamed, that he was not . . . cool enough to be perfectly master of himself.'

Tom Killigrew, dramatist and royal jester

There was another side to his drinking which made 'St Evremond' declare that it was not for every man to venture a debauch with him; 'for a jest or a diversion, he would often hazard his life, and that many would think paying too dear for his conversation'. But in the stories which have survived it is others, rather than Rochester, whose lives seem to have been at stake. In a brawl at Epsom, it was Rochester's friend, Downes, who died, and in another story of a jest at a Thames-side inn it is again Rochester's companions who were in danger:

> The late Lord Rochester being, upon a freak with some of his companions, at the Bear at the Bridge-foot, among their music, they had an hump-back'd fiddler, whom they called His Honour. To humour the frolic, they all agreed to leap into the Thames, and it came to Lord Rochester's turn to do it at last; but his Lordship seeing the rest in, and not at all liking the frolic, set the crooked fiddler at the brink of the balcony, and push'd him in, crying out – I can't come myself, gentlemen, but I've sent my honour.

That wine sometimes lent him an angel's tongue can be seen in a letter to Henry Savile, his fat, patient and disreputable friend:

> Mr Savile,
>
> Do a charity becoming one of your pious principles, in preserving your humble servant Rochester from the imminent peril of sobriety; which, for want of good wine more than company (for I can drink like a hermit betwixt God and my own conscience) is very like to befall me. Remember what pains I have formerly taken to wean you from your pernicious resolutions of discretion and wisdom! And, if you have a grateful heart (which is a miracle amongst you statesmen), show it, by directing the bearer to the best wine in town: and pray let not this highest point of sacred friendship be perform'd lightly, but go about it with all due deliberation and care, as holy priests to sacrifice, or as discreet thieves to the wary performance of burglary and shop-lifting. Let your well-discerning palate (the best judge about you) travel from cellar to cellar, and then from piece to piece, till it has lighted on wine fit for its noble choice and my approbation. To engage you the more in this matter, know, I have laid a plot may very probably betray you to the drinking of it. My Lord —— will inform you at large.
>
> Dear Savile! as ever thou dost hope to outdo Machiavel, or equal me, send some good wine! So may thy wearied soul at last find rest, no longer hov'ring twixt th' unequal choice of politics and lewdness! Mayst thou be admir'd and lov'd for thy domestic wit, belov'd and cherish'd for thy foreign interest and intelligence.
>
> Rochester.

Drink, which at first brought him happiness, poetry, fantastic fancies, soon combined with disease to attack his health, sour his tongue, make restless his conscience, and embitter his poetry. The

contrast can be seen in two poems; one, the famous 'Upon Drinking
in a Bowl', which begins:

> Vulcan contrive me such a cup
>   As Nestor us'd of old:
> Shew all thy skill to trim it up;
>   Damask it round with gold.
>
> Make it so large that, fill'd with sack
>   Up to the swelling brim,
> Vast toasts, on the delicious lake,
>   Like ships at sea may swim;

the other, the bitter, unhappy 'To a Lady: in a Letter', with its
ironic echo of Lovelace:

> Let us, since wit has taught us how,
>   Raise pleasure to the top:
> You rival bottle must allow,
>   I'll suffer rival fop. . . .
>
> There's not a brisk insipid spark,
>   That flutters in the town,
> But with your wanton eyes you mark
>   Him out to be your own. . . .
>
> All this you freely may confess,
>   Yet we'll not disagree:
> For did you love your pleasures less,
>   You were no match for me.

Rochester's manuscript: the changes in the printed version are to the benefit of the poem, including the omission of the last verse

A sad speculation is why the hero of the defeats at Bergen and the Downs, the man who could regard the fascinating Charles with a cold clear eye, who knew genuine love, with its mingling of poetry, fantasy, humour and fear so well that he wrote one of the most perfect analyses of it in the song beginning:

> An age in her embraces past,
> Would seem a winter's day

why, of all at Court, it was Rochester who chose to follow Buckingham, 'the lord of useless thousands', along his dismal road?

Many possible answers can be advanced: an inheritance from his father, the fashion of the times, the particular example of his friends; and that clear eye for others' character and his own, which made him so good a satirist, may have inclined him to despair. Buckhurst was a light-hearted debauchee into whose charming verse seriousness seldom entered; Savile, outside of politics, a good-humoured Falstaff, with a shrewd eye to the limits of drinking; Rochester was the only one of the three conscious of an ideal morality. He confessed to Burnet that all his life long he had 'a secret value and reverence for an honest man and loved morality in others'. His defence of his satires, 'that there were some persons that could not be kept in order, or admonished, but in this way', was not hypocritical, though the spoiled Puritan who spoke was quickly succeeded by the wit and poet who told Burnet that 'the lies in these libels came often in as ornaments, that could not be spared without spoiling the beauty of the poem'.

Debauchery did not come to him in the beautiful beguiling guise of Madam Rampant and the ladies of the town in his friend Etherege's *She Would If She Could*. If he inherited his taste for debauch from his father, there was enough of his stern mother in him to make him see clearly what ugliness he preferred to the 'love, peace and truth' that waited him at Adderbury. Not even that upright, prejudiced woman could have condemned 'Corinna' to a more moral ending than did her son, but there is a hint of a guilty man's compassion for a fellow debauchee in the lines:

> Gay were the hours, and wing'd with joy they flew,
> When first the town her early beauties knew:
> Courted, admir'd, and lov'd, with presents fed,
> Youth in her looks, and pleasure in her bed:
> Till fate, or her ill angel, thought it fit
> To make her doat upon a man of wit:
> Who found 'twas dull to love above a day,
> Made his ill-natur'd jest, and went away.
> Now scorn'd of all, forsaken and opprest,
> She's a *Memento Mori* to the rest:
> Diseas'd, decay'd, to take up half a crown

Must mortgage her long scarf and manto gown:
Poor creature, who unheard of, as a fly
In some dark hole, must all the winter lie:
And want, and dirt, endure a whole half year,
That, for one month, she tawdry may appear.

He did not spare himself if one can take 'The Debauchee' as a self-portrait.

I rise at eleven, I dine about two,
I get drunk before seven, and the next thing I do,
I send for my whore, when for fear of a clap,
I dally about her, and spew in her lap;
There we quarrel and scold till I fall asleep,
When the jilt growing bold, to my pocket does creep;
Then slyly she leaves me, and to revenge the affront,
At once both my lass and my money I want.
If by chance then I wake, hot-headed and drunk,

What a coyl do I make for the loss of my punk?
I storm, and I roar, and I fall in a rage,
And missing my lass, I fall on my page:
Then crop-sick, all morning I rail at my men,
And in bed I lie yawning till eleven again.

So the war went between the Puritan mother, with her gift of
railing, and the fuddled 'good fellow', his father. Rochester could
have declared like the Shropshire lad:

They cease not fighting, east and west,
On the marches of my breast.

At last the body worn out, the fight ended from exhaustion, and
the victory was his mother's.

The sombre desperate mood in which his poetry seems usually
to have been composed was aided by the general disillusionment of
the time. So much had been expected of the Restoration and so
little had come of it; so much had been expected of the war with
Holland, and it brought only disgrace. Vast hopes disappointed
are apt to leave an overmastering weariness behind, and war is not
usually followed by peace of mind. The excitement of war is a drug
that we miss in the dull days after. Spleen was the disease which
ran through the literature of the succeeding quieter years, and
my generation is in a good position to understand it. In a letter to
Savile Rochester wrote: 'The world, ever since I can remember, has
been still so insupportably the same, that 'twere vain to hope there
were any alterations.' Disillusionment, monotony, boredom preyed
worst on the finest spirits. The less sensitive were more easily
contented with the small scandals that took the place of adventure
and wide hopes.

Such a one was Henry Savile, the 'fat boy' of the Court. His
latest exploit was always good for a laugh at the expense of his
unwieldy flesh. In September 1671 John Muddyman, writing to
Rochester, sick in the country, recounted the tale of his attempt on
the virtue of Lady Northumberland.

Edward Hyde, First Earl
of Clarendon

The lady was at my Lord Sunderland's, and the knight errant lodged
in a convenient apartment, from whence in the dead night, tempted
by his evil genius or the earthy part of his love, he made a sally into
her bedchamber, having the day before stole away the bolt so that
there was nothing but a latch to lift, but whether offering any ruder
proofs of his passion or contenting himself with a simple, though
unseasonable declaration of it, her scrupulous virtue was so alarmed
that she rang a little bell that hung unfortunately at her bed's head
with that violence as if not only a poor lover's heart but the whole
house had been on fire. Whereupon her servant coming into the
room our disconsolate lover retired overwhelmed with despair and
so forth. The family breathe nothing but battle, murder and sudden

death, so that either way we are like to lose a very honest fellow, but I hope shall gain this wholesome document; how necessary it is for every man to stick to his own calling.

Life has somehow to be lived, and Rochester drank to make it endurable; he wrote to purge himself of his unhappiness; he tried to supply artificially the adventures which no longer came to him in war and acted the innkeeper and the astrologer; he flung himself, the better to forget the world, into the two extremes, love and hate. Sir Car Scrope, that 'purblind knight', and the Earl of Mulgrave, the King himself, were for him as much the instruments of a passion to escape as were Mrs Barry, Mrs Boutel, Mrs Roberts, and slatternly Nell Browne of Woodstock.

James Scott, Duke of Monmouth

[2] The passion of hate began early. Coupled as it was to ingratitude, one suspects that drink may already have affected Rochester's character by the end of 1667, within ten months of his marriage. On 5 October he had been summoned to the House of Lords with his future arch-enemy, the Earl of Mulgrave. It was a sign of the King's special favour, for both men were under twenty-one years, and they did not take their seats without opposition. On 8 November

in the Lords' house great difficulty hath arisen upon further enquiry whether lords that are under age can even by the King's writ be called to sit there. The case is my Lord Mulgrave and my Lord Rochester, the latter of whom is already in the house by such a writ, and its doubted that, upon the Judges' opinions that a minor cannot be a Judge in a Court of Judicature, they will be refused place and suffrage there.

But the King's will had its way, and in 1670 the Duke of Monmouth was called to the House while still a minor without a voice being raised. Rochester's status as a member of the House of Lords enabled him on 20 November to sign a protest in favour of the Commons' impeachment of the Earl of Clarendon. The occasion marks the first deviation from the high standard of conduct he had set himself in the Dutch War.

In one thing above all others the old Chancellor had been preeminently successful. He had alienated almost every party in the State. Except for the Bench of Bishops, whom he had enabled to take an Oriental revenge on the Nonconformists, there was none to regret his fall or willing to raise a voice to prevent it. The Commons were his enemies because of his support of the Royal prerogative; the Cavaliers hated him as the author of the Act of Indemnity and Oblivion, known by them as an Act of Oblivion for the King's friends and of Indemnity for his enemies; to the

Puritans and Catholics he was the man who had let the Anglican hounds off their leash.

The King had more intimate reasons for disliking the Minister who had done more than any man for his restoration. It was not only that his bearing was magisterial and that he upbraided the King openly for his loose living and neglect of public business; what damaged him more was the report that he had persuaded Mrs Stewart, the Lady-in-Waiting whom the King coveted, secretly to marry the Duke of Richmond. The 'merry gang', of course, were against him. Buckingham when with the King would caricature the gait and manners of the Chancellor and strut with a pair of tongs. The Chancellor's only retort to that melancholy pursuer of pleasure was open contempt. Charges in plenty could be found to fling at his head: he had married the King to a barren woman, so that his own daughter, the Duchess of York, might become queen; he had sold Dunkirk to the French for his private enrichment; he had used the stones of St Paul's to build himself a house.

While the Duke of York was ill of smallpox, the Commons sent to the Lords a general impeachment of the Chancellor for treason. Distrust of the Lower House was greater than the Lords' hatred of the Chancellor, and the impeachment was refused, but a powerful minority, headed by Buckingham and Bristol and including Rochester, signed a protest in favour of impeachment. Clarendon was induced by the King to leave the country in order that the breach between the Houses might be healed. This final proof of loyalty was treated as a confession of guilt, and an Act banished him for ever from the King's dominions.

His fall gave cause for rejoicing to those whom Evelyn called 'the buffoons and ladies of pleasure' and Pepys more particularly 'Bab May, my Lady Castlemaine, and that wicked crew'. Rochester was inspired to one poem on the fall of Clarendon and it is the least happy of his verses in the satiric vein.

> Pride, lust, ambition, and the people's hate,
> The Kingdom's broker, ruin of the State,
> Dunkirk's sad loss, divider of the fleet,
> Tangier's compounder for a barren sheet:
> This shrub of gentry, marry'd to the Crown
> His daughter to the heir, is tumbled down;
> The grand despiser of the nobles lies
> Groveling in dust, as a just sacrifice. . . .

Rochester had made a long journey in a short time from Degree Day at Oxford and the Chancellor's kiss.

But Rochester's most enduring and cherished enmity was for the Earl of Mulgrave, John Sheffield, later Duke of Buckinghamshire.[1] This quarrel was to become part of the literary politics of the age

[1] Not to be confused with the Duke of Buckingham, Rochester's boon companion

76

and led finally in 1678, if rumour is to be believed, to the assault on Dryden. But between the attack on Clarendon and the quarrel with Mulgrave came one of the sudden outbursts of irritation which were to become more frequent as Rochester's health failed. On 17 February 1669 Pepys recorded:

> The King dining yesterday at the Dutch Ambassador's, after dinner they drank and were pretty merry; and among the rest of the King's company, there was that worthy fellow my Lord of Rochester, and Tom Killigrew, whose mirth and raillery offended the former so much, that he did give Tom Killigrew a box on the ear in the King's presence, which do give much offence to the people here at Court, to see how cheap the King makes himself, and the more, for that the King hath not only passed by the thing, and pardoned it to Rochester already, but this very morning the King did publicly walk up and down, and Rochester I saw with him as fine as ever, to the King's everlasting shame, to have so idle a rogue his companion. How Tom Killigrew takes it I do not hear.

That Rochester was drunk we learn from a letter of Lady Sunderland who wrote: 'This has been a very quarrelsome week; before the King my Lord of Rochester forgot his duty so much as to strike Tom Killigrew. He was in a case not to know what he did, but he is forbid the Court.'

The attack was unwise, for Tom Killigrew could claim his jests had royal licence, not only on the stage, where his *Parson's Wedding* proved one of the most amusing and one of the most indecent of Restoration comedies, but at Court. At Court his jests had sometimes a moral tone – which might have proved dangerous with any other King. Pinkethman records how 'King Charles II, being in company with the Lord Rochester and others of the nobility, who had been drinking the best part of the night, Killigrew came in, – Now, says the King, we shall hear of our faults. – No, faith, says Killigrew, I don't care to trouble my head with that which all the town talks of.'

Caution after this quarrel might have advised Rochester to retire for a little into the country, but caution was alien to his nature, and a newsletter of 11 March shows him again in trouble. His friend Savile had been sent to the Tower after carrying a challenge from Buckingham to Sir William Coventry. 'On Tuesday night', the letter states, 'there was a quarrel between the Duke of Richmond and Mr James Hamilton, after they had well dined at the Tower with Sir Henry Savile. They had chosen their seconds, but the Lord General sent for the principals, and put them on their honours not to prosecute it. The Earl of Rochester was one of the party, who, upon his disgrace at Court, intends to go to France for some time.'

He was gone 'upon more sober advice' within ten days, after solemnly asking pardon of Harry Killigrew for the affront he had offered his father.[1]

It was universally assumed that Rochester left for France in disgrace with the King. The King himself may have publicly encouraged the notion, unwilling openly to leave Rochester's offence unpunished, but the disgrace was superficial. The quarrel at the Tower occurred on 9 March and three days later the King was writing from Newmarket to his sister, the Duchess of Orleans: 'This bearer, my Lord Rochester, has a mind to make a little journey to Paris, and would not kiss your hands without a letter from me; pray use him as one I have a very good opinion of; you will find him not to want wit, and did behave himself, in all the Dutch war, as well as any body, as a volunteer.'

It was five years since Rochester had last 'kissed the hands' of the Duchess of Orleans, Charles's 'dear dear sister', to whom the King was more devoted than to any of his mistresses. The next summer she was to visit England to conclude that alliance between England and France against Holland known as the *Traité de Madame*. A little more than three weeks later she was dead and her husband suspected of the murder. Her legacy to her brother was Louise de Kéroualle, later Duchess of Portsmouth, the supplanter of Lady Castlemaine. Burnet described Charles's sister as 'a woman of fine wit, great gallantry, but of keen resentment where she thought herself slighted'; Rochester wrote to his wife, on the news of her death, with feeling not disguised by epigram: 'She died the most lamented (both in France and England) since dying has been the fashion.'

Rochester's stay in France, though according to the English Ambassador he lived discreetly, was not entirely uneventful.

On 1 May William Perwich, the English agent in Paris, wrote to Sir Joseph Williamson: 'On Monday this Court went to St Germains, where the King made a general muster of all his Army, with the ceremony of great guns in the field, and that night he went hence my Lord Rochester was robbed in a chaise (of some 20 pistols and his periwig).'

Another incident during his stay gives credit to his courage, which later in the same year was to be impugned by Lord Mulgrave. Also in Paris at the time was Lord Cavendish, later Duke of Devonshire. On 21 August 1669 Sir John Clayton wrote to Sir Robert Paston that there was

> news from Paris of my Lord Cavendish, his being dangerously ill of seven wounds received in a quarrel which happened in the playhouse when Scaramuchio acted, my Lord Rochester only being in his company; it is said my Lord Cavendish has killed two of the Frenchmen. The story is too long to acquaint you with every particular,

[1] Harry Killigrew shared the family trait of an indiscreet tongue. It was not long since he had been in disgrace for saying that Lady Castlemaine was a little wanton when she was young ('when she was young' being the core of the offence), and before Rochester returned from France he was to be found lying in a hackney coach, half dead, stabbed in nine places by footmen in the pay of Lady Shrewsbury and, as it was believed, her lover, the Duke of Buckingham.

Henrietta Anne, Duchess of
Orleans, Charles's 'dear
dear sister'

but so horrid you never heard of the like, and much to the advantage
of the English; the King of France is so enraged at it as he intends to
hang all the French that were concerned in it, there being at the
least six or seven of them in the business.

Lord Cavendish recovered from his wounds, nor were the
Frenchmen in any danger of their lives. The Ambassador wrote to
Lord Arlington:

The King has put the people in prison that injured my Lord
Cavendish and my Lord Rochester, and has expressed a great
displeasure against them; and the least that will happen to them they
say is losing their employments; but all their friends having spoke

Louis XIV among the ladies of his Court

to me to speak for them to the King, and my Lord Cavendish desiring it too, I spoke to his most Christian Majesty, and entreated him to forgive them, the English having had all the satisfaction that could be desired. He returned me a great many expressions how sorry he was such a thing should happen to be done by his officers to any strangers, much more to the English and to people of that quality; so I believe after some few days they may be forgiven.

In England Elizabeth was expecting her first child. A brief cool letter survives from her husband in Paris, dated 22 April 1669: 'I should be infinitely pleased (Madam) with the news of your health. Hitherto I have not been so fortunate to hear any of you but assure yourself my wishes are of your side as much as is possible and pray only that they may be effectual, and you will not want for happiness.'

As the date of delivery approached Rochester made preparations to return, and applied to the Secretary of State, Arlington, indirectly through the English Ambassador, who wrote on 15 July:

> The reasons of my Lord Rochester's coming into France, I suppose, are not unknown to your Lordship; upon his return into England I believe there is nothing he is more desirous of than your Lordship's favour and countenance; and if hereafter he continues to live as discreetly as he has done ever since he was here, he has other good qualities enough to deserve it, and to make himself acceptable wherever he comes.

This testimonial to discretion comes a little ironically from the Ambassador who was to seduce Lady Sussex in Paris 'to the wonder of the French Court and the high displeasure of this', as Savile wrote to Rochester.

On 30 August Rochester's first child, Anne, was baptized, and it is reasonable to suppose that by that time he was back in England.

[3] At the end of November came the strange affair of the frustrated duel with the Earl of Mulgrave which did more than anything to injure Rochester's reputation for courage, though it is difficult to understand why.

Mulgrave was a man as young as Rochester himself, not yet twenty-three, but his pride was a byword at Court. Rochester was later to lampoon him under the title of 'Monster All-Pride', and his nicknames included 'Haughty' and 'King John'. John Macky in his *Memoirs of the Secret Service* described him as he had become in the fullness of years.

> He is a nobleman of learning, and good natural parts, but of no principles. Violent for the High Church, yet seldom goes to it. Very proud, insolent and covetous, and takes all advantages. In paying his debts unwilling; and is neither esteemed nor beloved: for notwithstanding his great interest at Court, it is certain he has none in either Houses of Parliament, or in the country.

Of his physical appearance Rochester wrote (and even an enemy's caricature must be based on truth if it is to strike home):

> With a red nose, splay foot and goggle eye,
> A plough man's looby mien, face all awry,
> With stinking breath, and ev'ry loathsome mark,
> This Punchinello sets up for a spark.

Mulgrave's hatred of Rochester survived his enemy's death and he flung at the dead man a double taunt in his reference to 'the nauseous songs which the late convert made'.

On the evening of 22 November notice was given at Court of some differences that had happened between the Earls, and an order was immediately made to secure them both. Neither was to be found at his lodgings, nor was any news to be had of them. Mulgrave had spent that night with his second in an inn at Knightsbridge, where they were thought to be highwaymen, but the landlord liked them the better for it. Mulgrave, in his memoirs, gives his own account of the meeting next day; of the cause he states only that he had been informed that the Earl of Rochester 'had said something of me, which, according to his custom, was very malicious'.

It had been arranged that the duel should take place on horseback and Rochester had told Mulgrave's second, Colonel Aston, 'a very mettled' man, that he would bring with him a certain James Porter. But at the place of meeting he appeared not with James Porter but with 'an errant Lifeguardsman whom nobody knew. To this Mr Aston took exception upon the account of his being no suitable adversary; especially considering how extremely well he was mounted, whereas we had only a couple of packs: upon which we all agreed to fight on foot.' Rochester then drew Mulgrave on one side and

> told me he was so weak with a distemper that he found himself unfit to fight at all in any way, much less a-foot. My anger against him being quite over, because I was satisfied that he never spoke those words I resented, I took the liberty of representing what a ridiculous story it would make if we returned without fighting, and therefore advised him for both our sakes, especially for his own, to consider better of it, since I must be obliged in my own defence to lay the fault on him by telling the truth of the matter. His answer was that he submitted to it.

Mulgrave adds, with malice prettily veiled under a show of impartiality, that this 'entirely ruined his reputation as to courage (of which I was really sorry to be the occasion) tho' nobody had still a greater as to wit; which supported him pretty well in the world, notwithstanding some more accidents of the same kind, that never fail to succeed one another when once people know a man's weakness'.

For this last accusation no evidence has come down to us; on at least one future occasion the unwillingness to fight was not on Rochester's side. Mulgrave had agreed to fight on horseback, and he arrived badly horsed. This looks very like an attempt to force Rochester, by the discrepancy of their mounts, to fight on foot. He succeeded in making Rochester withdraw from the duel, for the sickness was not feigned, though the vague word 'distemper' covered an attack of the pox caught perhaps, in spite of his discretion, in Paris. He had been treated with mercury at Mrs Fourcard's 'Baths' in Leather Lane, Hatton Garden, a month before.

A quarrel in those days was quickest ended by the drawing of blood, and the undignified events of 23 November left neither party satisfied. Malice on both sides increased, until it burst out again ten years later in Mulgrave's *Essay on Satire* and involved Dryden just as Rochester's friendship involved Harry Savile, who in December 1674 seems to have attempted to make the long-lived quarrel his own.

> On Sunday night last, King being at supper at Treasurer's, Harry Savile being very drunk, fell so fouly on Lord Mulgrave, that King commanded Savile to be gone out of his presence. However the next day Mulgrave sent him a challenge by Lord Middleton; Rochester was second to the other side. There was no harm done; but D[anby] hath interested himself and prevailed with King to forbid Savile his presence.

John, Earl of Mulgrave, Lord Chamberlain 1688

'Monster All-Pride', John, Earl of Mulgrave

83

The History of the Insipids.

Chast, pious, prudent Charles the Second
The miracle of thy Restoration
may like to that of David be restored
ruined our Israelitish nation.

2
He's veran in thee Charles in true
altho' thy Countenance be an odd peice
prove thee as true a god vicegerent
as ere was harry with ye Codpiece
for Chastity & pious deeds
his Grandsir Harry Charles exceeds

Our Romish bondage breaker Harry
Spowded halfe a douzen wives
Charles only one resolved to marry
& other mens honour swives
yet he hath sonns & daughters more
then ere had harry by threescore

4
Never was such a faith's defender
he like a politick prince & pious
gives Liberty to Consciences tender
& doth to no religion tye us
Jews Christians Turks Papists hee's pleas'd
with Moses, Mahomett or Jesus.

5
In all affairs of Church & State
he very Zealous is & able
devout at prayers, & prettys tale
& ye Caball Counsell Table.
his very Dog at Counsell board
sits grave & wise as any Lord.

6
Let Charles's policy noe man flout
the wisest Kings have all some folly
nor let his piety any doubt
Charles like a Sovraigne wise & holy
makes young men Judges of the bench
and Bishops those that love a wench.

7
his father's foes he doth reward
preserving those that cutt off's head
old Cavaliers the Crownes best guard
he lets them starve for want of bread
never was any King endued
with soe much grace & gratitude.

8
Blood that wears treason in his face
Villaine Compleat in Parsons gowne
how much is he at Court in grace
for stealing Ormond & the Crowne
since Loyalty doth noe man good
lett's steale the King & outdoe Blood.

9
A Parliament of knaves & sotts
members by name wee must not mention
he boughts to pay & buys their votes
here with a place there will a pension
when he with money can't Colloque them
he doth with frowns prorogue prorogue them.

10
But they long since by too much giving
undid, betrayd & sold ye nation;
making their memberships a living
better then ere was sequestration
God give thee Charles a Resolution
to damn ye knaves by dissolution.

11
ffame is not grounded on successe
the victorys were Cæsars glory
lost battells made not pompey lesse
but left him still great in story.
malicious fate doth oft devise
to beate ye brave, & foole ye wise.

12
Charles in the first Dutch warr stood faire
to have been Soveraigne of the Deep,
when Opdam blowne up in the aire,
had not his highnesse gone to sleep,
our fleet slack tacks so let spareing by waking
the Dutch had else been in sad takeing

13
The Burgen busnesse was well layd.
tho' we paied deare for that designe
had we not three days of parling stayd
the Dutch fleet Charley there had been thine
tho' the falser Dane resolved to sell them
to Chevadeny & saved St Kolem.

14
Had not Charles sweetly chows'd the states
by Bergen Battle growne more wise
& made them shitt as small as Ratts
by their rich Smyrna fleet surprize
that hang'elty Holmes but sailed in spraig
Hans had been put into a bagg.

15
misse, stormes, shole virtually, adverse winds,
& once ye enemyes wise Division;
defeated Charles his best designes
till he became his foes division
but he had swinged the Dutch at Chatam
had he had ships but to some at them

v The Poet and the King

The encounter with Mulgrave, and the lies spread of his cowardice, may well have been the final cause of Rochester's quarrel with the world. The world despised him – very well, he would despise the world. His pen should return the strokes he suffered from men's tongues.

> Oh, but the world will take offence hereby!
> Why then the world shall suffer for't, not I.

Hatred sharpened his wit, his Puritan inheritance lent him moral fervour, and his life gave him the words, words from the taverns and the stews of Whetstone Park, seldom heard before in serious literature.

He had not far to look for subjects in the Stuart London of narrow streets, the Stuart Parliaments of narrow minds. Everywhere was vice, incompetence, physical ugliness. With the patriotism of the volunteer who had witnessed in the Downs the Navy broken and in flight, because the ships were undermanned and the men ill-fed, he singled out the King's mistresses who were absorbing both his treasure and his vitality; soon Charles himself was the victim of his pen.

> Chaste, pious, prudent C—— the Second,
>   The miracle of thy restoration
> May like to that of quails be reckon'd,
>   Rain'd on the Israelitish nation;
> The wish'd for blessing from Heav'n sent
> Became their curse and punishment.

He was banished the Court for this poem, 'The History of Insipids', but while they were the wittiest, they were not the strongest terms in which he wrote of the King.

> Restless he rolls about from whore to whore,
> A merry monarch, scandalous and poor.

> Nor are his high desires above his strength;
> His sceptre and his —— are of a length.

With a mingling of hate (it was his Puritan upbringing) and envy

most Magnificent Riding of Charles ye II to the Parliament — De Konincklijcke rijding van Carolis de II tot sijn Parlem
The Kings Majesty   D Lord Chancelor   A de Konincklijcke Majesteyt   D de heer Kanselier
The Duke of Yorke   E Duke of Bukingam   B de Hartogh van Iorck   E de Hartogh van Bockenga
the Duke of Albemarle, leading his   F Duke of Ormond   C de Generael Monck   F de Hartogh van Ormond
majesties Horse of State   G Captaine of the guard   ... het wijamt Paert   G de Kapetijn van de Gaerd

Charles II's progress to parliament

'Nor are his high desires
        above his strength;
His sceptre and his —
        are of a length.'

(he was the son of Henry Wilmot) he followed the King's pleasures.

> So well, alas! the fatal bait is known,
> Which Rowley does so greedily take down;
> And howe'er weak and slender be the string,
> Bait it with whore and it will hold a king.

Under any other sovereign, Rochester's career would have prematurely ended, but wit in the days of Charles could cover even treason. Reflections on the King and his mistresses which cost Sir John Coventry his nose cost Rochester, time and again, no more than a few weeks' banishment from Court. The relations of the King and the poet were strange ones. Up to the last years of his life the Earl was receiving many favours from the King, whom he continued to lampoon. He can be compared with the medieval jester speaking bitter truths and receiving sometimes gold and sometimes cuffs. Hamilton states that he was banished from Court once a year; this is probably a humorous exaggeration, but it seems likely that he was banished on at least three occasions for poems on the King and his mistresses.

What did Rochester owe the King? The list of benefits is a long one. In 1664 Charles had recommended him as a suitor to Elizabeth Mallet: the next year he granted him £750 after the Bergen expedition. In 1666 he appointed him a Gentleman of the Bedchamber with a pension of £1,000 a year and summoned him in 1667 to the House of Lords, although Rochester was not of age. In February 1668 he appointed him Keeper of the King's Game in the County of Oxford, and in April Rochester was petitioning for a grant of the offices of four bailiwicks in Whittlewood Forest. In 1673 he was granted, in company with Laurence Hyde (Master of the Robes) and the notorious royal pimp William Chiffinch (Keeper of the Closet), the park or late park of Bestwood and the four loads of hay out of Lenton Mead, Nottinghamshire, to be held by them for ever in free and common socage at the rent of £5; 'being granted to them as a mark of the King's favour and bounty in consideration of many and faithful services'. In 1674 Rochester was appointed Keeper and Ranger of Woodstock Park, with a lodge called High Lodge for residence. (This was in some ways the most important favour the King granted him and it revoked the appointment in 1670 of Lord Lovelace. Woodstock from that time shared with Adderbury the Earl's summers, and it was there that he died in the great gloomy bed long shown to visitors.)[1]

In April of the next year he again shared an appointment with Chiffinch, on the surrender of Sir Allen and Sir Peter Apsley. This was the Mastership of the King's Hawks, and on 23 June a Royal Warrant was issued him for a grant of the manors of Twickenham and Edmonton, the manor of East and West Deeping, Lincs., and the manor of Chertsey, for forty-one years. (Three days later he was drunk and tearing down the rare dial in the Privy Garden.)

It is more difficult to understand what Charles owed Rochester, what induced the King to endure for so long the complete lack of respect. Perhaps only in the King's abysmal cynicism can an

[1] Some anger seems to have been caused by the Royal grant. On 28 March William Harbord wrote to the Earl of Essex that 'Arlington had a cruel dispute with Anglesey yesterday and told him that he was a knave, which is too true.' That this dispute concerned Rochester is known from Anglesey's diary. Arlington was a proud, capable man, who knew how to manage the King, while Anglesey was generally discredited, 'for he sold everything in his power, and himself, so oft, that at last the price fell so low that he grew useless and contemptible'. In his diary under date 27 March this man who 'stuck at nothing' records: 'After Council, Lord Arlington, upon my passing Lord Rochester's grant by the King's command, said, before Lord Keeper and many more, that I understood not the duty of my place; that he never looked for better from me, that by God I served everybody so, and would do so to the end of the chapter.'

The High Lodge, Woodstock Park, granted to Rochester by the King

explanation be found. We have Burnet's word for that. 'He thought no man sincere, nor woman honest, out of principle; but that whenever they proved so, humour or vanity was at the bottom of it. No one, he fancied, served him out of love, and therefore he endeavoured to be quits with the world by loving others as little as he thought they loved him.' To be quits with the world – it was a phrase Rochester might have used, but there was a difference. Rochester remained an idealist. He loved morality in others, and there was an ideal of Kingship to which Charles did not attain.

Only occasionally do we catch glimpses of friendliness for Charles Stuart the man, who loved music and appreciated wit. 'The best present I can make at this time', Rochester writes to Savile, 'is the bearer, whom I beg you to take care of, that the King may hear his tunes, when he is easy and private, because I am sure they will divert him extremely', and one hears from Savile how Charles 'has heard with very great delight Paisible's new compositions, and was not less pleased at all the compliments you bestowed upon him; but I would not have you think he takes so much pleasure in your good wishes as in your good company'. Burnet thought otherwise, that 'the King loved his company for the diversion it afforded better than his person. And there was no love lost between them. He took his revenges in many libels.'

Contemporaries are often blinded by propinquity. Rochester had been Charles's pimp (it was his own description) and his jester, but it is difficult to believe there was no fondness at all between them. His wit was not always used at the King's expense but sometimes purely for his diversion. The famous extempore epitaph:

> Here lies a great and mighty king,
>   Whose promise none relies on;
> He never said a foolish thing,
>   Nor ever did a wise one,

evoked the more witty reply that 'My words are my own, but my acts are my ministers'.' Another occasion of extempore wit, with good humour uppermost, is recorded by Hearne.

King Charles II, Duke of York, Duke of Monmouth, Laurendine, and Frazier (the King's physician) being in company, my Lord Rochester upon the King's request, made the following verses:

> Here's Monmouth the witty,
> Laurendine the pretty,
>   And Frazier the great physician;
> But as for the rest,
> Take York for a jest,
>   And yourself for a great politician.

The Royal BANQUETING-HOUSE in Whitehal.

Hearne explains the point of the verses in a series of footnotes: Monmouth was 'a half witted man', Laurendine 'a deformed person', Frazier 'a mean empty physician'; York 'would not take a jest', while the King 'was negligent and careless'. And in an eighteenth-century commonplace book can be found these lines ascribed to Rochester. They have a country ring about them, as though indeed they might have been written by the Rochester of Adderbury:

> Under King Charles II's Picture.
> 'I John Roberts writ this same,
> I pasted it and plaistered it, and put it in a frame.
> In honour of my master's master,
> King Charles the Second by name.'

In a volume entitled *Mr Waller's Letters to M. St Evremond* a scene is described in which Rochester's wit is shown at its friendliest, coaxing Charles Stuart from tired anger to amusement. It is more than doubtful whether Waller ever wrote these letters, but the scene may not on that account be wholly fictitious; some of the phrases bear the stamp of the real Rochester.

Last night I supped at Lord Rochester's with a select party: on such occasions he is not ambitious of shining; he is rather pleasant than not: he is comparatively reserved; but you find something in that restraint, which is more agreeable than the utmost exertions of talent in others. . . . The most perfect good-humour was supported through the whole evening; nor was it in the least disturbed when unexpectedly towards the end of it the King came in. 'Something has vexed him,' said Rochester, 'he never does me this honour, but when he is in an ill-humour.'

The following dialogue then ensued:

The King: How the devil have I got here? The knaves have sold every cloak in the wardrobe.

Rochester: Those knaves are fools. That is a part of dress, which, for their own sakes, your Majesty ought never to be without.

The King: Pshaw! I'm vexed.

Rochester: I hate still-life – I'm glad of it. Your Majesty is never so entertaining as when –

The King: Ridiculous! I believe the English are the most intractable people upon earth.

Rochester: I most humbly beg your Majesty's pardon if I presume in that respect.

The King: You would find them so were you in my place and obliged to govern.

Rochester: Were I in your Majesty's place I would not govern at all.

The King: How then?

Rochester: I would send for my good Lord Rochester and command him to govern.

The King: But the singular modesty of that nobleman –

Rochester: He would certainly conform himself to your Majesty's bright example. How gloriously would the two grand social virtues flourish under his auspices!

The King: O, *prisca fides*! What can these be?

Rochester: The love of wine and women.

The King: God bless your Majesty!

Rochester: These attachments keep the world in good humour, and therefore I say they are social virtues. Let the Bishop of Salisbury deny it if he can.

The King: He died last night; have you a mind to succeed him?

Rochester: On condition that I shall neither be called upon to preach on the thirtieth of January [the date of Charles I's execution], nor on the twenty-ninth of May [the date of the Restoration].

The King: These conditions are curious. You object to the first, I suppose, because it would be a melancholy subject, but the other –

Rochester: Would be a melancholy subject too.

The King: That is too much –

Rochester: Nay, I only mean that the business would be a little too grave for the day. Nothing but the indulgence of the two grand social virtues could be a proper testimony of my joy upon that occasion.

The King: Thou art the happiest fellow in my dominions. Let me perish if I do not envy thee thy impudence.

Note the true Rochester ring of 'I hate still-life.'

That the King on at least one occasion did visit Rochester's lodgings and there 'make merry' is known. In February 1677 Lord Buckingham, with Salisbury, Shaftesbury, and Wharton, was committed to the Tower. They had argued that Parliament was *ipso facto* dissolved by a prorogation of more than a year, and had refused to ask pardon of the King and the House. It was a peculiarly muddled occasion. Buckingham and Shaftesbury had been bribed by Louis, Charles's secret ally, to get rid of a Parliament from which Danby, Charles's Treasurer, had promised the King to obtain supplies if he would break with France. Charles, his foot in either camp, watched his minister commit the Lords to the Tower with mixed feelings. Expediency, the code by which he ruled, seemed to point in two directions. It was the moment for intervention by the 'merry gang', and on 2 August W. Fall was writing to Sir Ralph Verney, Rochester's former guardian,

> The great discourse of the town is that the Duke of Bucks shall be restored to favour and be Lord Steward of the Household in place of the Duke of Ormond; but of this they are very silent at Court, only his sacred Majesty and his Grace (I hear) were very merry one night at Lord Rochester's lodgings, which, I conceive, created this discourse . . .

and on 7 August in a letter from Andrew Marvell to Sir Edward Harley the influence of Rochester's circle is revealed:

Rochester (left) followed Buckingham 'the lord of useless thousands', along his dismal road

The Duke of Buckingham petitioned only that he had laid so long, had contracted several indispositions, and desired a month's air. This was by Nelly, Middlesex, Rochester and the merry gang easily procured with presumption to make it an entire liberty. Hereupon he laid constantly at Whitehall at my Lord Rochester's lodgings, leading the usual life. The Duke of York, the Treasurer, and, they tell me, the Duke of Monmouth remonstrated to the King that this was to leap over all rules of decency and to suffer his authority to be trampled on, but if he had a favour for him he might do it in a regular way. Nevertheless it was for some days a moot point betwixt the Ministers of State and ministers of pleasure who should carry it. At last Buckingham was advertised that he should retire out of Whitehall. He obeyed and since presented they say a more acknowledging petition than either Salisbury's or Wharton's. Whereupon I hear that he was yesterday by the same rule dismissed.

Save when he spoke against the Bill for excluding the Duke of York from the throne this is the only occasion on which Rochester is known to have played a political part, but the operations of the merry gang were perforce carried on by candlelight, when the wine was on the table.

It was in his relations with the King that the mountebank element in Rochester's character emerged. As a jester softens his jibe with a tumble, so Rochester would come again into favour with a piece of play-acting. One may see here some resemblance to his father, dressed in his yellow periwig, talking French, and disclosing the nature of his disguise at every tavern. So the son too discloses himself, whether he is playing an innkeeper on the Newmarket Road, a City gentleman, a quack selling his wares on Tower Hill. He reveals himself by the strain of seriousness in his acting: the Newmarket adventure ends in tragedy, the City gentleman inveighs in Rochester's own accents against the follies of the Court, the quack in his broadside satirizes all London. In these adventures no less than in the lampoons, the spoiled Puritan is disclosed: the man who hated immorality in others, who might have been a second Donne with his twisted, passionate, metaphysical mind, if he had not lived in a time when Hobbes was all the fashion, when the ghosts of men slain in battle did not return to give notice of a future state.

[2] The dates of these desperate attempts to find amusement are matter for conjecture, as are the causes which led to them. The Newmarket exploit rests solely on the evidence of 'St Evremond', but it is not intrinsically unlikely. Burnet does not record it, but there are many stories which he does not detail belonging to this instinct for masquerade. 'He had not been long there [at Court]

before he gave himself up to all sorts of extravagance, to gross impiety and profaneness, and committed the wildest frolics that a wanton fancy could devise; for he would have gone about the streets as a beggar, made love as a porter, set up a stage as a mountebank. . . .'

The story tells how Buckingham and Rochester, happening to be in disgrace at Court at the same time, became landlords of an inn on the Newmarket Road. It has been identified, I do not know on what evidence, by Hore, the historian of the turf, as the Green Mare Inn at Six Mile Bottom. Here they dispensed such generous hospitality that all the husbands in the neighbourhood came there to drink and brought their wives. While the husbands grew drunk, Rochester and Buckingham courted the women. But one old man, who was married to a young and beautiful wife, came every evening alone, leaving his wife at home in the care of his sister. Rochester's interest was aroused by the difficulty of the conquest. One night, while Buckingham plied the old man with drink, the Earl dressed himself in women's clothes and knocked at the door of the house. The old sister opened it and Rochester drew from his skirts a bottle of cordial which he said her brother had sent her from the inn. She had no sooner admitted him, when he was overtaken by sickness and fell in an apparent faint to the floor. The wife and sister carried him upstairs and laid him on a bed and poured some of his own spirits down his throat. For this bottle he substituted a bottle of opium, which set the old sister when she tasted it fast asleep, and the wife began to complain of her husband, who, too

A seventeenth-century inn

93

old to give her pleasure himself, shut her within doors. Rochester soon learned from her complaints that there would be no danger in discovering himself, and after they had enjoyed each other, he persuaded her to return with him to the inn, but first she broke open her husband's boxes and took his savings. On their way to the inn, as they were crossing a field, they saw the husband returning and lay down to escape detection. He passed close by but did not see them, and they repeated their enjoyment before he was out of

¶ Certaine wholesome Observations and

Rules fo Jnne-keepers, and also for their Guests, meet to be fixed vpon the wall of euery Chamber in the house ; but meant more specially for the good of M.ͬ *Henry Hunter* and his wife, of *Smithfield,* his louing brother and sister, and of the Guests which vse their house.

1. WE Reade of Inkeepers that they were of ancient time, as in *Ios.* 2. *Iudg.* 19. verse. 21.22.
2. Our Sauiour in the Gospel commends the vse of Innes. *Luke* 10. ver. 34. and brought to an Inne.
3. Yea Christ himselfe by his owne presence did sanctifie the vse of Innes by eating his passeouer there. *Mat.* 26. 18.
4. In *Acts* 28. there is expresse mention of an Inne with approbation and liking. They came to meet vs at the market of *Appius,* and at the three Tauerns.
5 Common experience sheweth all men what vse there is of Innes for ease of Trauailers, that their bodies which are the members of Christ, and Temples of the holy ghost appointed to a glorious resurrection, may be refreshed after wearisome labour.
6 It must not be accounted a small matter to affoord house roome, lodging, rest and food to the comforts of Gods children.

Rules for Innekeepers.

1. THough your house (as an Inne) bee open for all men to come vnto , yet account honest men your best guests : euer hold their company better then their roomes.
2 Amongst honest men, et such as be religious withal, be most welcome. The feet of the Saints are blessed, and often leaue b essings behind them , as we read of *Ioseph. Gen.* 39. 45.
3. Of religious and godly men let faithfull Ministers haue heartiest intertainement. The feet of such as bring glad tidings of peace and good things, oh how beautifull are they. *Rom.* 10. Such as receiue a Prophet in the name of a Prophet shal haue a Prophets reward. *Mat.* 10. Be not so glad of your gain, as that you may pleasure such.
4 Because your guests be Gods children, and their bodies the members of Christ, let their vsage for meat, lodging, diet, and sleepe bee such as becomes such ; worthy personages , as bee heires with God, euen fellow heires. with Christ. *Rom.* 8.
5. In seruing and louing your guests, remember you do serue and loue God, who takes all as done to himselfe, which for his sake is done to his. *Mat.* 25. 34. 33. 36.
6. Content your selues with an honest gaine, so vsing your guests as they may haue an appetite to returne to you when they are gone from you.
7 Make choice of good seruants , such as know God and make conscience of their waies: for these are likeliest to be true, faithfull, diligent, and cheerefull in their seruice; also such will best please your best guests, and will not iustly offend your worst Moreouer, God will cause your busines to prosper best in the hands of such.
8. Giue your seruants no euill example in word or deed, beare not with their lying, deceit, swearing, prophaning of the Sabbath, or wantonnes. Cause them to keepe the Lords day holy, going to the Church by turnes : examine them how they profit by Sermons; loue such seruants best, as most loue Gods word.

Rules for Guests.

1. VSe an Inne not as your owne house, but as an Inne; not to dwell in but to rest for such time as ye haue iust and needfull occasion and then to returne to your owne families.
2. Remember ye are in the world as in an Inne to tarry for a short space; and then to be gone hence.
3. At night when ye come to your Inne thanke God for your Preseruation : next morning pray for a good Iourney.
4. Eat and drinke for necessity and strength, and not for lust.
5. At table let your talke be powdred with the salt of heauenly wisedome, as your meat is seasoned with material and earthly salt.
6. Aboue all abhorre all oathes, cursing and blasphemy, for God will not hold him guiltlesse which taketh his name in vaine.

FINIS.   T.W.

Rochester's poetry in the eighteenth century was illustrated by cheap cuts which often, as in this case, bore no relation to the text

sight. When they reached the inn, Buckingham took her in his turn, but the interest of the adventure was over, and they sent the girl to London with the suggestion that she find another husband. The one she had betrayed, discovering his wife gone and his savings stolen, hanged himself from a beam. Soon afterwards Charles and the Court arrived at the inn on the way to Newmarket; Buckingham and Rochester disclosed themselves, and their story atoned for their offence.

Newmarket was a town of mirth and legend. Foreign observers watched with some awe how the Court amused itself there, sometimes three times in the year, noticing that 'the stables are all wainscoted and sculptured, and . . . horses are fed with new-laid eggs and Spanish wine'. The King rode his own horses, sometimes to victory, got drunk on the road and made the fiddlers at his inn sing all the obscene songs they knew, watched Lord Digby walk five miles within the hour over the heath 'stark naked and barefoot', met the jockeys at supper.

According to Theophilus Cibber it was at Newmarket that Rochester contrived with one of Charles's mistresses a stratagem to cure the King of 'nocturnal rambles'.

He agreed to go out one night with him to visit a celebrated house of intrigue, where he told his Majesty the finest women in England were to be found. The King made no scruple to assume his usual disguise and accompany him, and while he was engaged with one of the ladies of pleasure, being before instructed by Rochester how to behave, she picked his pocket of all his money and watch, which the King did not immediately miss. Neither the people of the house, nor the girl herself was made acquainted with the quality of their visitor, nor had the least suspicion who he was. When the intrigue was ended, the King enquired for Rochester but was told he had quitted the house, without taking leave: but into what embarrassment was he thrown when upon searching his pockets, in order to discharge the reckoning, he found his money gone? He was then reduced to ask the favour of the Jezebel to give him credit till tomorrow as the gentleman who had gone in with him had not returned, who was to have pay'd for both. The consequence of this request was, he was abused and laughed at; and the old woman told him that she had often been served such dirty tricks, and would not permit him to stir till the reckoning was paid, and then called one of her bullies to take care of him. . . . After many altercations, the King at last proposed, that she should accept a ring which he then took off his finger, in pledge for her money, which she likewise refused, and told him, that as she was no judge of the value of the ring, she did not choose to accept such pledges. The King then desired that a jeweller might be called to give his opinion of the value of it, but he was answered that the expedient was impracticable, as no jeweller could then be supposed to be out of bed. After much entreaty his Majesty at last prevailed upon the fellow to knock up a jeweller and show him the ring, which as soon as he had inspected, he stood amazed, and inquired with eyes fixed upon the fellow, who he had got in his house? to which he answered, a black-looking ugly son of a w——, who had no money in his pocket, and was obliged to pawn his ring. The ring, says the jeweller, is so immensely rich, that but one man in the nation could afford to wear it; and that one is the King. The jeweller, being astonished at this accident, went out with the bully, in order to be fully satisfied of so extraordinary an affair; and as soon as he entered the room, he fell on his knees, and with the utmost respect presented the ring to his Majesty. The old Jezebel and the bully, finding the extraordinary quality of their guest, were now confounded, and asked pardon most submissively on their knees. The King in the best-natured manner forgave them, and laughing asked them whether the ring would not bear another bottle.

[3] If his cynicism caused the King to endure Rochester's jests and satires, he must often have been urged to harshness by his mistresses. Nell Gwyn remained Rochester's friend, the Duchess of Cleveland (the former Castlemaine pensioned off in 1670 as a Duchess) and Louise de Kéroualle, the Duchess of Portsmouth, became his enemies. It was Cleveland who is said to have boxed his ears when he attempted to kiss her as she alighted from her carriage and received the impromptu witticism:

> By Heavens! 'Twas bravely done!
> First, to attempt the Chariot of the Sun,
> And then to fall like Phaeton.

In 1678 Rochester's letters to Savile show that the Duchess of Portsmouth was using her influence with the King against him: 'she has ne'er accused me of any crime, but of being cunning: and

'Chaste, pious, prudent Charles the Second'

(overleaf) Mr Rose, the royal gardener, presenting Charles II with the first pineapple successfully raised in England

I told her, somebody had been cunninger than I to persuade her so', and again with growing uneasiness: 'I do not know how to assure myself the D. will spare me to the King who would not to you.'

But it was the rather miserable, ageing band of the King's mistresses who had most cause to be uneasy, as each gave way in turn to a younger rival, losing their looks with miscarriages and high living. Age was an implacable and incorruptible enemy, and they found his minor victories, the falling of the hair, the wrinkles, the decaying teeth, recorded in a merciless poetic gazette.

The Duchess of Cleveland was the first to fail. She was Rochester's kinswoman, she had furthered his marriage, but he had not spared her; he had followed all her infidelities to Charles and had recorded them; Monmouth and Cavendish, Henningham and Scrope, 'scabby Ned', 'sturdy Franck'.

> When she has jaded quite,
> Her almost boundless appetite . . .
> She'll still drudge on in tasteless vice,
> As if she sinn'd for exercise.

His information may have been derived in the way Burnet describes. 'To gain him intelligence there [at Court] he employed a footman, who knew almost everybody, to stand, all winter long, every night as a sentinel at such ladies' doors as he believed might be in any intrigues. By this means he made many discoveries, and when he was thus furnished with materials, he retired in the country and wrote libels.'

There was no safety for the royal mistresses. While the three-cornered contest went on, Cleveland against Portsmouth, and age against them both, they must always have been aware of this poetic spy, this Protean adversary from whom there was no safety. He had vanished from London – but their maids might be telling their mistresses' secrets to a doctor on Tower Hill; he was in the country, but his footmen were at Court, and his friends were writing him letters: 'My Lady Portsmouth has been ill to the greatest degree. The King imputes her cure to his drops, but her confessor to the Virgin Mary, to whom he is said to have promised in her name that in case of recovery she should have no more commerce with that known enemy to virginity and chastity, the Monarch of Great Britain.'

He was never without material. And there were times when he struck, not in the more or less hidden form of lampoons, which might not reach the King's eyes, but in the open Court. There was the occasion when Elkanah Settle's *Empress of Morocco* was performed at Court, in 1671. The Duchess of Cleveland was on the point of final defeat. Shaken two years before by the arrival of

Louise de Kéroualle, Duchess of Portsmouth
'To varnish and smooth o'er those graces, You rubb'd off in your night embraces: To set your hair, your eyes and teeth, And all those powers you conquer with.'

101

Barbara Villiers, Duchess of
Cleveland and Countess of
Castlemaine, as Minerva
'[Cleveland] I say is
        much to be admir'd,
Although she ne're was
            satisfied or tired.
Full forty men a day
    provided for this whore,
Yet like a bitch she
    wags her tail for more.'

Nell Gwyn she was to be beaten off the field by the end of 1671 by
Louise de Kéroualle. So the old mistress sat with her successful
rivals and heard Lady Elizabeth Howard speak Rochester's Prologue
to the play. The claws were veiled, the occasion was polite, but
the irony must have been none the less evident to Cleveland. The
Prologue was addressed directly to the King.

> To you (Great SIR) my message hither tends,
> From youth and beauty, your allies and friends.
> See my credentials written in my face.
> They challenge your protection in this place,
> And hither come with such a force of charms,
> As may give check ev'n to your prosperous arms. . . .
> Nor can you 'scape our soft captivity,
> From which old age alone must set you free.
> Then tremble at the fatal consequence,
> Since 'tis well known, for your own part, great Prince,
> 'Gainst us still you have made a weak defence.

Nell Gwyn
'She's now the darling
strumpet of the crowd.'

The conquering beauties may have applauded the lines, but the
defeated and ageing Cleveland perhaps preferred Rochester in his
more brutal mood, which recognized at least her importance.

> Who can abstain from satire in this age?
> What nature wants I find supply'd by rage.
> Some do for pimping, some for treach'ry use;
> But none's made great for being good or wise.
> Deserve a dungeon, if you would be great,
> Rogues always are our ministers of state;
> Mean prostrate bitches, for a Bridewell fit,
> With England's wretched Queen must equal sit.

It was his cruel veracious answer to Lovel's question in Shadwell's *Sullen Lovers*: 'Why dost thou abuse this age so? Methinks
it's as pretty an honest, drinking, whoring age as a man would
wish to live in.'

VI The Affray at Epsom

Meanwhile the five years of continual drunkenness passed on towards their tragic climax at Epsom. There were quarrels during those years of which we know no more than such bare facts as are provided in news-sheets; that, for instance, of 25 March 1673 which states that 'a duel between the Earl of Rochester and Lord Dunbar has been prevented by the timely intervention of the Earl Marshal'. The drunken frolics grew more senseless and more mischievous. On 26 June 1675 a letter is sent to Edinburgh telling how: 'My Lord Rochester in a frolic after a rant did yesterday beat down the dial which stood in the middle of the Privy Garden, which was esteemed the rarest in Europe. I do not know if upon that account he will be found impertinent, or if it is by the fall beat in pieces.' The same 'frolic' is mentioned by Sir Francis Fane the Elder, in his Commonplace Book. Lord Rochester's companions were Lord Middlesex, Lord Sussex and Harry Savile and they had been 'deboshing all night with the King'. When they came to the dial, on the way to their lodgings, they remarked 'Kings and Kingdoms tumble down and so shall thou' and took it in their arms and flung it down.

The youth who twelve years before had arrived at Court and charmed all with his wit, beauty and learning had become a vexation. He had alienated the King's mistresses with his satires (all except the easy-going Nell Gwyn); the King admired his wit but was weary of offering himself as a subject of it; to such sober men as Evelyn he was no more than a 'profane wit', and profanity was going out of fashion. In the sixties there had been a time for mirth; now in the seventies was a time for seriousness. Sedley and Buckhurst, who had shown themselves naked on an inn balcony in Covent Garden, were turning to politics, even fat merry Savile became an ambassador. His friends were growing as weary of Rochester as he had grown of mankind, and some, like Greenhill, the painter, who was found drunk and dying in a ditch, were finished with the world. Disease was darkening Rochester's mind, which yet remained, next to Dryden's, the most acute critic of the age. Others had danced upon the ice, but he had always known what dwelt below, the horrors of incompetency and sadism which

Dr Alexander Bendo, The Noble Mountebank

105

emerged in the terror of the Popish Plot. With the exception of Buckingham, and in the affray at Epsom Etherege, the companions of his frolics had become very obscure, a certain Captain Bridges, a Mr William Jepson, a Mr Downes.

All these three were with him at Epsom (the same town where Buckhurst and Sedley and Nell Gwyn kept 'merry house' in the more carefree days) in the summer of 1676. On 29 June Charles Hatton in a letter to his brother told the whole story:

> Mr Downes is dead. The Lord Rochester doth abscond, and so doth Etherege and Capt. Bridges who occasioned the riot Sunday sennight. They were tossing some fiddlers in a blanket for refusing to play, and a barber, upon the noise, going to see what the matter, they seized upon him, and, to free himself from them, he offered to carry them to the handsomest woman in Epsom, and directed them to the constable's house, who demanding what they came for, they told him a whore and, he refusing to let them in, they broke open his doors and broke his head, and beat him very seriously. At last, he made his escape, called his watch, and Etherege made a submissive oration to them and so far appeased them that the constable dismissed his watch. But presently after, the Lord Rochester drew upon the constable. Mr Downes, to prevent his pass, seized on him, the constable cried out murther, and, the watch returning, one came behind Mr Downes and with a spittle staff cleft his skull. The Lord Rochester and the rest run away, and Downes, having no sword, snatched up a stick and striking at them, they run him into the side with a half pike, and so bruised his arm that he was never able to stir it after.

Rochester had gone too far at last. For some time it was thought that he would be put on trial for murder. The Earl of Anglesey in a letter to Essex on 27 June stated that he was to be tried, and on 1 July Harbord wrote to Essex: 'Yesterday, the Lord Cornwallis was tried by his peers. . . . My Lord Rochester's turn will be next.' But the trial never took place; Rochester had absconded, and by the time he returned to Court, he had earned his forgiveness from the King.

Where had Rochester gone? In August he was at Adderbury, but by that time the storm had passed. It seems probable that the interval was filled by the best authenticated of his masquerades and that during July he played the part of doctor and astrologer on Tower Hill. For his adventure as an innkeeper there is only 'St Evremond's' word, but the story of 'Alexander Bendo' is told by Anthony Hamilton, though he includes details which belong to another occasion and another quack; the broadside which Rochester is said to have issued advertising his cures is to be found printed as early as 1710 in a collection of Sedley's poems, and best of all

The Famous Pathologist

or the

Noble Mountebank

represented

In a true Copy of an Originall

Bill,

sett forth by Doct.ᵣ Alexandᵣ Bendo
when he aim'd at Phisical Practise,
and shott his Experimental Darts,
at the Greedy to be Wounded.

To Henry Bayton Esq.ʳ

and the

Lady Ann his Wife

at Farely Castle

upon

New Years day. 1687.

Si populus vult decipi
decipiantur.

D.ᵣ Rabelais.

authentications, the masquerade is mentioned by Dr Burnet:[1]

> For his other studies, they were divided between the comical and witty writings of the ancients and moderns, the Roman authors, and books of physic: which the ill state of health he was fallen into made more necessary to himself: and which qualified him for an odd adventure, which I shall but just mention. Being under an unlucky accident, which obliged him to keep out of the way, he disguised himself, so that his nearest friends could not have known him, and set up in Tower-street for an Italian mountebank, where he practised physic for some weeks not without success.

The passage is of importance in attempting to fix the date and the cause of the adventure. It has generally been assumed that a lampoon had led on this occasion to his banishment from Court; there is in an early edition of his works a poem on the King and his mistresses entitled 'A Satire on King Charles II for which he was banished the Court and set up as a mountebank on Tower Hill.' But a lampoon seems hardly to fit Burnet's phrase 'an unlucky accident, which obliged him to keep out of the way'. It is true that there had been, in the case of another poem, something of an unlucky accident, when the King asked for some verses on the ladies of the Court and was handed an attack on himself, perhaps the verses entitled 'A Satire the King took out of his Pocket', which contains the following exhortation:

> Go read what Mahomet did (that was a thing
> Did well become the grandeur of a King)
> Who all transported with his mistress' charms,
> And never pleas'd but in her lovely arms;
> Yet, when his janizaries wish't her dead,
> With his own hand cut off Irene's head.

But a lampoon, however bitterly phrased, entailed at worst a retirement into the country. The phrase 'unlucky accident' better fits the death of Downes at Epsom.

Alexander Bendo in his 'Advertisement' declares: 'The knowledge of these secrets I gathered in my travels abroad (where I have spent my time ever since I was fifteen years old, to this my nine and twentieth year) in France and Italy.' It would not be out of keeping with the general tenor of the broadside to find in it some autobiographical truth. Rochester had gone abroad to France and Italy when he was, if not fifteen, at any rate fourteen years and seven months old, and if at the time of the masquerade he was twenty-nine, it must have taken place in 1676, the year of the affray at Epsom.

It is likely enough then that he disappeared from his home in London to reappear in a complete disguise 'so that his nearest

[1] Professor Pinto has in fact provided the best verification of all by discovering a copy of the original bill made by Rochester's servant Alcock for Rochester's eldest daughter, Lady Anne Baynton, in 1687. Where Alcock's copy differs from that of 1710, I have made changes, but it is remarkable how small these are. (1973)

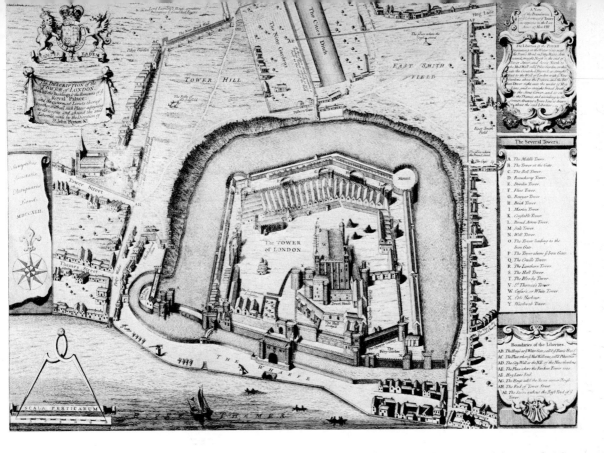

friends could not have known him', at lodgings in Tower Street,
'next door to the sign of the Black Swan at a goldsmith's house.
There from three of the clock in the afternoon till eight at night'
he dispensed cures and simples, cures for the 'Labes Britannica or
grand English disease, the scurvy', and particularly cures for the
diseases of women. 'The green-sickness, weaknesses, inflammations,
or obstructions in the stomach, reins, liver, spleen, etc. (For I
would put no word in my bill that bears any unclean sound; it is
enough that I make myself understood; I have seen physicians'
bills as bawdy as Aretine's dialogues; which no man that walks
warily before God can approve of.)'

It was not only the sick that came to him on Tower Hill. He
appealed also to the sound, especially to women. He offered to tell
the future from the stars and from dreams:

As to astrological predictions, physiognomy, divination by dreams,
and otherwise (palmistry I have not faith in, because there can be no
reason be alledg'd for it) my own experience has convinc'd me more
of their considerable effects, and marvellous operations, chiefly in
the directions of future proceedings, to the avoiding of dangers that
threaten, and laying hold of advantages that might offer themselves.
I say, my own practice has convinc'd me more than all the sage and
wise writings extant of those matters: for I might say this for myself
(did it not look like ostentation) that I have very seldom failed in my

predictions, and often been very serviceable in my advice; how far I am capable in this way, I am sure is not fit to be delivered in print.

Did he remember when penning these confident lines how he had waited after Bergen for the return of Wyndham's ghost and been disappointed and how he felt his faith shaken (for Wyndham had bound himself 'not without ceremonies of religion'), although he had seen the presages of death fulfilled? There had been another occasion, too, which he may have had in mind when he spoke of his own experience. He was to tell the story later to Burnet.

> He told me of another odd presage that one had of his approaching death in the Lady Warre, his mother-in-law's, house: the chaplain had dreamt that such a day he should die, but being by all the family put out of the belief of it, he had almost forgot it: till the evening before at supper, there being thirteen at table; according to a fond conceit that one of these must soon die, one of the young ladies pointed to him, that he was to die. He, remembering his dream fell into some disorder, and the Lady Warre reproving him for his superstition, he said he was confident he was to die before morning, but he being in perfect health, it was not much minded. He went to his chamber and sate up late, as appeared by the burning of his candle, and he had been preparing his notes for his sermon, but was found dead in his bed the next morning.

These were the cracks in the universe of Hobbes, the disturbing doubts in his disbelief, which may have been in Rochester's mind even in the midst of his masquerade, so riddled is the broadsheet with half-truths. But he turned from them to more amusing matters, the question of women's complexions, paragraphs which must have brought him more custom than all his promises of physic for the scurvy.

> Those that have travell'd in Italy will tell you to what a miracle art does there assist nature in the preservation of beauty; how women of forty bear the same countenance with those of fifteen; ages are there

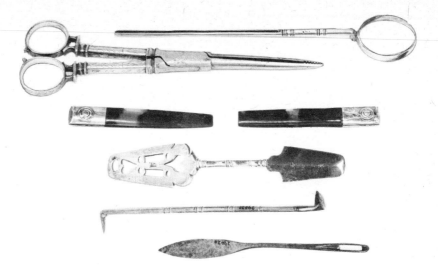

A pocket set of surgical instruments

A London prostitute

no ways distinguish'd by faces: whereas here in England, look a horse in the mouth, and a woman in the face, you presently know both their ages to a year. I will therefore give you such remedies, that without destroying your complexion (as most of your paints and daubings do) shall render them purely fair, cleaning and preserving them from all spots, freckles, heats and pimples, nay marks of the small-pox, or any other accidental ones, so the face be not seam'd nor scarr'd. I will also cleanse and preserve your teeth, white and round as pearls, fastning them that are loose; your gums shall be kept entire and red as coral, your lips of the same colour, and soft as you could wish your lawful kisses. . . . I will besides (if it be desired) take away from their fatness who have overmuch, and add flesh to those that want it, without the least detriment to their constitutions. Now should Galen himself look out of his grave, and tell me these were baubles below the profession of a physician, I would coldly answer him, that I take more glory in preserving God's image in its unblemish'd beauty, upon one good face, than I should do in patching up all the decay'd carcasses in the world.

In his answer to the charge of being a mountebank the unmistakable Rochester breaks through the jargon of the quack.

If I appear to anyone like a counterfeit, ev'n for the sake of that chiefly, ought I to be constru'd a true man, who is the counterfeit's example, his original, and that which he imploys his industry and pains to imitate and copy: is it therefore my fault, if the cheat by his wits and endeavours makes himself so like me, that consequently I cannot avoid resembling him? Consider, pray, the valiant and the coward, the wealthy merchant and the bankrupt, the politician and the fool; they are the same in many things, and differ in but *one* alone: the valiant man holds up his head, looks confidently round about him, wears a sword, courts a Lord's wife and owns it; so does the coward; one only point of honour, and that's courage (which, like false metal, one only trial can discover) makes the distinction.

111

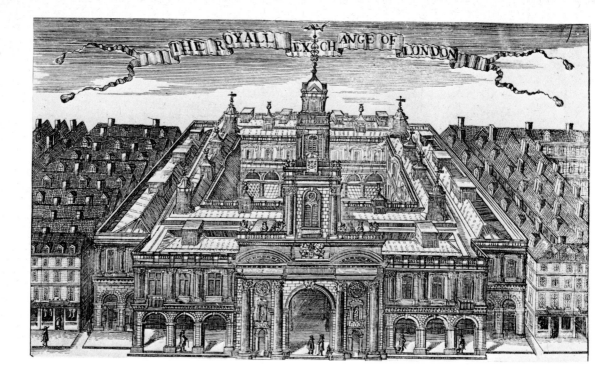

The bankrupt walks the Exchange, buys bargains, draws bills, and accepts them with the richest, whilst paper and credit are current coin: that which makes the difference is real cash, a great difference indeed, and yet but one, and that the last found out, and till then the least perceiv'd.

Now for the politician, he is a grave, deliberating, close, prying man: pray, are there not grave, deliberating, close, prying fools? If, then, the difference betwixt all these (though infinite in effect) be so nice in all appearance, will you expect it should be otherwise betwixt the false physician, astrologer, etc. and the true? The first calls himself learned doctor, sends forth his bills, gives physic and counsel, tells and foretells; the other is found to do just as much; 'tis only your experience must distinguish betwixt them: to which I willingly submit myself: I'll only say something to the honour of the mountebank, in case you discover me to be one.

Reflect a little what kind of creature 'tis: he is one then who is fain to supply some higher ability he pretends to, with craft: he draws great companies to him, by undertaking strange things which can never be effected.

The politician (by his example, no doubt) finding how the people are taken with specious, miraculous impossibilities, plays the same game, protests, declares, promises I know not what things, which he's sure can ne'er be brought about: the people believe, are deluded, and pleas'd. The expectation of a future good, which shall never befall them, draws their eyes off a present evil. Thus are *they* kept and establish'd in subjection, peace, and obedience, *he* in greatness, wealth and power: so you see the politician is, and must be a mountebank in state affairs, and the mountebank (no doubt if he thrives) is an arrant politician in physic.

If the authenticity of this address had ever been seriously questioned, the Biblical phrase – 'He draws great companies to him' – would be worth noting as a parallel to passages in letters to Mrs Barry and Savile. The language of the Bible, however satirically used, is part of Rochester's style. What is more worthy of note is the passage relating to the valiant man and the coward. If I am right he had just fled from Epsom where his companion lay dead; men were already assuming his cowardice who knew nothing of the details of the affray, of how dark the night was, how inflamed with wine the senses. He had a contempt for easy judgments, for a division into white and black without a knowledge of the minuteness of the shades of colouring between. Now in the address he reverts to the same theme: 'One only point of honour and that's courage . . . makes the distinction.'

There is one more indication that 1676 was the date of the masquerade. In a letter to Rochester dated from Whitehall 15 August 1676 ('to be left with the postmaster of Banbury in Oxfordshire'), Harry Savile writes (the letter is much mutilated and the meaning obscure):

> . . . this being the critical time . . .ke your fortune, for Monsieur Rabell is so . . . [fav]ourite of his Majesty and your Lordship of Monsieur Rabell that I do not see you can ever have a better opportunity of doing your business; now your chemical knowledge will give you entrance to a place where Manchester himself is kept out for his ignorance which hitherto has carried him through all; in a word the days of learning are coming upon us, and under a receipt for the worms no man will be admitted so far as the privy chamber. Pray for your friends my most dear Lord in this day of trial, and if I come in danger, send me a 4 for a purge or upon my expulsion hence prepare to receive me for a lead lap. . . .

Monsieur Rabell was a famous empiric, the numeral 4 was an astrological symbol and stood for the word 'recipe'. It seems highly likely that these references are to Rochester's exploit as a doctor and astrologer.

To the same occasion belongs Hamilton's story of his stay in the city among the merchants and their wives. According to the author of the *Gramont Memoirs*, Rochester before becoming Alexander Bendo took on the habit and manner of a wealthy middle-class citizen, criticized the extravagance of the Government with the aldermen, and the vices of the Court ladies and the King's mistresses with their wives. With the latter he became popular by comparing them favourably with the Court beauties, exclaiming that fire from Heaven ought surely to fall on Whitehall for harbouring such ruffians as Rochester and Killigrew who declared that all husbands in London wore horns and all the wives paint.

[2] He had saved himself from a trial for murder and had won the King's forgiveness by his masquerade, but he returned to Court to find that he had played into his enemies' hands. Never before had he given them such an opportunity; the evaded duel with Mulgrave was a trifle compared with the desertion of Downes. He had drawn his sword on the constable, after the watch had been dismissed, and had left his friend to pay the penalty. It was remembered that in his 'Satire against Mankind', printed as a broadside the year before, he had written:

> The good he acts, the ill he does endure,
> 'Tis all from fear, to make himself secure.
> Merely for safety, after fame they thirst;
> For all men would be cowards if they durst.

(One remembers Stevenson's character in *The Suicide Club*: 'Envy me, envy me, I am a coward.')

It is difficult to accuse Rochester with any certainty of following his own paradox. If he acted as a coward, and not merely as a man confused with drink and darkness, the same must be said of Etherege. Etherege, however, was a man of many friends, Rochester of many enemies. One in particular came forward at this moment and dared to challenge him with his chosen weapon, words, and met with no mean success. This was Sir Car Scrope, a man noted for the ugliness of his squint, his conceit, and his rather squalid love affairs. In 'A Defence of Satire' he included an unmistakable reference to the affray at Epsom:

> He who can push into a midnight fray
> His brave companion, and then run away,
> Leaving him to be murder'd in the street,
> Then put it off with some buffoon conceit;
> Him, thus dishonour'd, for a wit you own,
> And count him as top fiddler of the town.

The challenge was promptly taken up by Rochester in a poem 'On the Supposed Author of a Late Poem in Defence of Satire'.

> To rack and torture thy unmeaning brain,
> In satyr's praise to a low untun'd strain,
> In thee was most impertinent and vain,
> When in thy poem we more clearly see
> That satyr's of divine authority,
> For God made one on Man when he made thee. . . .
> Curse on that silly hour that first inspir'd

Thy madness, to pretend to be admir'd,
To paint thy grizly face, to dance, to dress,
And all those awkward follies that express
Thy loathsome love, and filthy daintiness.
Who needs will be an ugly *beau-garçon*,
Spit at, and shun'd by ev'ry girl in town:
Where dreadfully love's scare-crow, thou art plac'd
To fright the tender flock that long to taste:
While ev'ry coming maid, when you appear,
Starts back for shame, and straight turns chaste for fear. . . .

One epithet in the poem seems to have struck home. Nell Gwyn in her only recorded letter wrote ironically: 'The Pall Mall is now to me a dismal place, since I have utterly lost Sir Car Scrope never to be recovered again, for he told me he could not live always at this rate and so begun to be a little uncivil, which I could not suffer from an ugly *beau garçon*.'

Rochester's was not the last word. Scrope replied briefly, with a point the satirist might have envied:

Rail on, poor feeble scribbler, speak of me
In as bad terms, as the world speaks of thee.
Sit swelling in thy hole, like a vext toad,
And full of pox and malice spit abroad.
Thou can'st hurt no man's fame with thy ill-word;
Thy pen is full as harmless as thy sword.

There was too much truth in the reply: no question now that the world was speaking ill of him. In a letter to Savile in 1677, written when 'almost blind and utterly lame', he spoke of himself as 'a man whom it is the great mode to hate'. Even if his sword were not harmless, he was becoming so little thought of that there was no disgrace in refusing to meet its point. In 1680, the last year of his life, he took up the cause of the Earl of Arran, whose courtship of Mistress Poulett had been thwarted by her uncle, Edward Seymour. Arran, a spendthrift foolish youth, after challenging Seymour to a duel, had been forced to flee to The Hague, and Rochester, although he was a sick man at the brink of death, took up the challenge and waited for Seymour at the rendezvous by Arlington Gardens three hours. Seymour thought it safe to ignore him, employing against him Mulgrave's old story.

An ingenious account of the affair was sent by Francis Gwyn to Lord Conway, who was also courting Mistress Poulett, on 9 March.

On Thursday last Mr Seymour sent for me in the morning and commanded me to go to my Lord Rochester, it having been publicly said at my Lord Sunderland's table that my Lord Rochester had used expressions to encourage my Lord Arran in this piece of insolency towards him before it was done and had spoke something of it since reflecting on Mr Seymour.

I went immediately and my Lord Rochester appointed to meet the next morning on horseback with his sword and pistol. His reason for it was as he told me because he had a weakness in his limbs, but he thought he could do very well on horseback, though I believe the true reason was that he thought it impossible horses and equipage should be provided for us all in so short a time without giving suspicion and so making a discovery, which in effect was the fate of it, though we had provided ours I am confident without the least discovery. But at two o'clock on Thursday night comes Mr Collingwood, who then was waiting to Mr Seymour, I being then with him, and told him the King had commanded him not to stir out of his house till he had sent to him to speak with him, which he would do next day in the evening. Mr Collingwood likewise told us that he had already been with the Lord Rochester with the same message, which occasioned my not going to my Lord to tell him we were prevented. And my Lord Rochester laid hold of it, and goes out the next morning, pretending the King's commands to him was only not to concern himself with any quarrel relating to the Lord Arran; when not finding anybody, which he very well knew he should not do, he came back, and first reported that he had been in the field and Mr Seymour did not appear, but that report is long ago stopped and we are at last in a state of quietness. Mr Seymour went out of town on Friday. This I know your Lordship would look upon as a strange piece of intelligence from a Clerk of the Council if you did not know the whole occasion, but that which suits better with my profession is that the matters have produced a proclamation against duelling, which is now in the press.

A note in Conway's hand throws a light on the too ingenious story. 'Giving an account of Sir Edward Seymour's heroic courage, a pack of the greatest lies that was ever told, for he durst not fight Lord Arran but was the jest of the Court on that occasion.'

There had been a time when Rochester's satires at least were feared. Even his friends were not safe from his pen. He had held a mirror up to his age, a mirror that distorted a little but in the cause of truth. His hatreds were not all personal, not all made up of such men as Mulgrave and Scrope. His surprise, when resentment was shown by one of 'the number of those fools his wit has made his enemies' (the words are Etherege's), was genuine. Savile wrote to him of the Duchess of Portsmouth's indignation and he replied without hypocrisy: 'By that God that made me, I have no more offended her in thought, word or deed, no more imagin'd or utter'd the least thought in her contempt or prejudice, than I have plotted treason, conceal'd arms, train'd regiments for a rebellion.' He had forgotten 'Portsmouth's Looking Glass'.

> Methinks I see you newly risen
> From your embroider'd bed and pissing,
> With studied mien, and much grimace
> Present yourself before your glass . . .
> Lay trains of love, and state-intrigues,
> In powders, trimmings and curl'd wigs:
> And nicely choose, and neatly spread,
> Upon your cheeks the best French red.

But to name those who crowded before that mirror would be to fill a page with names: 'scabby Villiers', 'prying Poultney', 'bully Carr', 'florid Huntington', 'cinder Nell', 'villain Franck', 'blund'ring Settle', 'chaste, pious prudent Charles the Second', the faces flow and pass into an anonymous multitude, become the whole seventeenth-century world.

> The general heads, under which this whole island may be considered, are spies, beggars, and rebels, the transpositions and mixtures of these, make an agreeable variety; busy fools, and cautious knaves are bred out of 'em, and set off wonderfully; tho' of this latter sort, we have fewer now than ever, hypocrisy being the only vice in decay amongst us. Few men here dissemble their being rascals, and no woman disowns being a whore.

The same spirit dominates his later poetry:

> Were I, who to my cost already am,
> One of those strange, prodigious creatures Man,
> A spirit free, to choose for my own share,
> What sort of flesh and blood I pleas'd to wear,
> I'd be a dog, a monkey or a bear,
> Or any thing, but that vain animal,
> Who is so proud of being rational.

To these final months belongs undoubtedly one of his darkest and finest poems 'Upon Nothing': 'Nothing! thou elder brother ev'n to shade.' In it his accumulated hatred of the world was poured out.

> Nothing, who dwell'st with fools in grave disguise,
> For whom they reverend shapes and forms devise,
> Lawn sleeves, and furs, and gowns, when they like thee look wise.
>
> French truth, Dutch prowess, British policy,
> Hibernian learning, Scotch civility,
> Spaniards dispatch, Danes wit, are mainly seen in thee.
>
> The great man's gratitude to his best friend,
> King's promises, whores vows, tow'rds thee they bend,
> Flow swiftly into thee, and in thee ever end.

He had reached even the end of hatred, and the same year the end of what seems to have been his deepest sexual passion – that for Elizabeth Barry.

VII Elizabeth Barry

Rochester's character as a lover was drawn by Sir George Etherege in *Sir Fopling Flutter or the Man of Mode* produced before the King at the Duke's Theatre on 11 March 1676. It was generally agreed that the hero, Dorimant, represented Etherege's friend. 'I know he is a Devil, but he has something of the Angel yet undefac'd in him.' Of the play's truth Langbaine wrote: 'This play is written with great art and judgment, and is acknowledged by all, to be a true comedy, and the characters as well drawn to the life, as any play that has been acted since the restoration of the English stage.' The identification of Rochester with Dorimant was made both by the critic John Dennis in *A Defence of Sir Fopling Flutter* (1722) and by 'St Evremond'.

'I remember very well,' Dennis wrote,

> that upon the first acting this comedy, it was generally believed to be an agreeable representation of the persons of condition of both sexes, both in Court and town; and that all the world was charmed with Dorimant; and that it was unanimously agreed that he had in him several of the qualities of Wilmot, Earl of Rochester, as, his wit, his spirit, his amorous temper, the charms that he had for the fair sex, his falsehood, and his inconstancy; the agreeable manner of his chiding his servants, which the late Bishop of Salisbury takes notice of in his life; and lastly, his repeating, on every occasion, the verses of Waller, for whom that noble lord had a very particular esteem.

And 'St Evremond': '[Rochester] was generally fickle in his amours, and made no great scruple of his oaths of fidelity. Sir George Etherege wrote Dorimant in *Sir Fopling*, in complement to him, as drawing his Lordship's character, and burnishing all the foibles of it, to make them shine like perfections.'

Many passages of dialogue may be picked out to illustrate not only this side of Rochester's character but the way in which it was burnished by the hand of his friend. Dorimant's attitude is summed up by himself: 'Next to the coming to a good understanding with a new mistress, I love a quarrel with an old one,' and his success as a lover is vouched for by his friends.

Townley: Pray, where's your friend, Mr Dorimant?
Medley: Soliciting his affairs, he's a man of great employment, has

The Duke's Theatre, Dorset Gardens

119

THE

Man of Mode,

OR,

Sʳ Fopling Flutter.

A

COMEDY.

Acted at the *Duke's Theatre.*

By *George Etherege* Esq;.

LICENSED,

June 3.
1676.   *Roger L'Eſtrange.*

LONDON,
Printed by *J. Macock*, for *Henry Herringman*, at the Sign of
the *Blew Anchor* in the Lower Walk of the
New Exchange, 1 6 7 6.

(left) Checks for the Theatre,
Dorset Gardens

> more mistresses now depending than the most eminent
> lawyer in England has causes.
>
> *Emilia:* Here has been Mrs Loveit, so uneasy and out of humour
> these two days.
>
> *Townley:* How strangely love and jealousy rage in that poor woman.
>
> *Medley:* She could not have picked out a devil upon earth so proper
> to torment her.

Here was the bright amusing side, the intrigues with ladies of the
Court; but there was a darker aspect and one which led Rochester
in due course to Mrs Fourcard's. Granger says of him that 'he was
ever engaged in some amour or other, and frequently with women
of the lowest order, and the vilest prostitutes of the town'. Granger's
word alone would not be sufficient. But there is the testimony of
Hearne, the conscientious antiquary, who states that he '(among
other girls) used the body of one Nell Browne of Woodstock, who,
tho' she look'd pretty well when clean, yet she was a very nasty,
ordinary, silly creature, which made people much admire'. An

enigmatic paragraph in a letter to Rochester from John Muddyman of September 1671 seems to refer to another common intrigue:

> Fate has taken care to vindicate your proceeding with Foster, who is discovered to be a damsel of low degree and very fit for the latter part of your treatment, no northern lass but a mere dresser at Hazard's school, her uncle a wite that wields the puissant spiggot at Kensington, debauched by Mr Butler, a gentleman of the cloak and gallow-shoe, an order of knighthood very fatal to maiden head.

One of the references to Rochester by Pepys deals with the same subject. The entry is dated 2 December 1668, less than two years after his marriage to Elizabeth Mallet:

> The play done, we to White Hall; where my wife stayed while I up to the Duchess's and Queen's side, to speak with the Duke of York: and here saw all the ladies, and heard the silly discourse of the King, with his people about him, telling a story of my Lord Rochester's having of his clothes stole, while he was with a wench; and his gold all gone, but his clothes found afterwards stuffed into a feather bed by the wench that stole them.

Etherege did not leave this side of his friend's sexual life untouched. One scene, which is of no dramatic significance, serves only to show that Dorimant does not confine his attentions to the Mrs Loveits of polite society.

> Enter a footman with a letter.
> *Footman:* Here's a letter, sir.
> *Dorimant:* The superscription's right; For Mr Dorimant.
> *Medley:* Let's see; the very scrawl and spelling of a true-bred whore.
> *Dorimant:* I know the hand; the style is admirable, I assure you.
> *Medley:* Prithee read it.
> *Dorimant* reads.
> 'I told a you you dud not love me, if you dud, you wou'd have seen me again e're now; I have no money and am very mallicolly; pray send me a guynie to see the operies.
> Your servant to command,
> Molly.'

We know the names of many of the bawds of the time, who have won an odd immortality in literature, Mrs Cresswell, Mrs Ross, Mrs Bennet, Mrs Foster and Betty Morris, who kept houses in Moorfields, Whetstone Park, and Dog & Bitch Yard. There are references to several of these women in Rochester's poems, and he records a retort of Betty Morris 'when a great woman called her Buckhurst's whore':

> I please one man of wit, am proud on't too,
> Let all the coxcombs dance to bed to you.

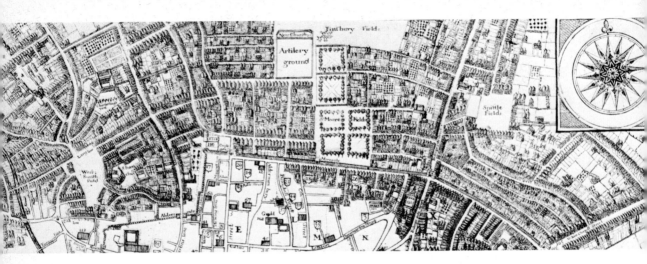

A part of London in 1666

She may indeed have been the 'bonny Black Bess' celebrated by Buckhurst:

> The ploughman and squire, the arranter clown,
> At home she subdu'd in her paragon gown;
> But now she adorns the boxes and pit,
> And the proudest town-gallants are forc'd to submit;
> All hearts fall a-leaping, wherever she comes
> And beat day and night, like my Lord Craven's drums.

With Rochester the prostitute was not a compensation for finer women whom he could not possess. He wrote to Savile: 'I have seriously consider'd one thing, that [of] the three businesses of this age, women, politics, and drinking, the last is the only exercise at which you and I have not prov'd ourselves arrant fumblers', but his successes at the first had not been few.

On 17 December 1677 Savile wrote to him:

> I had almost forgot for another argument to bring you to town that a French troop of comedians bound for Nimeguen were by adverse winds cast into this hospitable port and do act at Whitehall so very well that it is a thousand pities they should not stay, especially a young wench of fifteen, who has more beauty and sweetness than ever was seen upon the stage since a friend of ours left it.[1] In good earnest you would be delighted above all things with her, and it were a shame to the nation she should carry away a maidenhead she pretends to have brought and that nobody here has either wit or address or money enough to go to the price of. The King sighs and despairs, and says nobody but Sir George Downing or my Lord Ranelagh can possibly purchase her.

In 1679 Savile writing from Paris, refers to 'two Caledonian Countesses who are most in your favour . . . for your Lordship's comfort and their honour, I cannot hear that either of them have

[1] Presumably Mrs Barry who was bearing Rochester's child.

any inclinations besides yourself.' One of these ladies is referred to in another letter as Lady Kinnoul. And in 1670 Savile had invoked his aid from Adderbury, where Rochester was spending January for the christening of his son, against the Customs, who had struck a lamented blow in the cause of morality by burning a consignment of dildoes. 'By this, my Lord, you see what things are done in your absence, and then pray consider whether it is fit for you to be blowing of coals in the country when there is a revenge due to the ashes of these martyrs. Your Lordship is chosen general in this war betwixt the Ballers and the farmers.' Savile's challenge was perhaps taken up in 'Signor Dildoe':

> This Signor is sound, safe, ready and dumb,
> As ever was candle, carrot or thumb;
> Then away with the nasty devices and show
> How you rate the just merit of Signor Dildoe.

Of the Ballers to whom Savile refers we know a little from Pepys, who on 30 May 1668, by the talk of Harry Killgrew and others at supper at the New Exchange, understood 'the meaning of the company that lately was called Ballers; Harris telling how it was by a meeting of some young blades, where he was among them, and my Lady Bennet and her ladies; and there dancing naked, and all the roguish things in the world'. My Lady Bennet was the Mrs Bennet already mentioned, the colleague of Betty Morris and Mrs Cresswell.

If Rochester's affairs included at one end of the social scale the inmates of Whetstone Park, at the other they numbered at least one of the Royal mistresses. Mrs Roberts was the daughter of a clergyman and she was to die a year before Rochester in very similar circumstances, under the spiritual care of Dr Burnet. She left the King 'for the possession of my lord's person and heart as he imagined. But he was soon cloyed with the enjoyment of any one woman, tho' the fairest in the world, and forsook her.' The words are 'St Evremond's' and they echo Rochester's own declaration to Burnet. 'The restraining of man from the use of women, except one in the way of marriage, and denying the remedy of divorce, he thought unreasonable impositions on the freedom of mankind.' Mrs Roberts found no great difficulty in retrieving the King's affections. Charles expected constancy in women as little as he practised it himself. He had no objection to being the third Charles in Nell Gwyn's favours, and allowed Lady Castlemaine to deceive him with a host of favourites, who are said to have ranged from Monmouth to Jacob Hall, a rope dancer.

Almost alone of the King's mistresses Mrs Roberts escaped Rochester's satire, and she seems to have remained on friendly terms with him. In July 1678, a year before her death, Savile wrote to the Earl from his cure in Leather Lane:

> I confess I wonder at myself, and that mass of mercury that has gone down my throat in seven months, but should wonder yet more was it not for Mrs Roberts, for behold a greater than I, she is in the same house and we have met here from several corners as mad folks do in Bedlam. What she has endur'd would make a dam'd soul fall a laughing at his lesser pains, it is so far beyond description or belief that till she tells it you herself I will not spoil her story by making it worse. . . .

A more notorious name has been coupled with Rochester, that of Nell Gwyn. No one has denied her the merit of fidelity after she became the King's mistress. Even Rochester, in his satires, accuses her of no inconstancy. The satires are less savage than those on Castlemaine and Portsmouth, and a certain poetry sometimes breaks in:

> From Oxford prison many did she free,
> There dy'd her father, and there glory'd she
> In giving others life and liberty,
> So pious a remembrance still she bore
> Ev'n to the fetters that her father wore.
> Nor was her mother's funeral less her care,
> No cost, no velvet did the daughter spare:
> Fine gilded scutcheons did the hearse enrich,
> To celebrate this martyr of the ditch;
> Burnt brandy did in flaming brimmers flow,
>   Drunk at her funeral; while her well-pleas'd shade
> Rejoic'd ev'n in the sober fields below
>   At all the drunkenness her death had made.

There is evidence in plenty that, in spite of his attack on 'the darling strumpet of the crowd', Rochester remained her friend. In the only letter of hers that survives he is one of the friends whose absence from Court she mourns, while in 1677 he acted as her trustee. When her good nature seemed likely to prove her worst enemy and introduce a rival to the King's affections, it was to Rochester that Savile wrote with anxiety:

> I will venture at one small piece of intelligence, because one who is always your friend and sometimes (especially now) mine, has a part in it that makes her now laughed at and may one day turn to her infinite disadvantage. The case stands thus if I am rightly informed:– My Lady Hervey, who always loves one civil plot more, is working body and soul to bring Mrs Jenny Middleton into play. How dangerous a new one is to all old ones I need not tell you, but her Ladyship, having little opportunity of seeing Charlemagne upon her own account, wheadles poor Mrs Nelly into supping twice or thrice a

week at W. C[hiffinch]'s and carrying her with her; so that in good earnest this poor creature is betrayed by her Ladyship to pimp against herself, for there her Ladyship whispers and contrives all matters to her own ends as the other might easily perceive if she were not too giddy to mistrust a false friend. This I thought it good for you to know, for though your Lordship and I have different friends in the Court, yet the friendship betwixt us ought to make me have an observing eye upon any accident that may wound any friend of yours as this may in the end possibly do her, who is so much your friend and who speaks obliging and charitable things of me in my present disgrace.[1]

But it was to a sick man, embittered with the world and his past, that Savile wrote. Nell Gwyn may have always been his friend, she may have been, as some have suggested, his mistress; the only advice he gives now comes from a savage cynicism:

My advice to the lady you wot of has ever been this, *Take your measures just contrary to your rivals, live in peace with all the world, and easily with the King: never be so ill-natur'd to stir up his anger against others, but let him forget the use of a passion, which is never to do you good: cherish his love wherever it inclines, and be assur'd you can't commit greater folly than pretending to be jealous; but, on the contrary, with hand, body, head, heart and all the faculties you have, contribute to his pleasure all you can, and comply with his desires throughout: and, for new intrigues, so you be at one end 'tis no matter which: make sport when you can, at other times help it.* Thus, I have giv'n you an account how unfit I am to give the advice you propos'd: besides this, you may judge, whether I was a good pimp, or no. But some thought otherwise; and so truly I have renounc'd business; let abler men try it.

Nell Gwyn reciting the epilogue to *Sir Patient Fancy* 'That we have nobler
   souls than you we prove,
By how much more we're
   sensible of love.'

It is possible to see in these lines of advice with their bitter conclusion traces of a tragic and ignoble sacrifice, to set that exclamation 'you may judge whether I was a good pimp or no' beside the lines written about this time from his version of Fletcher's *Valentinian*, where the Emperor musters his bawds to procure him the body of Lucina:

Go, call your wives to counsel, and prepare
To tempt, dissemble, promise, fawn and swear,
To make faith look like folly use your skill,
Virtue an ill-bred crossness in the will,
Fame, the loose breathings of a clamorous crowd –
Ever in lies most confident and loud!
Honour a notion! Piety a cheat!
And if you prove successful bawds, be great

but there is little real evidence that Nell Gwyn was ever Rochester's mistress. In the Victoria and Albert Museum is a pamphlet entitled *Poetical Epistle from the Earl of Rochester to Nell Gwyn*. Published by an unknown editor in the middle of the eighteenth century it

[1] He had been banished from Court after a quarrel with Lauderdale.

purports to be copied from three manuscript volumes of Rochester's works in the French King's library, a present from Charles II. The poem opens 'Nelly, my life, tho' now thou'rt full fifteen' and proceeds, with an indecency which rivals the more notorious *Sodom*, to describe Nell Gwyn's body and the poet's intimacy with it. If genuine it would provide certain evidence that the actress was once Rochester's mistress, but for the poem's authenticity there is only internal evidence. From its style one can say it is not unworthy of Rochester; it is possible too, with Alexander Bendo in mind, to point to the chemical knowledge shown by the author and his intimacy with obscure beauty preparations.

As for other evidence there is a poem quoted by the pornographer 'Captain' Alexander Smith in his book of Court scandals, *The School of Venus*, and attributed by him to Etherege, which contains one line on which the whole story may have been constructed. The theme of the poem is described in the opening lines:

> The life of Nelly truly shown,
> From coal-yard and cellar to the throne,
> Till into the grave she tumbled down.

The poem, after describing how the actor Charles Hart relinquished Nelly to Lord Buckhurst, continues:

> To B—— thus resigned in friendly wise,
> Our glaring lass begins again to rise,
> Distributing her favours very thick,
> And sometimes witty Wilmot had a lick.

To such stories Rochester may have referred when he wrote, with irony:

> Much did she suffer, first on bulk and stage,
> From the blackguard and bullies of the age;
> Much more her growing virtue did sustain
> While dear Charles Hart and Buckhurst su'd in vain.
> In vain they su'd; curs'd be the envious tongue
> That her undoubted chastity would wrong;
> For should we fame believe, we then might say
> That thousands lay with her as well as they.

In the *Memoirs of Nell Gwyn* which are reprinted in Tom Davies's edition of Downes's *Roscius Anglicanus* it is stated: 'It noways appear that Lord Rochester was ever enamoured of her. Mrs Barry was his passion, and Mrs Boutel antecedently to Mrs Barry, at the time when Mrs Gwyn trod the stage.' Of Mrs Boutel little is known. She was celebrated in her day for the gentler parts in tragedy although she played Cleopatra in *All for Love*, in contrast with St Catherine in *Tyrranick Love*.

Of these women none has left such certain traces in Rochester's life as Mrs Barry. It was thought that 'he never loved any person so sincerely as he did Mrs Barry', and the conjecture is borne out by the letters which survive and trace his love through the stages of passion, tenderness, jealousy and disillusion. A woman of exquisite charm in conversation, Mrs Barry was not beautiful, but her face was expressive, her manner graceful. She claimed to be the daughter of Colonel Robert Barry, a barrister, and according to one story, she was recommended to the stage by her friend, Lady Davenant. Her first appearance in 1674 was unsuccessful, and the players despaired of ever making her a passable actress. It was then that Rochester is said to have intervened and offered a wager that in six months she would be one of the most approved performers at the Dorset Gardens Theatre. He took her with him into the country and taught her to use her naturally musical voice to good effect.

> Mrs Barry had an excellent understanding, but not a musical ear; so that she could not catch the sounds or emphases taught her; but fell into a disagreeable tone, the fault of most young stage-adventurers. To cure her of this defect, Lord Rochester caused her to enter into the meaning of every sentiment; he taught her not only the proper cadence or sounding of the voice, but to seize also the passions, and adapt her whole behaviour to the situations of the characters. It is said that in order to accomplish his intention, besides the many private instructions he gave her, he caused her to rehearse the part no less than thirty times upon the stage, and of these, about twelve times in the dress in which she was to play.

He won his wager. In 1675 he had begun to take an interest in the poet Otway, and through his influence that author's first play *Alcibiades* was performed at the Dorset Gardens Theatre, with Mrs Barry in the cast. She took the small part of Drailla, but gave undoubted indications of her merit. To place one's mistress upon the stage was to place her in the market place, fair game for any man with money in his pouch. The limit of Rochester's own desire had hitherto marked the period of his love; now he was to love on, and watch another's desire alter.

He could declare disagreements and jealousy to be the mark of true love:

> Alas! 'tis sacred jealousy,
>   Love rais'd to an extreme;
> The only proof twixt them and me,
>   We love, and do not dream . . .

and treat jealousy with self-mockery and tenderness:

> Madam, now as I love you, I think I have reason to be jealous; your neighbour came in last night with all the marks and behaviour of a

Leave this gawdy guilded Stage
From custome more than use frequented
Where forces of either sex and age
Crowd to see themselves presented
To loves Theatre the Bed
youth and beauty fly together
And Act soe well it may be said
The Lawrell there was due to either
Twixt strifes of love & war Thindifference
lies in this
when neither overcomes Loves triumph
greater is

Poem in Rochester's hand:
'Leave this gawdy guilded
stage'

spy, every word and look implied that she came to solicit your love, or constancy: may her endeavours prove as vain as I wish my fears. May no man share the blessings I enjoy, without my curses; and if they fall on him alone, without touching you, I am happy, though he deserves 'em not: but should you be concerned, they'll all fly back upon myself; for he, whom you are kind to, is so blest, he may safely stand the curses of all the world without repining

but it cannot have been long before he knew how any man in town might enjoy her, if he had the money. 'In the art of exciting pity,' it was said of her performance by Colley Cibber, 'she had a power beyond all the actresses I have yet seen, or what your imagination can conceive', but for feeling compassion she had none. The stage was not a school of virtue, but of all the actresses of the time, Mrs Barry became the most notorious for her combination of immorality and coldness. It is a strange contrast: on the one hand the actress, who drew tears from her audience with the pathos of Otway's lines, revealing 'in characters of greatness a presence of elevated dignity, her mien and motion superb and gracefully majestic, her voice full, clear and strong, so that no violence of passion could be too much for her; and when distress or tenderness possessed her' subsiding 'into the most affecting melody and soft-

128

ness'; on the other 'that mercenary prostituting dame', of whom Tom Brown wrote, 'should you lie with her all night, she would not know you next morning, unless you had another five pounds at her service'. Through life the same accusation pursued her, so that many years after Rochester's death it was still being written:

> But slattern Betty Barry next appears
> Whom every fop upon the stage admires. . . .
> At thirty-eight a very hopeful whore,
> The only one o' th' trade that's not profuse,
> A policy was taught her by the Jews,
> Tho' still the highest bidder she will choose.

To follow the stages of Rochester's love is easy. There is a letter printed by 'Captain' Alexander Smith, with Mrs Barry's reply, which is not included in Charles Gildon's edition of Rochester's letters, but it may well be a genuine one. It shows Rochester as an importunate lover, using well-worn phrases.

> Since I am out of your presence (which is more intolerable to me than the sweetest death) I cannot live without a sight of you; so I wait your directions how I may once more be happy in the enjoyment of your company, which if you forbid me, you stick a dagger to my heart, which now bleeds for you.

Mrs Barry's answer is short and to the point: 'Sir, Tomorrow the Earl of P——ke goes out of town, and at ten in the morning I will meet your Lordship in the long Piazza in Covent-garden; till then farewell my dear, my dearest Rochester. Barry.'

In the letters printed by Gildon a change is evident. We are now in the period of possession. Passion is not always predominant, there is tenderness, increasingly there is jealousy, finally almost hatred.

First one hears Rochester with laughing solemnity (he calls

Piazza in Covent Garden

himself 'the wildest and most fantastical odd man alive'), abjuring her to remember

> the hour of a strict account, when both hearts are to be open, and we oblig'd to speak freely, as you order'd it yesterday, for so I must ever call the day I saw you last, since all time between that and the next visit, is no part of my life, or at least like a long fit of the falling-sickness, wherein I am dead to all joy and happiness. Here's a damn'd impertinent fool bolted in, that hinders me from ending my letter; the plague of —— take him, and any man or woman alive that take my thoughts off of you: but in the evening I will see you, and be happy in spite of all the fools in the world.

The mocking echo of religion with which the quotation opens is one of the unmistakable marks of Rochester's style. To Savile he once ended a letter 'Libera nos a malo – For Thine is my Kingdom, Power and Glory, for ever and ever', while on another occasion he altered Quarles's religious poem 'Why dost thou shade thy lovely face?' by the mere substitution of 'Love' for 'Lord' into an address to his mistress.

> Dissolve thy sunbeams, close thy wings and stay!
> See, see how I am blind, and dead, and stray!
> . . . O thou, that art my life, my light, my way!

It is possible that this tender blasphemy may belong to the same year as the letter, and the subject be the same, the woman who would lie with any man for five pounds.

Thirty-four undated letters to Mrs Barry survive, in print, though not in manuscript. Their relations may have opened in 1674; they certainly closed in 1678, soon after the birth of a child. The order of the letters seems to have no connection with their probable dates, and I think it is justifiable to shift them until a thread is revealed, leading from the tenderness and humour of the first letter to the harshness of the last. To the early time belongs undoubtedly this letter:

> Madam, There is now no minute of my life that does not afford me some new argument how much I love you; the little joy I take in every thing wherein you are not concern'd, the pleasing perplexity of endless thought, which I fall into, wherever you are brought to my remembrance; and lastly, the continual disquiet I am in, during your absence, convince me sufficiently that I do you justice in loving you, so as woman was never loved before.

These are not the letters of a lover in the first blind stages of passion; they are almost the letters of a married man, who has learned unselfishness, simplicity and tenderness. His heart no longer 'bleeds', her answers are no longer sentences of life or death, she is no longer the life and joy of his soul – no need to declaim of souls when bodies are so much at one. Instead she is 'Dearest of all that ever was dearest to me', 'Dearest of all pleasures'. He can write, without symbols or metaphors, 'Nothing can ever be so dear to me as you are.'

To read these letters and hear them fall into a sort of order is like sitting for a while in the old house in St James's where he lodged, listening through the stillness to the voice of ghosts, imploring, upbraiding, stammering with tenderness, mocking, blaspheming with a lover's blasphemy, quarrelling. The quarrels at first are without bitterness or reality; quarrels that tease him into greater love. It is she who pretends jealousy at first, so that he protests, 'The complaint you spoke to me, concerning Miss, I know nothing of, for she is as great a stranger to me, as she can be to you. So, thou pretty creature, farewell'; 'My visit yesterday was intended to tell you, I had not dined in company of women'; and sometimes the retort is angry, 'Madam, I found you in a chiding humour today, and so I left you; tomorrow I hope for better luck: till when, neither you, nor any you can employ, shall know whether I am under or above ground; therefore lie still, and satisfy yourself, that you are not, nor can be half so kind to Mrs [Barry] as I am; Good night.'

At first it is not of men that he is jealous, but only of women and their tales of him, especially 'the lean lady'.

> I know not well who has the worst on't, you, who love but a little, or I, who doat to an extravagance; sure, to be half kind is as bad as to be half witted; and madness, both in love and reason, bears a better character than a moderate state of either. Would I could bring you to my opinion, in this point; I would then confidently pretend you had too just exceptions either against me or my passion, the flesh and the devil; I mean, all the fools of my own sex, and that fat, with the other lean one of yours, whose prudent advice is daily concerning you, how dangerous it is to be kind to the man, upon earth, who loves you best. I, who still persuade myself, by all the arguments I can bring, that I am happy, find this none of the best, that you are too unlike these people every way, to agree with 'em in any particular. This is writ between sleeping and waking, and I will not answer for its being sense; but I, dreaming you were at Mrs N——'s, with five or six fools, and the lean lady, waked, in one of your horrors, and in amaze, fright and confusion, send this to beg a kind one from you, that may remove my fears, and make me as happy as I am faithful.

It was still possible to remove his fears, while they were caused by dreams and women, the fat one, the lean one, the neighbour who came in with the marks and behaviour of a spy. He would break out sometimes with angry words in Elizabeth Barry's company, but by the time he reached home he would be contrite and his repentance would be phrased in another of his parodies of religion:

Madam, till I have mended my manners, I am ashamed to look you in the face; but seeing you is as necessary to my life as breathing; so that I must see you, or be yours no more; for that's the image I have of dying. The sight of you, then, being my life, I cannot but confess, with an humble and sincere repentance, that I have hitherto lived very ill; receive my confession, and let the promise of my future zeal and devotion obtain my pardon, for last night's blasphemy against you, my Heaven; so shall I hope, hereafter, to be made partaker of such joys, in your arms, as meeting tongues but faintly can express, Amen.

This was the very sacredness of jealousy, 'kind jealous doubts, tormenting fears'. There was as little harshness in the upbraiding, as there was belief in the cause. Perhaps it was then he wrote his famous 'Song,'

My dear mistress has a heart
  Soft as those kind looks she gave me;
When with love's resistless art,
  And her eyes, she did enslave me.
But her constancy's so weak,
  She's so wild, and apt to wander;
That my jealous heart wou'd break,
  Should we live one day asunder.

Or that more perfect poem:

An age in her embraces past
  Would seem a winter's day,
Where life and light with envious haste
  Are torn and snatch'd away.

But, oh! how slowly minutes roll,
  When absent from her eyes,
That fed my love, which is my soul;
  It languishes and dies.

For then no more a soul but shade,
  It mournfully does move;
And haunts my breast, by absence made
  The living tomb of love.

You wiser men despise me not,
  Whose love-sick fancy raves
On shades of souls, and heav'n knows what;
  Short ages live in graves.

Whene'er those wounding eyes, so full
  Of sweetness, you did see,
Had you not been profoundly dull,
  You had gone mad like me.

Elizabeth Barry: 'I thank God I can distinguish, I can see very woman in you, and from yourself am convinc'd I have never been in the wrong in my opinion of women: 'Tis impossible for me to curse you; but give me leave to pity myself, which is more than ever you will do for me.'

(overleaf) Nell Gwyn
  'curs'd be the envious tongue
That her undoubted chastity
  wou'd wrong.'

132

Nor censure us, you who perceive
　　My best belov'd and me
Sigh and lament, complain and grieve,
　　You think we disagree.

Alas! 'tis sacred jealousy,
　　Love rais'd to an extreme,
The only proof, 'twixt them and me,
　　We love, and do not dream.

Fantastic fancies fondly move,
　　And in frail joys believe,
Taking false pleasure for true love;
　　But pain can ne'er deceive.

Kind jealous doubts, tormenting fears,
　　And anxious cares, when past,
Prove our heart's treasure fix'd and dear,
　　And make us blest at last.

In December 1677 a child was born. Rochester was sick in the country; two months before he had referred to himself in a letter to Savile as 'almost blind, utterly lame, and scarce within the reasonable hopes of ever seeing London again'. The news came to him in a letter from Savile, not without reproaches.

> The greatest news I can send you from hence is what the King told me last night, that your Lordship has a daughter borne by the body of Mrs Barry of which I give your honour joy. I doubt she does not lie in much state, for a friend and protectress of hers in the Mall [was it the lean lady, the fat lady or the spying neighbour?] was much lamenting her poverty very lately, not without some gentle reflections on your Lordship's want either of generosity or bowels towards a lady who had not refused you the full enjoyment of her charms.

The fault was not one of meanness or of waning affection. Rochester was not only a sick man, he was a man pursued by creditors. He had never been rich, for his father had squandered the estate; he had married an heiress, but he was her honest steward. His own fortunes depended on the King. As Gentleman of the Bedchamber he received a pension of £1,000 a year; the Rangership of Woodstock brought him a little more; he had occasional grants from the King. It was little enough on which to live at Court, and in the year when Mrs Barry bore his child, his creditors were attacking the very source of his income. A number of petitions were sent to the Lord Treasurer, of which it will be sufficient to give one instance, that of Agnes Curson, who showed that the Earl, after being indebted to her for £100, 'after a long solicitation and attendance at last the Earl was pleased to grant an assignment for

'This Lord . . . used sometimes, with others of his companions, to run naked, and particularly they did so once in Woodstock Park, upon a Sunday in the afternoon.' (Thomas Hearne)

137

the said sum (which is all the security she has for her debts) out of his pension; she humbly begs Treasurer Danby's favour in this particular. Resolution hereon: nil.'

He could not send Mrs Barry money, but he did not neglect her.

> Madam, [he wrote] Your safe delivery has deliver'd me too from fears for your sake, which were, I'll promise you, as burthensome to me, as your great belly could be to you. Every thing has fallen out to my wish, for you are out of danger, and the child is of the soft sex I love. Shortly my hopes are to see you, and in a little while after to look on you with all your beauty about you. Pray let no body but yourself open the box I sent you; I did not know, but that in lying-in you might have use of those trifles; sick and in bed, as I am, I could come at no more of 'em; but if you find 'em, or whatever is in my power of use, to your service, let me know it.

By 1678 the shadows had begun to fall, not only on Rochester who in the spring had been at the point of death – indeed his end was prematurely announced – but on all England. In October Sir Edmund Berry Godfrey was found murdered near Somerset House and the 'Popish Plot' was launched. Rochester was sick, poor and in hourly danger, for he had reason to fear what informers might learn of certain earlier doings in Somerset, when his wife had become a Catholic. Perhaps all 'the Hound of Heaven' needed now was a complete disillusionment with his mistress to bring him to his knees in the company of Dr Burnet and the Reverend Robert Parsons.

The disillusionment emerged slowly. First it was impatience which took the place of tenderness. It is no longer of the fat or the lean woman he speaks but of other men. Harsh words are no longer quickly repented, they are explained and justified, but there is still sufficient love for him to date his letter 'An hour after I left you.'

> Madam, Tho' not for real kindness sake, at least to make your own words good, (which is a point of honour proper for a woman) endeavour to give me some undeniable proofs that you love me. If there be any in my power which I have yet neither given nor offer'd, you must explain yourself; I am perhaps very dull, but withal very sincere: I could wish, for your sake, and my own, that your failings were such; but be they what they will, since I must love you, allow me the liberty of telling you sometimes unmannerly truths, when my zeal for your service causes, and your own interest requires it: these inconveniences you must bear with from those that love you, with greater regard to you than themselves; such a one I pretend to be, and I hope if you do not yet believe it, you will in time find it.
>
> You have said something that has made me fancy tomorrow will prove a happy day to me; however, pray let me see you before you

speak with any other man, there are reasons for it, dearest of all my desires. I expect your commands.

'Unmannerly truths' became common.

> Madam, my faults are such, as, among reasonable people, will ever find excuse; but to you I will make none, you are so very full of mystery: I believe you make your court with good success, at least I wish it; and as the kindest thing I can say, do assure you, you shall never be my pattern, either in good-nature or friendship, for I will be after my own rate, not yours,
>
> Your humble servant.

There had been a time, earlier in their love, when he had declared that the greatness of her spirit distinguished her in love, as in all things else, from womankind. The end now had almost come, and although, writing to her at three o'clock in the morning, he still declared, 'Anger, spleen, revenge and shame, are not yet so powerful with me as to make me disown this great truth, that I love you above all things in the world', he writes almost in terms of hatred:

> I thank God I can distinguish, I can see very woman in you, and from yourself am convinc'd I have never been in the wrong in my opinion of women: 'Tis impossible for me to curse you; but give me leave to pity myself, which is more than ever you will do for me. You have a character, and you maintain it; but I am sorry you make me an example to prove it: it seems (as you excel in everything) you scorn to grow less in that noble quality of using your servants very hardly; you do well not to forget it, and rather practise upon me, than lose the habit of being very severe; for you that choose rather to be wise than just or good-natur'd may freely dispose of all things in your power, without regard to one or the other. As I admire you, I would be glad I could imitate you; it were but manners to endeavour it; which, since I am not able to perform, I confess you are in the right to call that rude which I call kind; and so keep me in the wrong for ever (which you cannot choose but take great delight in): you need but continue to make it fit for me not to love you, and you can never want something to upbraid me with.

If to the beginning of his love for Mrs Barry may be ascribed 'A Pastoral Dialogue' written in 1674:

> There sighs not on the plain
> So lost a swain as I;

it is not unreasonable to attribute to this bitter ending the poem 'Upon his Leaving his Mistress':

> 'Tis not that I am weary grown
> Of being yours, and yours alone:
> But with what face can I incline,
> To damn you to be only mine?

Elizabeth Barry offers a
cornucopia to William III

You, whom some kinder pow'r did fashion,
By merit, and by inclination,
The joy at least of a whole nation.

Let meaner spirits of your sex
With humble aims their thoughts perplex:
And boast, if by their arts they can
Contrive to make *one* happy man,
While, mov'd by an impartial sense,
Favours, like Nature, you dispense
With universal influence.

There remained to be considered the child 'of the soft sex I love',
who had been christened by her mother's name. Rochester was
fond of his children, and now that the mother's infidelity was
certain he took the child from her.

Madam [he wrote] I am far from delighting in the grief I have given
you, by taking away the child: and you, who made it so absolutely
necessary for me to do so, must take that excuse from me, for all the
ill nature of it: on the other side, pray be assur'd, I love Betty so well,
that you need not apprehend any neglect from those I employ; and I
hope very shortly to restore her to you a finer girl than ever. In the
mean time you would do well to think of the advice I gave you, for

how little show soever my prudence makes in my own affairs, in yours it will prove very successful, if you please to follow it; and since discretion is the thing alone you are like to want, pray study to get it.

There is a finality in the last phrase that makes it doubtful whether this quarrel was ever healed. Of the child we know for certain only that she died at the age of fourteen, and was buried where her mother later lay at Acton. In his will he bequeathed 'to an infant child by the name of Elizabeth Clarke forty pounds annuity; to commence from the day of my decease, and to continue during her life; to the payment of which I bind the manor of Sutton-Mallet'. It seems probable that this was Mrs Barry's child: one is less ready to believe in 'Captain' Alexander Smith's story of a Madam Clark and of her peculiarly brutal rape a year before Rochester's death.

Near this Place
Lies the Body of
ELIZABETH BARRY
of the Parish of S^t
MARY SAVOY who
Departed, this life
y^e 7th of November 1713
Aged 55 years.

TO
THE MEMORY OF
CRAYLE CRAYLE Esq^R
WHO DIED 2^D OCTO^R 1780
AGED 58 YEARS
AND
WAS INTERRD IN THE
FAMILY VAULT
NEAR THIS
PLACE.

An affectionate remembrance
of two beloved Relatives;
ELIZABETH,
Wife of JAMES BRAMALL TOOSEY,
died May 31st 1826, in her 53^d Year;
d of ELIZABETH SARAH, their Daughter,
died June 15th 1826, in her 27th Year,
s surviving her Parent only fifteen days

HUNTING ye HARE
with deep mouthed hounds

VIII Stttt-life

Mrs Barry and Mrs Roberts and Mrs Boutel belonged to London and to the house in St James's; the country seems to have been associated in Rochester's mind with his wife and children. He hadn't the usual courtier's scornful idea of country life, briefly expressed by Sir Robert Bulkeley in a letter to Rochester: 'Whenever I leave London (which is a sort of dying)'. Gramont, according to Anthony Hamilton, called the country 'a young person's gibbet and galleys'. With the difficulties of communication, the lack of amusement (whether theatre or stews), the backwardness of the inhabitants, Oxfordshire was as remote from London as the Orkneys today are from Edinburgh. The comedies of the period are full of country knights and country wives who arrive in London wearing uncouth garments and with manners which belong to a strange and uncivilized realm. Stanford in Shadwell's *Sullen Lovers*, after railing at life in city and Court, is advised to try the country: 'There you may be free.' 'Free!' he exclaims, 'yes, to be drunk with March beer, and wine worse than ever was served in at Pye-corner at the eating of pigs; and hear no other discourse but of horses, dogs and hawks.'

But Rochester had been brought up as a child in the country, he had known nothing of cities before he went to Oxford, and seldom a year passed but he retired to it – whether to write, to recover from sickness, or simply for contemplation. In a letter to Savile he said of the country that it was 'where only one can think; for you at Court think not at all; or, at least, as if you were shut up in a drum; you can think of nothing, but the noise that is made about you'. He needed too at times to limit his 'fury of wine and fury of women' of which Nathaniel Lee wrote, though he did not always find escape from that fury in the country. In his last work, the remodelling for the Restoration stage of Fletcher's *Valentinian*, he introduced lines which were clearly autobiographical:

> Discourteous nymphs! who own these murmuring floods
> And you unkind divinities o' th' woods!
> When to your banks and bowers I came distrest,
> Half dead through absence, seeking peace and rest,
> Why would you not protect by these your streams

A sleeping wretch from such wild dismal dreams?
Mishapen monsters round in measures went,
Horrid in form with gestures insolent;
Grinning through goatish beards with half clos'd eyes,
They look'd me in the face, frighted to rise!

So may have grinned from the walls of High Lodge, Woodstock, the figures of fauns and satyrs in the indecent pictures, which, according to Aubrey, he had painted there. For he brought with him into the country some of the practices of town, but there was a sharp division between Woodstock, his official residence as Ranger from 1674, and Adderbury, the home where his wife chiefly lived. Savile described that division between two houses not fifteen miles apart when he referred to 'the sobriety of Adderbury and the debauchery of Woodstock'. It was at Woodstock that he enjoyed Nell Browne, it was at Woodstock that Buckingham sometimes paid him a visit, on one occasion with 'the best pack of hounds that ever ran upon English ground'. It was at Woodstock that he entertained his wilder companions; it was only on the decorous occasions of christenings that Savile or Buckhurst was to be seen at Adderbury. It may have been these two who were concerned in a story recorded by Hearne.

Once the wild Earl of Rochester, and some of his companions, a little way from Woodstock, meeting in a morning with a fine young maid going with butter to market, they bought all the butter of her, and paid her for it, and afterwards stuck it up against a tree, which the maid perceiving, after they were gone, she went and took it off, thinking it pity that it should be quite spoiled. They observed her, and riding after her, soon overtook her, and as a punishment, set her upon her head, and clapt the butter upon her breach.

A vagrant

144

The only escapades recorded of him at Adderbury are very harmless and are only based on oral tradition. He is said once to have dressed himself as a tinker and walked to the neighbouring hamlet of Barford St John. Here, when the people gave him their pots and pans to mend, he knocked out the bottoms. They put him in the stocks for it, but he sent a man with a note addressed to Lord Rochester at Adderbury, and presently his coach and four horses drove into the village, and he was released. The tradition is a kindly one, for he is said to have sent the villagers new pots and pans. Another day he dressed as a tramp (one is reminded of Burnet's statement that 'he would have gone about the streets as a beggar'), and meeting another tramp, asked him whither he was going. The man said that he was going to Lord Rochester's, though it was useless, for he never gave anything. The Earl accompanied him and while the tramp went to the back of the house, he went to the front and gave orders to his servants how they were to receive him. They seized him and put him in a barrel of beer, and every time he raised his head Rochester knocked it down again. Presently he was released, given a meal and a new suit of clothes, and told never again to say that Lord Rochester gave nothing away.

The division between Woodstock and Adderbury, between the 'rake-hells', as he himself called them, and his wife and children, was usually complete. But on one occasion the sinister Woodstock house with its lascivious pictures and the memories of Nell Browne, and the park which had been the scene of drunken dancing, saw an innocent intruder. 'An old woman of Woodstock', Hearne entered in his journal, 'told me yesterday that when the Duke of Monmouth was at Port-Meadow race, and afterwards went to my Lord Rochester's at Woodstock, when the Duke, the Earl, and the child (the said Charles) walk'd in the park, the Duke gave the boy the right hand, and she thought him the finest boy she ever beheld with her eyes. The Duke made him a present of a fine little horse.'

Even here there is no mention of Lady Rochester at Woodstock, and the meeting between the young Lord Wilmot and the Duke of Monmouth may have occurred after his father had fetched him from his mother, who was probably at her Somerset home, to have him touched for the King's Evil. The only mention of Wood-stock in connection with Lady Rochester comes in a short undated letter to her husband in which it is not fanciful to distinguish an accent of despairing affection:

> Though I cannot flatter myself so much as to expect it, yet give me leave to wish that you would dine tomorrow at Cornbury where necessity forces
>
> your faithful humble Wife,
E. Rochester.
>
> if you sent to command me to Woodstock when I am so near as Cornbury I shall not be a little rejoiced.

Hearne tells how 'they said he was very barbarous to his own lady, tho' so very fine a woman', but infidelity was the full extent of his barbarity. A love story, eclipsing more placid affections, may have lain hidden between these two young, witty and unhappy people. It would be wrong to think of her always as the suffering wife living alone with her children in the great dull house at Adderbury. There were times no doubt when she came to London, though the only record of such a visit is early in her married life. In a letter dated from Westminster on 4 March 1671 Lady Mary Bertie wrote to a friend: 'I was with my Lady Rochester and my Lady Betty Howard and Mrs Lee at a play, and afterwards I supped at my Lady Rochester's and came not home till almost 12 aclock.' There were times of gaiety at Adderbury, too, which offer a contrast to the festivities of Woodstock. Lady Mary Bertie was staying there on 17 June 1672 and wrote to the same friend: 'Lady Rochester kept my brother's birthday with great solemnity, causing the bell to be rung and making a great dinner. We concluded it by dancing 16 dances after supper, and because the weather was hot, we danced some of them in the forecourt, some in the garden and the rest in the hall.' The same summer, one learns from Lady Mary, Rochester was in Somerset with his wife, and in the autumn he was made a Deputy-Lieutenant for Somerset. The next September festivities were again held at Adderbury, when Thomas Wharton married old Lady Rochester's grand-daughter, Anne Lee, the beginning of an unhappy marriage.

Most years Rochester spent some part of the summer with his wife; that he was at Adderbury with her in 1676 and 1678 is known from Lord Anglesey's diary, while every September there was racing at Woodstock for the plate (the plate was won on 16 September 1679 by Rochester with a grey). There were other breaks too in the monotony of country life. In 1673 George Fox, the wild Quaker, had 'a large and precious meeting' at Adderbury and stayed the night with Bray D'Oyley in what is now known as the Old Manor House; 'as I sate at supper, I saw I was taken; and I saw I had a suffering to undergo', he wrote later to his wife from

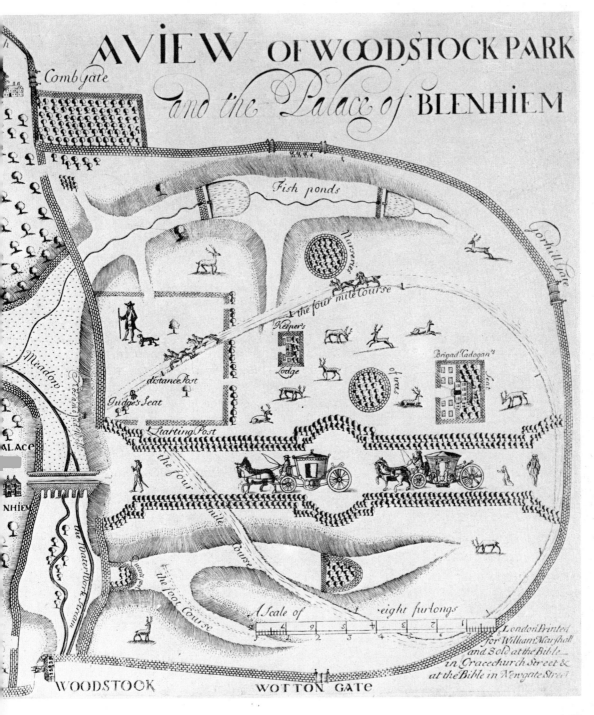

Worcester Gaol. He was not arrested at Adderbury, however, but the next day, at Armscot, in Worcestershire. And in the first year of Rochester's marriage, in 1667, was published a quarto tract: *God's Terrible Judgment in Oxfordshire. A True Relation of a Woman of Adderbury having used divers horrible wishes and imprecations, was suddenly burnt to ashes on one side of her body, when there was no fire near her.* Adderbury had preserved into the Restoration something of that dark element of Puritanism, which had led in the Civil War to fighting in the village streets and to the murder of the parson at the door of his house.

Then there were the celebrations at Adderbury of the children's baptisms: in August 1669 of Anne, a ceremony at which the father was probably present, newly come from Paris, and in January 1671 of Charles, his only son, who was to outlive him by but a year, a beautiful child, one of the handsomest in England according to Hearne, and his portrait bears the antiquary out. Of his christening we know a little from a letter of Henry Savile apologizing for his absence: 'My most deplorable excuse was made why I was not at the christening of my Lord Wilmot by my Lord Buckhurst and Sedley. It is a ceremony I was sorry to miss, but your Lordship staying much with your Lady will I presume once a year furnish us with such solemnities, and for the next I hope I shall have no reason to fail paying my attendance.' Savile's assumption was not quite justified. The next baptism, that of Elizabeth, took place in July 1674, and that of his last child, Mallet, in January 1675, the year in which Rochester is said to have been banished from Court for writing 'The History of Insipids'. All these baptisms must have been the occasions of some festivity, the house would have been lit up to welcome the nobles from London, and perhaps in 1669 and 1674 there was dancing on the lawn.

Rochester loved these children, who inherited their parents' beauty, though Charles inherited his father's ill-health. Hearne has something to say of the daughters' looks.

As for his three daughters, the eldest Anne was a tall, handsome body, married first to Henry Bainton in com. Wilts. Esq., and afterwards to Francis Grevil (eldest son to Foulk, Lord Brooks) by whom she had, among other children, William, the present Lord Brooke, who though he has aim'd to be wicked like his grandfather, that Lord Rochester, yet wants his parts. The second daughter, the Lady Elizabeth, she was a pretty little body, and was married to Edward Montagu, Earl of Sandwich [this was the son of the unsuccessful suitor of Elizabeth Mallet]. . . . I cannot learn anything of Woodstock people about the Lady Mallet, what sort of person she was, any further than that she was not so handsome as the other two; but I find by the Peerage of England that she was married to (John) Vaughan, Baron Lisburne, in Ireland.

Lady Elizabeth Wilmot: 'she was a pretty little body'. (Thomas Hearne)

A corner of Adderbury Churchyard: the tomb of a tender nurse

In a corner of Adderbury Churchyard there is a small gravestone with this inscription under the puffed cheeks of cherubim: 'In Full and Certaine Hope of the second coming of Christ Resteth Here the Body of Mary late wife of John Swift and Tender Nurse to the Right Honourable Ladyes Elizabeth and Mallett Willmott she suffered Her mortal change November the 28 In the Year 1687.' Mary Swift may be numbered with John Cary and his wife among the faithful servants of the estate who won more affection from old Lady Rochester than any but her children and grandchildren.

For his children Rochester had the love of a man who sees in them the only form of immortality in which he can believe. Often in his letters to his wife he asks to be remembered to them. 'Remember me to Nan and my Lord Wilmot'; 'My humble service to my aunt Rogers and Nan'; 'Pray bid my daughter Betty present my duty to my daughter Mallet'; 'God bless you and the children whate'er becomes of your humble servant'. There is a dispute with his wife over the health of his son. 'I am extremely troubled for the sickness of your son as well in consideration of the affliction it gives you, as the dearness I have for him myself', he writes when he hears of it, and later: 'T'was very well for your son, as ill as you took it, that I sent him to Adderbury, for it proves at least to be the King's evil that troubles him; and he comes up to London this week to be touch't.' It is a pity that we have no light on Charles's arrival in London and his stay with his father and how the London house, the scene of many meetings of the 'merry gang', appeared to the curious, clear-sighted eyes of a child. Two letters from his father survive, full of the pathetic wisdom of the man who on his deathbed was to express the hope that his son would never be a wit. He had always possessed the power of being wise for others.

A letter from Rochester to his wife

Charles, I take it very kindly that you write to me (tho' seldom) and wish heartily you would behave yourself so, as that I might show how much I love you without being ashamed. Obedience to your grandmother, and those who instruct you in good things, is the way to make you happy here, and for ever. Avoid idleness, scorn lying, and God will bless you: For which I pray, Rochester.

I hope, Charles, when you receive this, and know that I have sent this gentleman to be your tutor, you will be very glad to see I take such care of you, and be very grateful; which is best shown in being obedient and diligent. You are now grown big enough to be a man, if you can be wise enough [the child was nine when his father died, who seems to have shared old Lady Rochester's impetuous ideas of maturity]; and the way to be truly wise, is, to serve God, learn your book, and observe the instructions of your parents first, and next your tutor, according as you employ that time, you are to be happy or unhappy for ever. But I have so good an opinion of you, that I am glad to think, you will never deceive me. Dear child, learn your book, and be obedient, and you shall see what a father I will be to you; you shall want no pleasure while you are good: And that you may be so, are my constant prayers, Rochester.

These are not the letters of a hypocrite. He did not wish his son to live as he lived or think as he thought; he wished his son to believe in God and not to follow his father into the cold of an atheist's universe. He told Burnet later that 'they were happy that believed: for it was not in every man's power', and he acknowledged that 'the whole system of religion, if believed, was a greater foundation of quiet than any other thing whatsoever'. He wanted for his child both happiness and quiet.

One would like to add to this picture of Rochester as a parent, some features of him as a countryman, as his mother's son. It would be strange if he had not received from her, as well as a love of the country, some of her power of management and her possessive love of acres. He had in his hands not only the care of Adderbury, where he was probably helped by his mother, but his wife's estates at Enmore in Somerset, which had made her so coveted an heiress. He seems to have managed the latter with ability and on the whole with remarkable honesty. He himself was continually in debt – he told Burnet of the shifts to which he and his friends were driven, 'their unjust usage of their creditors, and putting them off by any deceitful promise they could invent, that might deliver them from present importunity' – but he does not seem to have drawn for his own expenses on his wife's estate without repayment. She may sometimes have needed money, but she was never reduced to such straits as when he wrote

Dear wife, I recover so slowly and relapse so continually that I am almost weary of myself. If I had the least strength I would come to

Anne Baynton

'The eldest Anne was a tall, handsome body.' (Thomas Hearne)

(overleaf left) Lord Charles Wilmot: 'Avoid idleness, scorn lying, and God will bless you: For which I pray, Rochester.'

(overleaf right) Lady Elizabeth and Lady Mallet Wilmot

Adderbury, but in the condition I am, Kensington and back is a voyage I can hardly support; I hope you excuse my sending you no money, for till I am well enough to fetch it myself they will not give me a farthing, and if I had not pawn'd my plate I believe I must have starv'd in my sickness.

It is true that he wrote once to her, 'It is now some weeks since I writ you word that there was money return'd out of Somerset for your use, which I desired you to send for by what sums yourself pleas'd. By this time I believe I have spent it half; however you must be supplied if you think fit to order it.' But the fault of this self-confessed embezzlement was partly his wife's, and there were other times when she expected from him more than he was able to perform.

I receive the compliment you make in desiring my company as I ought to do. But I have a poor living to get that I may be less burdensome to your Ladyship. If your Ladyship had return'd money out of Somerset for the buying these things you sent for they might have been had by this time. But the little I get here will very hardly serve my own turn; however I must tell you that 'twas Blancourt's fault you had not Holland and other things sent you a fortnight ago.

On another occasion he certainly borrowed without leave from her Somerset revenue:

You have I hear done me the favour to expect me long in the country where I intended to have been long ago, but Court affairs are more hardly solicited now than ever, and having follow'd them till I had spent all my own money and yours too, I was forced to stay something longer here till I had contriv'd a supply, which being now dispatch'd I have nothing to hinder me from what I heartily desire which is to wait on your Ladyship at Adderbury.

She was a favoured creditor, and his final estimate of himself as a steward does not seem unduly biased:

I know not who has persuaded you that you want five pounds to pay the servants' wages, but next week Blancourt is going into the west, at whose return you may expect an account of your entire revenue, which I will be bound to say has hitherto, and shall (as long as I can get bread without it) been wholly employ'd to the use of yourself and those who depend on you; if I prove an ill steward at least you never had a better, which is some kind of satisfaction to your humble servant.

Adderbury House, Oxfordshire: 'because the weather was hot, we danced some of them in the forecourt, some in the garden and the rest in the hall.'

All the same there were times when the household at Adderbury lacked ordinary comfort: 'Whatever coal you order I shall return money for upon notice; ready cash I have but little, 'tis hard to come by, but when Mr Cary comes down he shall furnish you with as much as I can procure; when you have more commands I am ready to receive 'em.'

Come and behold ᵉ salvation of ᵞ Lord.

HEAVEN SHALL TURN THY WEAPONS AGAINST

The wrath of God is upon all they
that conspire against his church

Thy crymes they aim'd at but the
king ᵞ heaven protects it

My testimony still triumphs

By our discoverys you may know
What damn'd Intreagues are hatch't below

E: xit Vsct Stafford

THE INFERNALL CONCLAVE

Behold th'Infernall Conclave, mett in state,
Contriving Englands, and its Monarchs Fate.
Assassinate the King Subvert his Laws,
They cry'd, and on their Ruin, build our Cause.

Pardons were streight prepar'd, and men made free
Of Heaven, to perpetrate their Villany
And thus secure, their Plotts went brisky on,
Against our fixed Laws, and settl'd Throne.

But he that sitts enthron'd, in mercy chose,
Those instruments, that did the whole disclose.
And thus to Oates and all the rest wee owe
The Kingdoms Peace, if wee can keep it so.

IX 'What Evil Angel Enemy...?'

For Rochester's relations with his wife the main evidence is their surviving correspondence, and the letters in no way bear out 'the brutal treatment' mentioned by Hearne.

In the letters he seldom appears as the happy lover, though once he wrote from Newmarket a few hurried lines: 'I'll hold you six to four I love you with all my heart, if I would bet with other people I'm sure I could get two to one'; and once with kind mockery:

> Madam, I received your three pictures, and am in a great fright lest they should be like you. By the bigness of the head, I should apprehend you far gone in the rickets: by the severity of the countenance, somewhat inclined to prayer and prophecy: yet there is an alacrity in your plump cheeks that seems to signify sack and sugar: and your sharp-sighted nose has borrowed quickness from the sweet-smelling eye. I never saw a chin smile before, a mouth frown, or a forehead mump. Truly the artist has done his part (God keep him humble) and a fine man he is if his excellence don't puff him up like his pictures. The next impertinence I have to tell you is that I am coming into the country; I have got horses, but want a coach: when that defect is supplied, you shall quickly have the trouble of Your humble servant, Rochester.

These letters were still in the mood of the marriage, of the elopement at Charing Cross, of the song to the 'live-long' minute; they were addressed to the high-spirited girl, who had summed up her lovers so bawdily and quaffed the big glass of claret in her stepfather's presence to the suitor of the moment. But there was much in their marriage to alter both of them.

Infidelity tormented Rochester's conscience. He could write with melancholy tenderness the song 'Absent from thee I languish still: Then ask me not, when I return?' or in a letter:

> I kiss my dear wife a thousand times, as much as imagination and wish will give me leave. Think upon me as long as it is pleasant and convenient to do so and afterwards forget me; for though I would fain make you the author and foundation of my happiness, yet would I not be the cause of your constraint and disturbance, for I love not myself as much as I do you; neither do I value my own satisfaction equally as I do yours. Farewell.

Once at least he owned his debt to her:

> 'Tis not an easy thing to be entirely happy, but to be kind is very
> easy, and that is the greatest measure of happiness. I say not this to
> put you in mind of being kind to me, you have practised that so long
> that I have a joyful confidence you will never forget it, but to show
> that I myself have a sense of what the methods of my life seem so
> utterly to contradict. I must not be too wise about my own follies,
> or else this letter had been a book dedicated to you, and published
> to the world.

Their marriage was not ruined. On what remained of the first
passion and tenderness enough affection remained to build again,
if they had been left alone to do it. But marriage had not brought
them solitude. Sir John and Lady Warre, who had stood between
Elizabeth Mallet and her lovers, who had tried, with the aid of her
grandfather, Lord Hawley, to sell her to the highest bidder, who
had advised and persuaded and reprimanded, still haunted their
daughter. They had not consented to the marriage, but they
accepted the accomplished fact. Lady Warre's visits were an annual
affair, and the result was always frayed nerves, impatience, angry
letters between husband and wife. 'The style of your Ladyships last,
though kinder than I deserve, is not without some alloy from your
late conversations with those whom I should extremely honour if
they would do me the right and you the virtue never to come near
you when I am really as well with you as I wish.' Where was the
virtue in confession and a plea for pardon, when every lapse had
already been recounted to his wife by Lady Warre?
After one such visit he wrote with self-torturing bitterness:

> My most neglected wife, till you are a much respected widow, I find
> you will scarce be a contented woman, and to say no more than the
> plain truth I do endeavour so fairly to do you that last good service
> that none but the most impatient would refuse to rest satisfied. What
> evil angel enemy to my repose does inspire my Lady Warre to visit
> you once a year and leave you bewitch'd for eleven months after?
> I thank my God that I have the torment of the stone upon me (which
> are no small ones) rather than that unspeakable one of being an
> eye-witness to your uneasiness. Do but propose to me any reasonable
> thing upon earth I can do to set you at quiet, but it is like a mad
> woman to lie roaring out of pain and never confess in what part it is;
> these three years have I heard you continually complain, nor has it
> ever been in my power to obtain the knowledge of any considerable
> cause with confidence. I shall not have the like affliction three years
> hence, but that repose I'll owe to a surer friend than you; when that
> time comes, you will grow wiser, though I fear not much happier.

She had been three years complaining, he declared, but the only
complaint which survives could hardly be described by any but a

man with a raw conscience and tortured nerves as the roaring of a mad woman.

> If I could have been troubled at any thing when I had the happiness of receiving a letter from you I should be so because you did not name a time when I might hope to see you: the uncertainty of which very much afflicts me. Whether this odd kind of proceeding be to try my patience or obedience I cannot guess, but I will never fail of either where my duty to you require them. I do not think you design staying at Bath now that it is like to be so full and God knows when you will find in your heart to leave the place you are in: pray consider with yourself whether this be a reasonable way of proceeding and be pleased to let me know what I am to expect, for there being so short a time betwixt this and the sitting of the Parliament I am confident you will find so much business as will not allow you to come into the country. Therefore pray lay your commands upon me what I am to do and, though it be to forget my children and the long hopes I have lived in of seeing you, yet I will endeavour to obey you or in the memory only torment myself without giving you the trouble of putting you in mind that there lives such a creature as your faithful humble ——.

This was mild enough, and perhaps the better to wound, but that she could claim still some of the old high spirit seems implied in a long letter from her husband:

> I cannot deny to you but that heroic resolutions in women are things of the which I have never been transported with great admiration; nor can be if my life lay on't, for I think it is a very impertinent virtue. . . . I infer that as heat in the feet makes cold in the head, so may it be with probability expected too, that greatness and meanness should be as oppositely seated and a heroic head is liker to be balanc'd with an humble tail. Besides reason, experience has furnish'd me with many examples of this kind, my Lady Montennell Villers and twenty others, whose honour was ever so excessive in their heads that they suffered a want of it in every other part. Thus it comes about Madam that I have no very great esteem for a high spirited lady and therefore should be glad that none of my friends thought it convenient to adorn their other perfections with that most transcendent accomplishment; it is tolerable only in a waiting gentlewoman who to prove herself lawfully descended from Sir Humphrey, her great uncle, is allowed the affectation of a high spirit, and a natural inclination towards a genteel converse. This now is a letter, and to make it a kind one I must assure you of all the dotage in the world, and then to make it a civil one, down at the bottom, with a great space between, I must write

> Madam

> I have too much respect for you to come near you whilst I am in disgrace but when I am a favourite again I will wait on you.

There is a poem attributed to Rochester in a commonplace book.

It reflects the same heavy unhappy irony as the close of this letter and is addressed 'To his More than Meritorious Wife':

> I am by fate slave to your will,
> And I will be obedient still,
> To show my love I will compose ye,
> For your fair fingers' ring a posie,
> In which shall be express'd my duty,
> And how I'll be for ever true t'ye,
> With low made legs and sugared speeches,
> Yielding to your fair bum the breeches,
> And show myself in all I can
> Your very humble servant Jan.

If the verses are his they are a startling contrast with that earlier song in which he had expressed his constancy.

> I cannot change, as others do,
>   Though you unjustly scorn:
> Since that poor swain that sighs for you,
>   For you alone was born.

He had reached the stage of railing against marriage.

> To all young men that live to woo,
> To kiss and dance, and tumble too;
> Draw near and counsel take of me,
> Your faithful pilot I will be;
> Kiss who you please, Joan, Kate or Mary,
> But still this counsel with you carry,
>   Never marry.

It was he rather than his wife who roared like a mad woman, and in 'A Satire Against Marriage' the roaring reached its highest pitch:

> Marriage, thou state of jealousy and care,
> The curse of wife, what flesh and blood can bear?
> She ever loads your head, and stuns your passive ear,
> And still the plague you feel, or still you fear.

And its conclusion

> Of all the Bedlams marriage is the worst,
> With endless cords, with endless keepers curst!
> Frantic in love you run, and rave about,
> Mad to get in, but hopeless to get out.

'Endless keepers', so he may well have thought of Sir John and Lady Warre. 'Mad to get in', was it a reference to the six armed men and the coach across the road and the midnight ride? What was it that ran like a poison in the veins? Love was still there, it showed itself in the one exquisite song of a tired man seeking his everlasting rest, it revealed itself again on his deathbed. There was his ruined health, the pox, the stone, the eyes that at times could hardly see – 'my eyes are almost out', he wrote to her, and again, 'I recover so slowly and relapse so continually that I am almost weary of myself'; there was his infidelity – 'lest once more wand'ring from that Heaven, I fall on some base heart unblest'; there were the Warres; but if we read the letters closely, something else emerges, something to which he may have referred in the first line of the satire: 'Marriage, thou state of jealousy and care'. He may not have been referring to his wife's jealousy but his own.

If he had cause to complain of Lady Warre, his wife had great cause to complain of his mother. Old Lady Rochester was a woman who needed an estate to manage. She had lost the children of her first marriage early, and when the grandchildren grew up, she lost the hobby which had been keeping her employed, the Ditchley estate. She had to have a home, and she came to her youngest son's house of Adderbury. He was complaisant, for he admired and probably a little feared his mother, who had set such an ineffaceable mark on his childhood. Her grandchild, Sir Edward Henry Lee, was born in 1663 and married at the age of fourteen in 1677. It was probably therefore in that year that old Lady Rochester descended on her son. Elizabeth was perhaps at Enmore, for her husband wrote to her, presumably from Adderbury, of the move that had been made.

The alteration of my mother's former resolutions (who is now resolv'd against ever moving from hence) puts me upon some thoughts which were almost quite out of my head; but you may be

Old Lady Rochester, a page from her account book and a carpenter's promise not to fish at Adderbury, his mark witnessed by the faithful agent, John Cary

sure I shall determine nothing that does not tend as much to your real happiness as lies in my power. I have therefore sent you this letter to prepare you for a remove first hither, and afterwards as fate shall direct which is (I find) the true disposer of things whatever we attribute to wisdom or providence. Be therefore in a readiness upon the first notice from me to put that in execution which I shall first inform you particularly of – let me have an answer and dispatch the messenger quickly. God bless you.

In another letter he writes hopefully that 'the happy conjunction of my mother and you can produce nothing but extreme good carriage to me as it has formerly done; you show yourself very discreet and kind in these and in other matters'. His letters from this time more frequently than not contain a message to his mother.

Old Lady Rochester was probably ill at ease, now that she was no longer head of a household. Her imagination must have set to work; her love for her son, her imperious, unbending disposition, her easily roused temper combined to invent stories of the wife to tell the husband, stories presumably meant to inspire jealousy. This seems evident from a letter of Rochester to his wife:

Wonder not that I have not writ to you all this while, for it was hard for me to know what to write, upon several accounts, but in this I will only desire you not to be too much amaz'd at the thoughts my mother has of you, since being mere imaginations they will as easily vanish as they were groundlessly created. For my own part I will make it my endeavour they may.

Perhaps another letter refers to his mother's accusations.

If you hear not from me it is not that I either want time or will to write to you, I am sufficiently at leisure and think very often of you, but could expect an account of what has befallen me, which is not yet fit for you to know; only thus much I will tell you, it was all in vindication of you.

If Rochester were a devil with 'something of the Angel yet un-defac'd in him', his mother was a good woman with a fund of Satanic malice. Five years after Rochester's death, at the age of seventy, it broke out in so extreme a fashion as by itself to vindicate her earlier victim. Her granddaughter, the Hon. Mrs Wharton, had died and left her fortune to her husband, a man for whom old Lady Rochester had an extreme hatred. 'A wickeder wretch was never borne than this bad man.' She accused him of forging his wife's will. 'Wharton can if he pleases counterfeit his wife's hand and so can a woman that waited upon her too.' Her accusations become almost unbalanced.

He gave her the pox a great many years ago and never told her of it, he kept another woman whom he had children by; in three years almost before she died, he never went in bed with her, and though she had been an hour together upon her knees to know his reason why he was angry with her he would never tell her to the last of her life.

One source of her hatred is plain. 'I hear Fanshawe is one of Wharton's great cronies and makes him friends at Court, but I know they must be pitiful ones, for he is a pitiful fellow, upon all accounts but mischief.' Fanshawe had been Rochester's friend who had visited him on his deathbed and afterwards spread the story that he was mad and that his repentance was no more than 'melancholy fancies'. For that she never forgave him. After Wharton had listened to so many accusations, one can hardly wonder at the postscript to one of her letters to her grandson, Lord Lichfield: 'I only desired a little picture my daughter Wharton had of my son Rochester, only set in a shagreen case and Mr Wharton denied it to me.'

She was old and pathetic, but masterful and dangerous, and she must share with Lady Warre the blame for much of the unhappiness which Rochester and Elizabeth Mallet found in their marriage. Elizabeth's dislike of her flared out in at least one letter, written presumably from Enmore. She had, probably with some thankfulness, left Adderbury and her children, including 'my Lady Anne', in the care of her mother-in-law, who had taken the opportunity of a visit from Rochester to fill him with fresh stories against his wife.

> The last letter [she writes] I received from your honour was something scandalous, so that I knew not well how to answer it. 'Twas my design to have writ to my Lady Anne Wilmot to intercede for me, but now with joy I find myself again in your favour, it shall be my endeavours to continue so, in order to which very shortly I will be with you. In the meantime my mother may be pleas'd to dispose of my children, and my chemists, and my little dogs and whatever is mine as she will. Only if I may have nothing about me that I like, it will be the cause of making the felicity of waiting on her befall me very seldom. Thus I remain with my duty to her, my service to you and all these things.

Had Lady Rochester criticized her for preferring her dogs to her children and suggested that she was not fit to bring them up? If so, she had the final victory, for Rochester's will appointed:

> For the better assurance of a happy correspondancy between my dear mother and my dear wife, I do appoint to my mother and wife the guardianship of my son till he attain the age of one and twenty, so long as my wife shall remain unmarried and friendlily live with my mother; always provided that if my wife shall marry or wilfully separate herself from my mother, that then this her guardianship shall determine.

Thus even after his death he bound the two women together.

She was not to marry again, if he could prevent it, nor were there to be any illicit contacts. His mother he left to see to that, as she had seen to it in life. He had once written to his wife with a humour, which perhaps only veiled a brutal truth:

> Run away like a rascal without taking leave, dear wife – it is an unpolished way of proceeding which a modest man ought to be asham'd of. I have left you a prey to your own imaginations, amongst my relations, the worst of damnations; but there will come an hour of deliverance. Till when may my mother be merciful unto you. So I commit you to what shall ensue, woman to woman, wife to mother, in hopes of a future appearance in glory.

As for the cause of his jealousy, the scrap of truth on which old Lady Rochester set her imagination to work, is there a hint of it in Elizabeth's letter? She leaves her mother-in-law to dispose of her dogs, her children and her 'chemists'. Old Lady Rochester took up her home at Adderbury in the last years not only of her son's life, but also of his wife's, who survived him by only a year, dying of 'apoplexy'. Her health had probably already begun to fail; she may have begun to dabble in 'chemists', quack doctors such as Rochester himself had once parodied. Perhaps it was on one of these men that his mother based her stories. Rochester himself was sick to death; in 1678 there had been a premature report of his death. The age of impotence had come upon him early, and those who can no longer give pleasure themselves are prone to believe that pleasure will be sought elsewhere. It is the stock situation of Restoration comedy. 'I profess it is a very sufficient vexation, for a man to have a handsome wife', declares Fondlewife in *The Old Batchelor* and is answered by Barnaby, 'Never, sir, but when the man is an insufficient husband. 'Tis then indeed, like the vanity of taking a fine house, and yet be forced to let lodgings, to help pay the rent.'

What is certain is that the coming of his mother to Adderbury led to no final rupture with Elizabeth. Tenderness was never lacking for long from his letters. 'I fear I must see London shortly,' he writes one Christmas, presumably from Woodstock, 'and begin to repent that I did not bring you with me; for since these rake-hells are not here to disturb us, you might have passed your devotions this holy season, as well in this place, as at Adderbury.'

Of the 'rake-hells' and of his own reputation he was growing heartily weary. As the sickness of his body increased, the more he desired quiet. Peace, along with love and truth, was a quality he sought in his most famous love song. Perhaps this letter was written at the end of 1677, for in October and November of that year he had entertained the Duke of Buckingham for a fortnight at Woodstock, and on 17 December he was still in the country, for Savile wrote to him that 'there is not one sinner in England now

A view of Woodstock

out of London but yourself'. It was the year too when he recognized himself with some bitterness as 'the man whom it is the great mode to hate'.

His reputation was dogging him. On 5 June Harry Savile had written from London to his brother, Lord Halifax:

> Last night also, Du Puis, a French cook in the Mall, was stabbed for some pert answer by one Mr Floyd, and because my Lord Rochester and my Lord Lumley were supping in the same house, though in both different rooms and companies, the good-nature of the town has reported it all this day that his Lordship was the stabber. He desired me therefore to write to you to stop that report from going northward, for he says if it once gets as far as York the truth will not be believed under two or three years.

And on 16 October Savile reported to Rochester another lie, this time based on a harmless incident in the country.

> I am induced to make more haste by the scurvy report of your being very ill of which I desire to know the truth from yourself who alone do speak true concerning yourself, all the rest of the world not being only apt to believe but very ready to make lies concerning you, and if your friends were like them there has been such a story made concerning your last adventure as would persuade us grave men that you had stripped yourself of all your prudence as well as of your breeches which you will give a man leave to think impossible who knows and admires your talents as much as I do. After all if you have not caught cold and made yourself sick with your race, it is not one pin matter for all the other circumstances of it, though the same advantages have been taken of it here that use to be on any unreasonable prank performed by your Lordship who have had experience

167

enough upon the like occasion to know that the best way is to make your personal appearance here which has never failed you.

Rochester replied, and the humorous *tu quoque* does not hide the growing weariness with his own reputation.

For the hideous deportment, which you have heard of, concerning running naked, so much is true, that we went into the river somewhat late in the year, and had a frisk for forty yards in the meadow, to dry ourselves. I will appeal to the King and the D. [Duke] if they had not done as much; nay, my Lord-Chancellor, and the Archbishops both, when they were schoolboys; and, at these years, I have heard the one declaimed like Cicero, the other preached like St Austin. Prudenter persons, I conclude, *they* were, even in hanging-sleeves, than any of the fleshy fry (of which I must own myself the most unsolid) can hope to appear, even in their ripest manhood. And now (Mr Savile) since you are pleas'd to quote yourself for a grave man and the number of the scandaliz'd, be pleas'd to call to mind the year 1676, when two large fat nudities led the coranto round Rosamond's fair fountain, while the poor violated nymph wept to behold the strange decay of manly parts, since the days of her dear Harry the Second. . . .

The story, trivial as it was, was not allowed to drop; Robert Harley wrote to his father Sir Edward Harley with some relish that Mr Martin would give him particulars of the 'beastly prank of my Lord Rochester and my Lord Lovelace and ten other men, which they committed on that Sabbath day which were at Estington, which was there running along Woodstock Park naked'. And the final, most heightened version, got into the pages of Hearne:

This Lord . . . used sometimes, with others of his companions, to run naked, and particularly they did so once in Woodstock Park, upon a Sunday in the afternoon, expecting that several of the female sex would have been spectators, but not one appear'd. The man that stript them and pull'd off their shirts, kept the shirts and did not deliver them any more, going off with them before they finished the race.

One may conclude the extracts from Rochester's letters to his wife with a brief note, as usual undated, but which one may assume with some confidence to belong to the last months of 1678 or to 1679: 'Dear Wife, I have no news for you, but that London grows very tiresome, and I long to see you; but things are now reduced to that extremity on all sides, that a man dares not turn his back for fear of being hanged: an ill accident to be avoided by all prudent persons, and therefore by your humble servant, Rochester.'

On Michaelmas Eve 1678, Titus Oates, the son of an Anabaptist preacher, a proud and ignorant man who had been dismissed from his chaplaincy in the Navy for sodomy, appeared before the Privy Council with the story of a Jesuit plot to kill the King, implicat-

TITUS OATES
Anagramma
TESTIS OVAT.

ing many of the chief men in the Kingdom. On 17 October a certain Mr Denton wrote to Sir Ralph Verney how 'Sir Edward Berry Godfrey went out about 9 on Saturday morning, told his servant that if any came to speak with him he would dine at home; he has not been since heard of.' Godfrey was the Justice of the Peace to whom Oates, before he appeared at the Council, had declared on oath the narratives he intended to make. On the same night as Mr Denton wrote his letter, Godfrey's body was found, with his sword thrust through it, in a ditch near St Pancras Church, but later evidence seemed to show that the murder had actually taken place in the neighbourhood of Somerset House.

Civilization died with him. No man dared turn his back, as Rochester wrote, for fear of the informers. Bedloe, Oates's chief associate, in December 1678, boasted of his intimacy with Buckhurst, Rochester and Sedley. It was probably no more than the confidence trick of a man who had always lived by his wits, and Rochester's fears indicate no alliance with the informers who now ruled the country. He was not one of the hunters; he had every reason to fear being one of the hunted. In the fury and falsity which fell like a pall over town and country, men with easier consciences than his were afraid, and found their fears justified by trial and death. The truth of those strange years is even now obscure; when the reaction came and the persecutors in turn were persecuted, many died with an air as innocent as that of their victims. Burnet's beautiful and impartial sentence stands still: 'Here are the last words of dying men against the last words of those who suffered; and in this mist of incertitude must matters be left till the great revelation of all secrets.'

Godfrey, who had won a knighthood for his courage during the plague, and who had been noted all his life for a moderate Protestant, was now canonized by the fanatics. But when his ghost walked, it was not for vengeance that it called.

> One Mrs Lamb, a kinswoman of the Bishop of Ely, being with two others in the garden at Somerset House, was desired to sing and did: the song had these words – 'Bleeding wounds do pity crave.' There happened in the staircase (all glass to the garden) a tall person in a shroud: all affrighted, they run away into the house. Some asked what they run for; they told what they saw. About nine persons looking through the glass staircase saw nothing: but desiring her to sing again, when she came to the former words, they all saw to their amazement the same apparition.

That Rochester had particular reasons for uneasiness appears from some enigmatic sentences in Burnet's account of his death:

> He told me, that he had thereupon received the sacrament with great satisfaction, and that was increased by the pleasure he had in his

lady's receiving it with him, who had been for some years misled in the communion of the Church of Rome, and he himself had been not a little instrumental in procuring it, as he freely acknowledged. So that it was one of the joyfullest things that befell him in his sickness, that he had seen that mischief removed, in which he had so great a hand.

It has been suggested that Rochester had induced his wife to turn Catholic for political motives, with an eye to the accession to the Duke of York. It is the most likely explanation. Certainly he never himself showed any inclination towards Catholicism. In 'The History of Insipids' he had warned Charles against his brother and his brother's religion, while his poem 'On Rome's Pardons' leaves no doubt that in that Church at least he would not find a rest.

> If Rome can pardon sins, as Romans hold,
> And if these pardons can be bought and sold,
> It were no sin, t'adore and worship gold. . . .
>
> When came this knack, or when did it begin?
> What author have they, or whom brought it in?
> Did Christ e'er keep a custom-house for Sin?

Some of the circumstances of his wife's conversion are known. It is a story, tantalizing for its *lacunae*, which introduces the ambiguous figure of Stanley College, the Protestant joiner. This 'active and hot man', in Burnet's phrase, who had often spoken ill of the King, was the first victim of the reaction against Oates and his anti-Catholic followers, which followed the dissolution of the Oxford Parliament. He was tried for an offence of which none deemed him guilty, of a plot to kill the King at Oxford and change the Government. So little was his guilt credited that the grand jury returned *Ignoramus*. The trial was then transferred to Oxford, and it was made quite clear to judge and witnesses that the King desired a verdict of guilty. The risk of an acquittal came from the sturdy Protestantism of the joiner's past, and it was the wish of the prosecution to discredit him in the eyes of religious sympathizers. It was in this connection that his strange association with Rochester was brought to light. Lady Rochester was dead, and the facts of her conversion emerge one by one from the depositions of various men.

On 24 August 1681 a certain Richard Crosse wrote from Thurloxton, near Taunton, to Sir Leoline Jenkins:

You desired to be informed by Col. Hawley and myself what we heard the late Lady Rochester say of College's being a Papist. The day before she fell sick she said that to her knowledge College was a Papist. Others heard it then and another time at Lady Warre's table. Sir Francis Warre can say more of it. I enclose a letter from William

Clarke, of Sandford, late a Justice of this county and formerly and now a trustee and steward to Lord Rochester's estate, which will inform you of what College confessed to him.

William Clarke to Richard Crosse:

I do not know that College was a Papist, but have heard him say that, being about 14 years since a trooper under the Earl of Rochester, my Lord employed him to bring Tomson, a priest, to his Lady to pervert her, and that he did so several times and by means of that priest she was perverted. This I believe to be the reason she took him to be a Papist, and this he declared to many others, who can be produced if necessary.

Another item in the story is supplied in the information of Thomas Harris, of Glaston, Somerset. In Michaelmas Term, 1677, he was lodging with Thomas Peter, a victualler, in Wych Street. One Sunday evening a person called College came in and entered into discourse concerning Lord Rochester and his lady, extolling the latter and vilifying the former.

I told him I heard my Lady was turned Papist. He asked me what I meant by a Papist. I answered one that maintained the tenets of the Church of Rome. He then undertook to defend the said tenets with great violence, telling me that he would bring books next day that should confute all arguments to the contrary. He likewise told me his name was Colledge, not College, and that he had wrought for Lord Rochester at Enmore.

College was condemned to die; it was the last mischief for which Rochester may be held partly responsible, this death of an innocent man.

The gallows at Tyburn

X The Literary Jungle

Dorimant's star had been short-lived. By the time that *Sir Fopling Flutter* was produced in 1676 Rochester was only twenty-nine, but the bright days were over. The events of Rochester's life in the later seventies appear like a fever chart hung at the bed of a patient condemned to die, but this patient could read his own chart. The eighteen-year-old hero of Bergen in 1665 had been accused ten years later, however unfairly, of cowardice by the ignoble Mulgrave. Next year the Epsom affray and the death of Downes was the occasion of a song, probably by Thomas D'Urfey:

> Room, room for a blade of the town,
>   That takes delight in roaring,
> Who all day long rambles up and down,
>   And at night in the street lies snoring.
>
> That for the noble name of spark
>   Does his companions rally;
> Commits an outrage in the dark,
>   Then slinks into an alley.[1]

The young man who had attempted to elope with Miss Mallet in 1665 was ten years afterwards a client of Mrs Fourcard's 'Baths' and the disillusioned lover of Mrs Barry.

The dramatist Nathaniel Lee wrote of him in the character of Rosidore after his death in 1680, 'Therefore, the fury of wine and fury of women possess me waking and sleeping', but in the last years of the seventies he had become an embittered and a thoughtful man who would die in 1680 of old age at thirty-three. Perhaps the most moving of all his poems is the ironic 'The Maim'd Debauchee', with its distant memory of Bergen and the battle in the Channel, and the brave defiance which turns sad and bitter in the last quatrain.

'I have languished for seven long tedious years of desire.' (Thomas Otway in a letter to Mrs Barry)

[1] Ironically this was included by John Hayward in the Nonesuch edition of Rochester's works as one of his own poems.

> As some brave admiral in former war
>   Depriv'd of force, but prest with courage still,
> Two rival fleets appearing from afar,
>   Crawls to the top of an adjacent hill,
>
> From whence (with thoughts full of concern) he views
>   The wise, and daring, conduct of the fight:

173

And each bold action to his mind renews,
  His present glory, and his past delight . . .

So when my days of impotence approach,
  And I'm, by love and wine's unlucky chance,
Driv'n from the pleasing billows of debauch
  On the dull shore of lazy temperance,

My pains at last some respite shall afford,
  While I behold the battles you maintain,
When fleets of glasses sail around the board,
  From whose broad-sides volley of wit shall rain.

Nor shall the sight of honourable scars,
  Which my too-forward valour did procure,
Frighten new-listed soldiers from the wars;
  Past joys have more than paid what I endure.

Should some brave youth (worth being drunk) prove nice,
  And from his fair inviter meanly shrink,
'Twould please the ghost of my departed vice,
  If, at my counsel, he repent and drink.

Or should some cold complexion'd sot forbid,
  With his dull morals, our night's brisk alarms,
I'll fire his blood by telling what I did,
  When I was strong and able to bear arms.

I'll tell of whores attack'd, their lords at home,
  Bawds' quarters beaten up, and fortress won,
Windows demolish'd, watches overcome,
  And handsome ills by my contrivance done.

With tales like these I will such heat inspire
  As to important mischief shall incline;
I'll make him long some ancient church to fire,
  And fear no lewdness they're called to by wine.

Thus statesman-like I'll saucily impose,
  And, safe from danger, valiantly advise;
Sheltered in impotence urge you to blows,
  And, being good for nothing else, be wise.

In what a different spirit he had written his poem on a passing
impotency, 'The Imperfect Enjoyment'.

  Naked she lay, claspt in my longing arms,
  I fill'd with love, and she all over charms,
  Both equally inspir'd with eager fire,
  Melting through kindness, flaming in desire;
  With arms, legs, lips close clinging to embrace,
  She clips me to her breast, and sucks me to her face.
  The nimble tongue (love's lesser lightning) play'd

Within my mouth, and to my thoughts convey'd
Swift orders, that I should prepare to throw
The all-dissolving thunderbolt below.
My flutt'ring soul, sprung with the pointed kiss,
Hangs hov'ring o're her balmy limbs of bliss.
But whilst her busy hand wou'd guide that part,
Which shou'd convey my soul up to her heart,
In liquid raptures I dissolve all o're,
Melt into sperm and spend at every pore.
A touch from any part of her had don't,
Her hand, her foot, her very looks a ——
Smiling, she chides in a kind murm'ring noise,
And sighs to feel the too too hasty joys;
When, with a thousand kisses wand'ring o're
My panting breast, and 'is there then no more?'
She cries: 'All this to love and rapture's due,
Must we not pay a debt to pleasure too?'
But I the most forlorn, lost man alive,
To shew my wisht obedience vainly swive,
I sigh alas! and kiss, but cannot drive.
Eager desires confound my first intent,
Succeeding shame does more success prevent,
And rage, at last, confirms me impotent.
Ev'n her fair hand, which might bid heat return
To frozen age, and make cold hermits burn,
Apply'd to my dead cinder, warms no more
Than fire to ashes cou'd past flames restore.
Trembling, confus'd, despairing, limber, dry,
A wishing, weak, unmoving lump I lie,
This dart of love, whose piercing point, oft try'd,
With virgin blood a hundred maids has dy'd,
Which nature still directed with such art,
That it through ev'ry port, reacht ev'ry heart,
Stiffly resolv'd, 'twould carelessly invade,
Woman or man, nor ought its fury staid;
Where e're it pierc'd, entrance it found or made—
Now languid lies, in this unhappy hour,
Shrunk up, and sapless, like a wither'd flow'r.
Thou treacherous, base, deserter of my flame,
False to my passion, fatal to my fame,
By what mistaken magic dost thou prove,
So true to lewdness, so untrue to love?
What oyster-cinder-beggar-common whore,
Didst thou e're fail in all thy life before?
When vice, disease and scandal led the way,
With what officious haste didst thou obey?
Like a rude, roaring hector in the streets
That scuffles, cuffs, and ruffles all he meets,
But if his king or country claim his aid,
The rascal villain shrinks and hides his head;

E'en so thy brutal valor is displaid
Breaks ev'ry stew, does each small crack invade,
But if great love the onset does command,
Base recreant to thy prince, thou dost not stand.
Worst part of me, and henceforth hated most,
Through all the town the common rubbing post,
On whom each wretch relieves her lustful ——
As hogs, on gates, do rub themselves and grunt,
May'st thou to rav'nous shankers be a prey,
Or in consuming weepings waste away.
May stranguries and stone thy days attend.
May'st thou ne'er piss, who didst refuse to spend,
When all my joys did on false thee depend.
And may ten thousand abler men agree
To do the wrong'd Corinna right for thee.

[2] Nothing was to do his reputation more harm with posterity than his breach with Dryden and the affair of Rose Alley when Dryden was cudgelled by hired bravos. It happened less than a year before he died, and if he were guilty it may seem remarkable that no hint of the guilt comes out in his dialogue with Dr Burnet, but did he necessarily feel any guilt? Lord Rochester could not fight a duel with Mr Dryden of Will's Coffee House. Not proven is the fairest verdict, but even if the verdict were guilty, a dying man could surely plead extreme provocation. The attack occurred on 12 December 1679 and Rochester lay dead in his Lodge in Woodstock Park on 26 July 1680.

To all of us today Dryden seems one of the great figures of our literature: the greatest of Restoration poets. To be the enemy of Dryden is to be like the poetaster Greene who criticized 'upstart Shake-scene'. But the term 'honest John' has covered from the eyes of posterity weaknesses which were evident to a contemporary. Dryden lacked the final greatness. He had not the strong belief in his own powers which enabled Milton to live with only Heaven and Hell for company. Not satisfied with his genius as a poet, he yearned to be known as a wit and a 'blade', a man of fashion, and he presented the ignoble picture of the greatest living dramatist, who among his own kind could rule with dignity from his summer and his winter seat at Will's Coffee House, haunting the wits with his presence, hanging to their skirts for what he could get from them.

Rochester's friendship with Dryden must have begun early if Malone's suggestion is correct and Rochester was partly responsible for Dryden's appointment as Poet Laureate in April 1668. In his dedication to *Marriage à la Mode* in 1673 Dryden states, 'You have not only been careful of my reputation, but of my fortune.' There can be no doubt that Dryden had real cause for gratitude. He writes that the play 'received amendment from your noble hands ere it was fit to be presented'. The wits were accustomed to take a hand in the writing of a play. Sir Charles Sedley had helped Shadwell with the writing of *Epsom Fair*, and the only fragment surviving of a prose play by Rochester shows a comic talent not unworthy of *Marriage à la Mode*. Rochester's share in the play's success is admitted by Dryden: 'You may please likewise to remember, with how much favour to the author, and indulgence to the play, you commended it to the view of his Majesty, then at Windsor, and, by his approbation of it in writing, made way for its kind reception in the theatre.'

Dryden continues by thanking Rochester for defending him from the meaner fry of wits, who 'can never be considerable enough to be talked of themselves, so that they are safe only in their obscurity, and grow mischievous to witty men, by the great diligence of their envy'. It is a theme harped on by most of the dramatists who dedicated their plays to Rochester; his taste seems to have been the fashionable taste and what he praised it was thought old-fashioned or presumptuous to criticize.

Dryden concludes his dedication with a tribute to Rochester's own verses:

> I have so much of self-interest, as to be content with reading some papers of your verses, without desiring you should proceed to a scene, or play; with the common prudence of those who are worsted in a duel, and declare they are satisfied, when they are first wounded. Your Lordship has but another step to make, and from the patron of wit, you may become its tyrant, and oppress our little reputations with more ease than you now protect them.

In all the careful prose it is hard to find a sentence written with sincerity, though in the letter, in which he thanked Rochester for his reply to the dedication, the mask is dropped for a moment when he refers to the reception at Oxford of one of his plays: 'Your Lordship will judge how easy 'tis to pass anything upon an University, and how gross flattery the learned will endure.' 'Gross flattery' may have been the order of the time, the patrons demanded it, and the dramatists supplied it, but they did not all supply it in the same measure. Compare Dryden's fifteen hundred words of servility in *Marriage à la Mode* with Shadwell's dozen lines before *The Sullen Lovers*, which are like the friendly growl of a great dog in return for his bone.

Almost at the same moment as Dryden, Elkanah Settle, the most conceited and the least worthy of Restoration tragedians, had won the patronage of Rochester and in 1671 the Earl contrived to have *The Empress of Morocco* performed at Court. If *The Conquest of*

Granada had shown the poor best to which the heroic tragedy, tethered to the heroic couplet, could rise, Settle's play showed the lowest point to which it could fall. It was unintentionally as devastating a parody of Dryden as Buckingham's *The Rehearsal*, which was produced at Drury Lane that winter with the great comic actor Joe Hayns as the poet Bayes.

The same year introduced another writer, who was never, like Dryden and Settle, to fall from Rochester's good graces. In the spring of 1671 Wycherley had become the lover of the Duchess of Cleveland and dreaded the anger of her former lover, the Duke of Buckingham.

> He applied himself therefore to Wilmot, Lord Rochester, and to Sir Charles Sedley, and entreated them to remonstrate to the Duke of Buckingham the mischief he was about to do to one who had not the honour to be known to him, and who had never offended him. Upon their opening the matter to the Duke, he cried out immediately that he did not blame Wycherley, he only accused his cousin. Ay but, they replied, by rendering him suspected of such an intrigue, you are about to ruin him, that is, your Grace is about to ruin a man with whose conversation you would be pleased above all things. Upon this occasion they said so much of the shining qualities of Mr Wycherley and of the charms of his conversation, that the Duke, who is as much in love with wit as with his kinswoman, was impatient till he should be brought to sup with him, which was in two or three nights. After supper Mr Wycherley, who was then in the height of his vigour both of body and of mind, thought himself obliged to exert himself, and the Duke was charmed to that degree that he cried out in a transport, 'By G———, my cousin was in the right of it' and from that very moment made a friend of a man whom he believed to be his happy rival.

Of Wycherley Rochester wrote with discrimination:

> Of all our modern wits none seems to me
> Once to have toucht upon true comedy
> But hasty Shadwell and slow Wycherley. . . .
> . . . Wycherley earns hard what e're he gains,
> He wants no judgment, and he spares no pains;
> He frequently excels, and, at the least,
> Makes fewer faults than any of the best.

Next among Rochester's following appeared, in 1672, John Crowne, a writer with some talent for comedy but none for tragedy, on which he spent too much of his life. He attracted Rochester's attention with a dedication to his *Charles the Eighth*.

John Crowne, starched and prim in his long cravat, John Dryden, Elkanah Settle, they were a strange trio to be found in the same patron's anteroom. Settle, a man of unbounded conceit, who was to end his days in making machinery for Bartholomew Fair and

Elkanah Settle's *Empress of Morocco*
'From breaths of fools thy commendation spreads, Fame sings thy praise with mouths of loggerheads.'
(John Dryden)

who as an old man acted in the *Droll of St George* in a dragon of green leather of his own invention, proved to be the unsettling element. The success of *The Empress of Morocco*, a hotchpotch of horrors, had gone to his head. Rochester's support made him the fashion with the young, and according to Dennis he became a formidable rival to Dryden; not only the town, but the University of Cambridge was much divided in their opinions about the preference that ought to be given to them, and in both places the younger fry inclined to Elkanah.

Settle in 1673, the same year as the dedication to *Marriage à la Mode*, printed his *Empress of Morocco* with a dedication which included an attack on Dryden. The next year Dryden replied in a pamphlet written in collaboration with Crowne and Shadwell. These lines were almost certainly not directed at Rochester, since Crowne and Shadwell were both his friends, but the patron who had recommended the performance of Settle's play at Whitehall cannot have read them with pleasure:

From breaths of fools thy commendation spreads,
Fame sings thy praise with mouths of loggerheads.
With noise and laughing each thy fustian greets,
'Tis clapt by quires of empty-headed cits.

179

It is not unlikely that the publication of the pamphlet lost Dryden his patron to the advantage of 'starched' Johnnie Crowne. Perhaps Rochester thought that to divide was to conquer. It was the Poet Laureate's privilege to write the masques which were occasionally performed at Whitehall by the Court. In 1675 Rochester exerted his influence and Dryden was passed over in favour of Crowne, who wrote *The Masque of Calisto*. Crowne was a genuinely modest dramatist. His Preface to the Reader gives a vivid impression of his dismay at an unexpected and unwanted honour. He was Dryden's friend and had no wish to supplant him: 'Had it been written by him, to whom by the double right of place and merit, the honour of the employment belonged, the pleasure had been in all kinds complete.' The masque, with the help of dancing and scenic effects, flights of nymphs descending from the skies, was a success. The Court could hardly have considered it otherwise, acted as it was by the royal Princesses. Only the author was dissatisfied, tinkered with the play even after the opening night, and finally found it necessary to apologize to the reader, whose expectations might have been aroused by accounts of Betterton's magnificent production.

> But you will be disappointed, you will find nothing here answer these swelling expectations. How it happens to be so, it is enough to tell you, that it was written by me, and it would be very strange, if a bad writer should write well; but, which was as great an unhappiness, I had not time enough allowed me to muster together, on so great an occasion, those few abilities I have. I was invaded on the sudden by a powerful command to prepare an entertainment for the Court, which was to be written, learnt, practised and performed, in less time than was necessary for the writing alone. . . . For my subject . . . I had but some few hours allow'd me to choose one. . . . I resolving to choose the first tolerable story I could meet with, unhappily encountered this where, by my own rashness, and the malice of Fortune, I involved myself before I was aware, in a difficulty greater than the invention of the Philosopher's Stone . . . to write a clean, decent, and inoffensive play, on the story of a rape.

Crowne was not too insignificant to rouse the great man's jealousy. Old Jacob Tonson told how 'even Dryden was very suspicious of rivals. He would compliment Crowne, when a play of his failed, but was cold to him if he met with success. He sometimes used to own that Crowne had some genius, but then he always added, that his father and Crowne's mother were very well acquainted.'

Between Rochester and Dryden there was no further friendship. *Aurengzebe*, published in 1675, was dedicated to Rochester's chief enemy, Lord Mulgrave. The same servile flattery which had been directed to Rochester was now directed to Rochester's enemy, the

John Dryden
'Dryden in vain tried
        this nice way of wit,
For he to be a tearing
        blade thought fit,
To give the ladies a dry
        bawdy bob,
And thus he got the name
        of Poet Squab.'

man who had accused him of cowardice over the botched duel. 'Contempt of popular applause', 'retired virtue', 'good nature', 'generosity', 'resolution and courage', it is difficult in any of these epithets to recognize the conceited and malicious Mulgrave. With something of a snarl Dryden refers to 'the character of a courtier without wit'. The abuse is as far off the mark as the praise.

> They fawn and crouch to men of parts, whom they cannot ruin, quote their wit when they are present, and when they are absent, steal their jests; but to those who are under them, and whom they can crush with ease, they show themselves in their natural antipathy; thence they treat wit like the common enemy, and giving no more quarter than a Dutchman would to an English vessel in the Indies, they strike sail where they know they shall be mastered and murder where they can with safety.

'Strike sail'? It was not a happy metaphor to direct against the man who had fought so well at Bergen.

[3] The year 1675, which saw the quarrel with Dryden and the elevation of Crowne, the birth of his third daughter and the rise of Mrs Barry, brought Rochester into relationship with three new dramatists, Otway, Nathaniel Lee and Sir Francis Fane.

Sir Francis Fane, a forgotten and unimportant writer, introduces a note of farce into these years which were hot, dusty and confused with literary quarrels. While the father was entering in his Commonplace Book the story of Rochester's drunken exploit in the Privy Garden, the son was engaged on a very tedious tragical comedy called *Love in the Dark*, which he dedicated to Rochester. He was evidently one of those who lived on the wits of others, who picked up others' jests and passed them as their own, who cocked their hats insolently in the pit at the play of a new author, but when Rochester, Sedley or Etherege praised, were afraid to damn. His admiration for Rochester was expressed in terms which were unlikely to please his agnostic patron.

> I must confess, I never return from your Lordship's most charming and instructive conversation, but I am inspired with a new genius, and improv'd in all those sciences I ever coveted the knowledge of. I find myself, not only a better poet, a better philosopher, but much more than these, a better Christian. Your Lordship's miraculous wit and intellectual powers being the greatest argument that ever I could meet with for the immateriality of the soul.

John Wilmot, Second Earl of Rochester: 'I know he is a Devil, but he has something of the Angel yet undefac'd in him.' (George Etherege)

Sir Francis Fane's hyperbole was to swell even further in the poem he wrote to Rochester, 'upon the report of his sickness in town, being newly recover'd by his lordship's advice in the country'.

> . . . Had credulous England, fond of foreign news,
> And from remotest parts the world above,
> Receiv'd the Indian faith, which none else does refuse,
> Did men believe, that after their remove
> From earth, they should enjoy the friends they love,
> With all their wit, their rhetoric, and sense,
> Which with immortal ease they could dispense,
> What crowds would leap into his funeral pile,
> London would desert, Kingless be the isle;
> The Strand instead of men would acorns yield,
> Whitehall a meadow lie, th' Exchange a field.

A poet of far greater promise, Nathaniel Lee, dedicated in 1675 his play *Nero* to Rochester. He ended his days in a madhouse, to

Nathaniel Lee: a poet in Bedlam

which, according to Sir Sidney Lee, he had been brought by a vicious life in the company of Rochester and his other patrons, but there is no evidence to show that Rochester had any influence for good or ill on the poet. The dedication to *Nero* (brief enough and confined to invoking Rochester's aid against the criticasters in the pit) is almost the sole record of their relationship. Rochester's patronage must have been brief-lived, for three years later he wrote of Lee in these terms:

> When Lee makes temperate Scipio fret and rave,
> And Hannibal a whining amorous slave,
> I laugh and wish the hot-brained fustian fool
> In Busby's hands, to be well lasht at school.

It was one of his few hasty judgments, and Lee seems to have borne him no ill-will. In *The Princess of Cleves*, written after Rochester's death, he pays him a moving tribute under the name of Count Rosidore. Nemours greets the Vidam of Chartres:

> Ha! my grave Lord of Chartres, welcome as health, as wine, and taking whores – and tell me now the business of the Court.
>
> *Vidam:*   Hold it, Nemours, for ever at defiance,
> Fogs of ill-humour, damps of melancholy,
> Old maids of fifty chok'd with eternal vapours,
> Stuff it with fulsome honour-dozing virtue,
> And everlasting dullness husk it round,
> Since he that was the life, the soul of pleasure,
> Count Rosidore, is dead.
>
> *Nemours:* Then we may say
> Wit was and satyr is a carcass now.
> I thought his last debauch would be his death –
> But is it certain?
>
> *Vidam:*   Yes, I saw him dust.
> I saw the mighty thing a nothing made,
> Huddled with worms, and swept to that cold den,
> Where kings lie crumbled, just like other men.
>
> *Nemours:* Nay then let's rave and elegize together,
> When Rosidore is now but common clay,
> Whom every wiser emmet bears away,
> And lays him up against a winter's day.

And Nemours concludes with a panegyric in prose:

> He was the spirit of wit and had such an art in gilding his failures, that it was hard not to love his faults. He never spoke a witty thing twice, though to different persons; his imperfections were catching, and his genius was so luxuriant, that he was forced to tame it with a hesitation in his speech to keep it in view. But oh how awkward, how insipid, how poor and wretchedly dull is the imitation of those that have all the affectation of his verse and none of his wit.

It is interesting to note that just before this scene Nemours quotes the speech inserted by Rochester into his revised version of Fletcher's *Valentinian*, which was still in manuscript:

> Nay, now thou puttest me in poetic rapture
> And I must quote Ronsard to punish thee:
> Call all your wives to counsel. . . .

Is Ronsard a printer's error for Rôsidore and had Lee seen the manuscript?

The last of the poets whom Rochester befriended in 1675 was Thomas Otway. He has eclipsed them all, though in the case of Nathaniel Lee not altogether justly. Otway conquered like Charles Lamb with pathos, and literature has never been entirely freed from his pernicious influence. Rochester was almost as unfortunate in befriending Otway as he was in quarrelling with Dryden. He has always been portrayed since as the villain in a triangle, the woman played by Mrs Barry, and the hero by the pathetic, the whimsical, the eternally unsuccessful playwright. When reading Sir Edmund Gosse's dramatic account of the affair (how the poet fell in love with Mrs Barry and was rejected, how the wicked Earl in revenge at his presumption ruined the unfortunate lover and drove him out of the country) it is difficult to realize that for Rochester's share in this tale there is no evidence whatever.

The facts are these. In 1675 Rochester recommended Otway's *Alcibiades* to the Court and the play was produced at the Dorset Gardens Theatre with a cast which included Mrs Barry. In the words of Otway himself in the Preface to *Don Carlos* in which he answers criticisms of the former play:

> I am well satisfied I had the greatest party of men of wit and sense on my side: amongst which I can never enough acknowledge the unspeakable obligations I received from the Earl of Rochester who, far above what I am ever able to deserve from him, seemed almost to make it his business to establish it in the good opinion of the King and his Royal Highness: from both of whom I have since received confirmation of their good liking of it, and encouragement to proceed. And it is to him I must in all gratitude confess, I owe the greatest part of my good success in this, and on whose indulgency I extremely build my hopes of a next.

After two years, years when Gosse would have had us believe that Otway was courting Mrs Barry and rousing Rochester's jealousy, he dedicated *Titus and Berenice* to the Earl in terms which show no abatement of good will. 'How great a hazard then does your Lordship run in so steadfastly protecting a poor exiled thing that has so many enemies.'

In May 1678, Otway was granted a commission in the Army and went soldiering in Flanders. He returned in the spring of 1679 'scabbed and lousy' in the words of Anthony Wood, and his condition inspired a verse in a satirical poem 'A Trial of the Poets for the Bays'.

> Tom Otway came next, Tom Shadwell's dear zany,
> And swears for heroics he writes best of any:
> Don Carlos his pockets so amply had filled,
> That his mange was quite cured, and his lice were all killed.

It is this poem which has caused the trouble. First published seventeen years after Rochester's death, it was attributed to Buckingham and Rochester. If Rochester had written it, then a quarrel of some kind must have divided poet and patron, but Professor Roswell Ham has shown that the evidence points unmistakably to Elkanah Settle as the author. For signs of a quarrel it is necessary to look elsewhere, this time in Otway's works, and there in 'The Poet's Complaint to his Muse' occurs the following verse:

> The first was he who stunk of that rank verse
> In which he wrote his Sodom farce,
> A wretch whom old diseases did so bite
> That he writ bawdy sure in spight,
> To ruin and disgrace it quite.

The play of *Sodom* is of a more pornographic character than any other work attributed to Rochester. The title page of the British Museum manuscript reads 'Sodom or the Quintessence of Debauchery by E of R Written for the Royall Company of

Whoremasters.' The play is said to have been acted at Court. The ascription is very doubtful. It was a common habit of the time to ascribe any poems of unusual indecency to Rochester. Contemporaries were not agreed that the play was by him; Anthony Wood was doubtful; the author, he wrote, was said to be 'one Fishbourne a wretched scribbler'. Professor Prinz, who shows little hesitation in claiming the poem for Rochester, brings forward no contemporary English authority except the notorious 'Captain' Alexander Smith. *Sodom* differs from Rochester's satires in its air of unreality; it is an obscene fairy story, oddly reminiscent of Thackeray's *The Rose and the Ring*. Those who believe Rochester to be the author have also to deny his authorship of the poem 'On the Author of a Play called Sodom':

> Weak feeble strainer at mere ribaldry,
> Whose muse is impotent to that degree
> That must, like age, be whipt to lechery.

So much for the evidence of any quarrel between the poets. The story of Otway's love for Mrs Barry is another matter. Otway's love letters to Mrs —— were published by Tom Brown in *Familiar Letters* in 1697, and Professor Ham has found an edition by the original publisher dated 1713, the year of Mrs Barry's death, in which her name is acknowledged. The evidence points to Mrs Barry as the person who gave the letters to be printed. Otway's, as one would expect from such an exploiter of pathos, are full of a sentimental tenderness (he pleads to her in the name of Rochester's child: 'By that sweet pledge of your first softest love', which is hardly the language of a rival). 'Though I have languished for seven long tedious years of desire' he writes, which seems to date the letters with some certainty after Rochester's death. But Mrs Barry was of a different metal. The 'mercenary, prostituting dame' demanded more from a lover than despairing words.

> That language of doting madness and despair [wrote Oldys], however it may succeed with raw girls, is seldom successful with such practitioners in that passion as Mrs Barry, since it only hardens their vanity. For she could get bastards with other men, though she would hardly condescend to grant Otway a kiss, who was as amiable in person and address as the best of them.

Rochester's patronage of Settle and Crowne, and even Lee, was certainly fickle; there is no sign of fickleness in his relations with Otway. The Earl's death, hemmed round by divines, putting up a last struggle for agnosticism against the attack of priest and prelate, is reflected in the climax of *Venice Preserved*. The play was printed in 1682, and the allusion to Rochester's death in 1680 is unmistakable. Pierre is on the scaffold awaiting execution when a priest is brought to him. He refuses to listen.

You want to lead
My reason blindfold, like a hamper'd lion,
Check'd of its nobler vigour then, when baited,
Down to obedient tameness, make it couch,
And show strange tricks which you call signs of faith.
So silly souls are gull'd and you get money.
Away, no more: Captain, I would hereafter
This fellow write no lies of my conversion,
Because he has crept upon my troubled hours.

It would be wrong to give the impression that Rochester was only the fickle patron of inferior poets. His admiration for Waller survived the old poet's senility and the friend of Etherege and Shadwell merited the elegies of Lee and Otway.

Shadwell mixed on terms of intimacy with the courtiers in a way that Dryden would have liked to do. 'My lord of Dorset', complained Nell Gwyn, 'appears once in three months, for he drinks ale with Shadwell and Mr Haris at the Duke's House all day long.' He has survived with difficulty Dryden's envious caricature of him as Og. A big, good-humoured, hard-drinking man, he was a careless, natural, diffuse dramatist. Rochester's praise of him is not exaggerated.

Sir Charles Sedley

> Shadwell's unfinish'd works do yet impart
> Great proofs of force of nature, none of art;
> With just bold strokes he dashes here and there,
> Shewing great mastery with little care.

Of Rochester's other literary friendships Buckhurst and Sedley take the chief places.

> For pointed satyrs I would Buckhurst choose,
> The best good man, with the worst natur'd muse,
> For songs and verses, mannerly obscene,
> That can stir nature up by spring unseen,
> And without forcing blushes please the Queen.
> Sedley has that prevailing, gentle art,
> That can with a resistless charm impart
> The loosest wishes to the chastest heart,
> Raise such a conflict, kindle such a fire
> Betwixt declining virtue and desire,
> Till the poor vanquish'd mind dissolves away
> In dreams all night, in sighs and tears all day.

In 1678 a new literary friendship was formed. Satirical poems and songs in manuscript had come to Rochester's attention, written by an usher named John Oldham in Archbishop Whitgift's free school at Croydon. According to Oldham's biographer Rochester visited the school with the Earl of Dorset and Sir Charles Sedley, but when he sent his servant in with his compliments, the message was received by the headmaster, who concluded it a mistake and took the honour to himself.

> The old gentleman immediately dressed himself in his summer Sabbath apparel, and repaired to the appointment. . . . When the tottering pedagogue made his entry, they were all on the laugh; he began with a stupid dull preface, of his sense of the honour they had done him; betraying at the same time his ignorance of such a visit, when Lord Dorset, observing the confusion of the man, and the laughing gravity of Lord Rochester, released him with a candid assurance their invitation was to Mr Oldham.

Oldham who at last appeared was 'tall and thin, which was much owing to a consumptive complaint, but was greatly increased by study. His face was long, his nose prominent, his aspect unpromising, but satire was in his eye.'

The encouragement which Oldham received from the visit ruined not only his modest career as a schoolmaster but his health. His 'noble visitors', his biographer states, had 'wit, wickedness, and money enough to debauch a saint. . . . With a small sum of money which he had saved in his tutorship, he posted to London, and became at once a votary of Bacchus and Venus.'

But Rochester with only two years to live can have had little to do with Oldham's seduction. On his patron's death Oldham wrote one of his few poems which lacks obscenity or satire and possesses a measure of tenderness.

> If I was reckoned not unblest in song,
> 'Tis what I owe to thy all-teaching tongue.
> Some of thy art, some of thy tuneful breath,
> Thou did'st, by will, to worthless me bequeath;
> Others, thy flocks, thy lands, thy riches have,
> To me, thou didst thy pipe and skill vouchsafe.

A coffee house

[4] The tributes of Etherege, Otway, Lee and Oldham have been forgotten by posterity, but not Rochester's quarrel with the great Dryden. It is only fair to look at that quarrel through the eyes of the Earl. Dryden's desertion had some of the quality of a military defection. The poets whom Rochester aided wrote under his banner. Rank came before genius. He had been insulted by a follower of inferior rank who had cause to be grateful. Sedley had an actor cudgelled in the park for imitating his dress, and a poet was not so far removed from a player.

Dryden in the years after the dedication of *Aurengzebe* must have felt a certain dread. What happened next, since Rochester was a poet as well as an Earl, was a masterly satire, 'An Allusion to Horace'. If we can put ourselves imaginatively into Rochester's place and remember how raw was the wound to his pride which Dryden had inflicted, we can only wonder at the poem's moderation.

On 1 November 1677 Savile wrote to Rochester that 'the whole tribe are alarumed at a libel against them lately sent by the post to Will's Coffee House. I am not happy enough to have seen it, but I hear it commended, and therefore the more probably thought to be composed at Woodstock.'

Rochester wrote back: 'For the libel you speak of upon that most unwitty generation the present poets, I rejoice in it with all my heart, and shall take it for a favour, if you will send me a copy. He cannot want wit utterly, that has a spleen to those rogues, tho' never so dully express'd.'

He had not denied he was the author, a curious omission considering Savile's direct attribution, and it seems more than likely that the libel which had alarmed Dryden and his followers at Will's was 'An Allusion to Horace'. The poem opens temperately enough:

> Well, sir, 'tis granted, I said Dryden's rhymes
> Were stol'n, unequal, nay dull many times.
> What foolish patron is there found of his,
> So blindly partial, to deny me this?
> But that his plays, embroider'd up and down
> With wit and learning, justly pleas'd the town,
> In the same paper, I as freely own.

He passes on to criticize Crowne and Settle, Flatman and Lee, and to express his admiration of Shadwell and Wycherley, Buckhurst and Sedley. It is only then that anger reveals itself in a personality:

> Dryden in vain tried this nice way of wit,
> For he to be a tearing blade thought fit,
> To give the ladies a dry bawdy bob,
> And thus he got the name of Poet Squab.

But to be just, 'twill to his praise be found,
His excellencies more than faults abound,
Nor dare I from his sacred temples tear
That laurel which he best deserves to wear.
But does not Dryden find ev'n Jonson dull?
Fletcher and Beaumont uncorrect and full
Of lewd lines, as he calls 'em? Shakespeare's style
Stiff and affected? to his own the while
Allowing all the justness that his pride
So arrogantly had to these denied?
And may not I have leave impartially
To search and censure Dryden's works and try
If these gross faults his choice pen does commit,
Proceed from want of judgment or of wit?

ALL FOR LOVE.
Her Nymph-like Nereids round her couch were plac'd,
Where she another Sea-born Venus lay.
Act 3.

Rochester was referring with some justice to Dryden's *Essay on the Dramatic Poetry of the Last Age* published five years before. In this Dryden had written: 'Let any man, who understands English, read diligently the works of Shakespeare and Fletcher, and I dare undertake, that he will find in every page either some solecism of speech, or some notorious flaw in sense; and yet these men are reverenced, when we are not forgiven. . . .'

Such criticism might possibly have been accepted from the future author of *All for Love* and *Don Sebastian*, but when he wrote the best Dryden could show was *The Conquest of Granada* and *Aurengzebe*. Except for the one flash of malice Rochester had shown justice and moderation. His criticism did not deserve the reply it received the next year in Dryden's Preface to *All for Love*: the mildness of the rebuke had encouraged the Laureate to a more than usually brutal attack.

Nor is every man, who loves tragedy, a sufficient judge of it; he must understand the excellencies of it too, or he will only prove a blind admirer, not a critic. From hence it comes that so many satires on poets, and censures of their writings, fly abroad. Men of pleasant conversation (at least esteemed so) and endued with a trifling kind of fancy, perhaps helped out with some smattering of Latin, are ambitious to distinguish themselves from the herd of gentlemen by their poetry. . . . And is not this a wretched affectation, not to be contented with what fortune has done for them, and sit down quietly with their estates, but they must call their wits in question, and needlessly expose their nakedness to public view? Not considering that they are not to expect the same approbation from sober men, which they have found from their flatterers after the third bottle.

He continues, with more direct reference to the offending poem:

They are persecutors even of Horace himself, as far as they are able, by their ignorant and vile imitations of him; by making an unjust use of his authority and turning his artillery against his friends. . . . With

192

what scorn would he look down on such miserable translators, who make doggerel of his Latin, mistake his meaning, misapply his censures, and often contradict their own? . . . For my part, I would wish no other revenge, either for myself, or the rest of the poets, from this rhyming judge of the twelvepenny gallery, this legitimate son of Sternhold,[1] than that he would subscribe his name to his censure, or (not to tax him beyond his learning) set his mark. For, should he own himself publicly, and come from behind the lion's skin, they whom he condemns would be thankful to him, they whom he praises would choose to be condemned; and the magistrates, whom he has elected, would modestly withdraw from their employment, to avoid the scandal of his nomination.

Dryden was perhaps trusting in the power of his patron to protect him, for Mulgrave now took a hand in the game of baiting the wit of whom the world had grown tired, whose health was gone, and whose power to hurt seemed departed. Manuscripts of Mulgrave's *Essay on Satire* were in circulation in 1679. The poem included attacks on the Duchess of Portsmouth and the Duchess of Cleveland:

> Was ever Prince by two at once misled,
> False, foolish, old, ill-natur'd and ill-bred;

but the greater part of his venom was reserved for Rochester. Mulgrave's authorship was disguised by a number of lines in praise of himself as a great lover. Suspicion rested at once on Dryden, although the poem had little merit. Contemporaries have a partial view of a poet's work; only posterity can realize the unlikelihood of Dryden's authorship. That Rochester, and probably the royal mistresses, assigned him the responsibility is evident from a letter to Savile in which Rochester writes:

> I have sent you herewith a libel, in which my own share is not the least; the King, having perus'd it, is no ways dissatisfied with his. The author is apparently Mr Dryden, his patron my Lord Mulgrave having a panegyric in the midst, upon which happen'd a handsome quarrel between his Lordship, and Mrs B—— at the Duchess of P——. She call'd him: The hero of the libel, and complimented him upon having made more cuckolds than any man alive. To which he answered, she very well knew one he never made, nor never car'd to be employ'd in making. Rogue and bitch ensued, till the King, taking his grandfather's character upon him, became the peace-maker.

These were the lines in which Rochester saw the whole shameful affair with Mulgrave reopened:

> Rochester I despise for's mere want of wit,
> Tho' thought to have a tail and cloven feet,
> For while he mischief means to all mankind,

[1] Joint author of a metrical version of the Psalms, whom Rochester had mocked at himself in verse.

Himself alone the ill effects does find. . . .
False are his words, affected is his wit,
So often does he aim, so seldom hit.
To every face he cringes while he speaks,
But when the back is turn'd, the head he breaks.
Mean in each action, lewd in every limb,
Manners themselves are mischievous in him,
A proof that chance alone makes every creature,
A very Killigrew without good nature.
For what a Bessus he has always liv'd
And his own kickings notably contriv'd;
For (there's the folly that's still mix'd with fear)
Cowards more blows than any hero bear.
Of fighting sparks fame may her pleasure say,
But 'tis a bolder thing to run away.
The world may well forgive him all his ill,
For every fault does prove his penance still.
Falsely he falls into some dangerous noose,
And then as meanly labours to get loose.
A life so infamous is better quitting,
Spent in base injury and low submitting.
I'd like to have left out his poetry,
Forgot by almost all as well as me.
Sometimes he has some humour, never wit:
And if it rarely, very rarely hit,
'Tis under such a nasty rubbish laid,
To find it out's the cinder-woman's trade,
Who for the wretched remnants of a fire,
Must toil all day in ashes and in mire.
So lewdly dull his idle works appear,
The wretched texts deserve no comments here.

Many years later Mulgrave gave the poem to Pope to alter in
preparation for a new edition. Pope did his best, cutting out the
whole senseless criticism of Rochester's poetry, inserting a couple
of lines of his own, and polishing the rest. One couplet remains
unaltered, and perhaps in those two lines the hand of Dryden may
be discerned:

> Mean in each action, lewd in every limb,
> Manners themselves are mischievous in him.

From High Lodge in Woodstock Park Rochester had written to
Savile on an earlier occasion:

You write me word that I'm out of favour with a certain poet, whom
I have ever admired, for the disproportion of him and his attributes.
He is a rarity, which I cannot but be fond of, as one would be of a
hog that could fiddle, or a singing owl. If he falls upon me at the
blunt, which is his very good weapon in wit, I will forgive him, if
you please, and leave the repartee to Black Will, with a cudgel.

194

On 18 December Black Will did his work in Rose Alley, close to Will's Coffee House.

In *Domestic Intelligence* number 49 of 23 December 1679, one reads:

> On the 18th instant in the evening, Mr Dryden, the great poet, was set upon in Rose-street, Covent Garden, by three persons who called him rogue and son of a whore, knocked him down and dangerously wounded him, but upon his crying out murder, they made their escape. It is conceived they had their pay before-hand, and designed not to rob him, but to execute on him some *feminine* if not *popish* vengeance.

The following advertisement appeared in the *London Gazette*:

> Whereas John Dryden Esq. was on Monday the 18th instant, at night, barbarously assaulted, and wounded, in Rose-street, in Covent Garden, by divers men unknown, if any person shall make discovery of the said offenders to the said Mr Dryden, or to any justice of the peace, he shall not only receive fifty pounds, which is deposited in the hands of Mr Blanchard, goldsmith, next door to Temple Bar, for the said purpose; but if he be a principal or an accessory, in the said fact, his Majesty is graciously pleased to promise him his pardon for the same.

No one claimed the reward.

The assault aroused little more than amusement among contemporaries. An anonymous writer referred to Dryden's translations from Latin:

> But what excuse, what preface can atone
> For crimes which guilty Bays has singly done,
> Bays whom Rose-alley ambuscade enjoin'd
> To be to vices which he practis'd kind?

Anthony Wood believed that Rochester acted in concert with the Duchess of Portsmouth; the two names remained linked even in Samuel Derrick's excellent collection of Dryden's poems published by Tonson nearly a century later, and the Rose Alley ambuscade became a symbol in the literature of the period for the perils of authorship.

Rochester had only eight months more to live when the attack occurred and his life was one of almost continuous pain. At this moment, when all the world was hateful to him, he found himself attacked, first as 'a rhyming judge of the twelvepenny gallery' in prose, and next as a coward in verse, and he believed both blows were dealt by the same hand, by the fat fellow who had been among his flatterers, whom he had helped with his influence at Court, whom he had watched making himself ridiculous in the effort to be a 'tearing blade' among the wits. Would it have been strange if he had had recourse to bravos and crab-tree cudgels?[1]

[1] Since this book was written in 1932 Professor J. H. Wilson has demonstrated that Rochester's 'Black Will' letter to Savile was probably written in 1676 three years before Mulgrave's satire was in circulation. Professor Pinto goes too far when he assumes that this dating of the letter proves the charge against Rochester to be 'wholly false'. The reference to Black Will is light-hearted, the quarrel with Dryden has only just begun with the dedication of *Aurengzebe* to Mulgrave. Mulgrave's satire may have made the sick man think more seriously of revenge. Rochester or the Duchess of Portsmouth or both? Neither can be acquitted or condemned.

XI *The Death of Dorimant*

In the spring of 1678 Anthony Wood entered in his journal: 'About 18 Apr., Th, John, Earl of Rochester, died at London aet 28 or thereabouts.' But a few days later he had to add the single word 'false'. It was not without reason that Nemours, hearing of Count Rosidore's death, asked 'But is it certain?'

Rumour anticipated his end by only two years. In April 1678 he had 'been at the gates of death'. Sickness as early as 1669 had forced him to attend Mrs Fourcard's 'Baths' for the mercury cure of venereal disease; in 1671 his eyes, he wrote, had been unable to endure wine or water; nearly every year since then had seen a relapse. To forswear wine and women might have saved him, but he had not the strength of will even if he had the inclination. The serious sickness from which he suffered in 1678 introduced a new element into the talk about him. Lady Chaworth wrote to Lord Roos that he was 'so penitent that he said he would be an example of penitence to the whole world and I hope he will be so'.

We know more of that first penitence from Burnet:

> When his spirits were so low and spent that he could not move nor stir, and he did not think to live an hour, he said, his reason and judgment was so clear and strong that from thence he was fully persuaded that death was not the spending or dissolution of the soul but only the separation of it from matter. He had in that sickness great remorses for his past life, but he afterwards told me, they were rather general and dark horrors than any convictions of sinning against God. He was sorry he had lived so as to waste his strength so soon, or that he had brought such an ill-name upon himself, and had an agony in his mind about it, which he knew not well how to express.

He partly recovered both from his sickness and his penitence, but a man who reads of his own death need never lack material for thought, and Rochester had heard the same news as Anthony Wood.

The bed in which Rochester died in High Lodge, Woodstock Park, 26 July 1680

[1] His successor as Ranger of Woodstock Park had been chosen.

This day I receiv'd the unhappy news of my own death and burial. But hearing what heirs and successors were decreed me in my place, and chiefly in my lodgings,[1] it was no small joy to me that these tidings prove untrue; my passion for living is so increased that I omit no care of myself, while before I never thought life worth the trouble of taking. The King, who knows me to be a very ill-natur'd man, will not think it an easy matter for me to die, now I live chiefly out of spite. Dear Mr Savile, afford me some news from your land of the living.

The brief penitence had not been a sudden conversion. He had always 'loved morality in others', and of late a new seriousness had shown itself, not the old destructive spirit of satire, which attacked vice wherever he saw it save in himself. His friends who had once been satisfied to drink with him were beginning to show that interest in affairs which was to convert them in the succeeding years from 'rake-hells' into statesmen and politicians. If Rochester had lived he might have taken the same road. His friend Robert Wolseley wrote:

> His wit began to frame and fashion itself to public business; he began to inform himself of the wisdom of our laws and the excellent constitution of the English Government; and to speak in the House of Peers with general approbation; he was inquisitive after all kind of histories that concerned England, both ancient and modern, and set himself to read the Journals of Parliament Proceedings.

In Lent, 1677, he had written to Savile: 'I would be glad to know if the Parliament be like to sit any time, for the Peers of England being grown of late years very considerable in the Government, I would make me at the session. Livy and sickness has a little inclin'd me to policy.' It is true he adds that when he comes to town, 'I make no question but to change that folly for some less; whether wine or women I know not; according as my constitution serves me.'

The renewed 'passion for living' left him only half a heart for folly, although he wrote, 'It is a miraculous thing (as the wise have it) when a man half in the grave cannot leave off playing the fool and the buffoon; but so it falls out to my comfort.'

The wind of death gave him the desire to express his love for Savile, one of the few friends whom he had not failed or who had not deserted him, now that it was the great mode to hate him.

> 'Tis not the least of my happiness that I think you love me, but the first of all my pretensions is to make it appear that I faithfully endeavour to deserve it. If there be a real good upon earth, 'tis in the name of friend, without which all others are merely fantastical. How few of us are fit stuff to make that thing, we have daily the melancholy experience. However, dear Harry! Let us not give out, nor despair of bringing that about, which as it is the most difficult, and rare accident of life, is also the best, nay (perhaps) the only good one. This thought has so entirely possessed me since I came in to the country (where only, one can think; for, you at Court think not at all; or, at least, as if you were shut up in a drum; you can think of nothing, but the noise that is made about you) that I have made many serious reflections upon it [but at this point his habitual cynicism

In the church vaults at Spelsbury the Rochester family is obscurely buried

198

takes control of his pen] and amongst others, gather'd one maxim, which I desire should be communicated to our friend Mr G——; That, we are bound in morality and common honesty, to endeavour after competent riches; since, it is certain, that few men, if any, uneasy in their fortunes, have proved firm and clear in their friendships. A very poor fellow is a very poor friend.

The 'passion for living' brought him back from the peace of Adderbury which might have offered him life to the death that London held out; he was not the first to die from too much living.

Oates had told his tale, the informers were abroad, and it was a serious, frightened London, without even the comfort of his friend's presence, for Savile had gone to France straight from Mrs Fourcard's establishment. 'Your Lordship is so well read,' he had written on 13 July 1679, 'that you cannot but have heard of an old Roman general, who was recalled from banishment to command the army, no other man in the Commonwealth being found so fit for it. I shall desire your Lordship to let that old gentleman put you in mind of me . . . for there being an affair of some difficulty to be performed in France, his Majesty sends me in all haste.' So while the sick Rochester steered his way through the dangers of the Popish Plot, his friend in letters from France wondered at the 'strange news' and complained of the small beer and that his sickness prevented him from indulging in the sole diversions of hunting and gaming.

In England the Protestant stars of Monmouth and Shaftesbury were in the ascendant, but the Duke of York remained the heir to the throne. Rochester in the past had not spared his attacks on the Duke; in 1674 he had warned Charles in a satire against his 'false brother and false friend', while in 'The History of Insipids' he had written:

> Then Charles beware of thy brother Y[ork]
>   Who to thy Government gives law.
> If once we fall to the old sport,
>   You must again both to Breda.

But the time had come when it was necessary for most men to make a bold decision. The House of Commons had gone too far in its support of Oates to be safe under a Catholic king, and Charles's health was failing. A Bill was therefore introduced to exclude the Duke from the Succession. Rochester's words when he addressed the House of Lords on this occasion were cleverly chosen. He supported the Duke's party by opposing the Bill, but for reasons which could not possibly raise the open opposition of the Whigs.

No tablet in the church records their presence, no long scroll of virtues in the manner of the century

Mr Speaker, Sir, [he said] although it hath been said that no good Protestant can speak against this Bill, yet, sir, I cannot forbear to offer some objections against it. I do not know that any of the King's

201

murderers were condemned without being heard, and must we deal thus with the brother of our King? It is such a severe way of proceeding that I think we cannot answer it to the world; and therefore it would consist much better with the justice of the House to impeach him and try him in a formal way, and then cut off his head, if he deserve it. I will not offer to dispute the power of Parliaments, but I question whether this law, if made, would be good in itself. Some laws have a natural weakness with them; I think that by which the old Long Parliament carried on their rebellion was judged afterwards void in law, because there was a power given which could not be taken from the Crown. For ought I know, when you have made this law, it may have the same flaw in it. If not, I am confident there are a loyal party, which will never obey, but will think themselves bound by their Oath of Allegiance and Duty, to pay obedience to the Duke, if ever he should come to be King, which must occasion a civil war. . . . Upon the whole matter, my humble motion is, that the Bill may be thrown out.

The next year, on 6 March, he took the oaths according to the Test Act, and the temporary improvement of his health and the new serious bent of his mind led him to hope for some official employment abroad. If he had ended his days as a Resident at some Prince's court or with the heavy Dutch drinking beer and regretting Whitehall he would have anticipated the career of his friend Etherege. What nature of post he expected is unknown. The only hint appears in a letter from Savile dated 16 April 1679 from Paris:

I shall not be one of those friends who would advise you to keep your temperance or your virtue longer. They are both excellent in the way to health, but base companions of it. You see, my Lord, I can not yet give in to the true and decent gravity of a minister, but I hope I shall mend against I see your Lordship at Boulogne, the certainty of which voyage does yet continue, though it is put a little farther off, because of a grave Spanish Ambassador who is yet at Brussels and comes [in] the pay of that country; but you shall be certainly informed of every alteration in that kind that may be of use to you for your coming upon that errand which I hope is already secured for you, for I have set my heart so much upon meeting you there that I shall run mad if anybody else should come in your place.

That Rochester in his own phrase had 'a great goggle-eye to business' is shown in the changed tone of his letters to Savile; the flippancies on the subject of drink and women almost disappear and give place to detailed accounts of political movements, the shufflings of Ministers, the activities of Oates. But his health was never to allow him to escape abroad, nor to see again the fat friend whom he had met first in the days of adventure, when his courage was unquestioned and his actions unhesitating. That autumn of 1679 he was again struggling up from the borders of death. In the days of his health he had been unable to resist the incitements of his Cavalier

'Strange news from England'

inheritance, but in sickness his mother's spirit held him in its Puritanical grasp. In October, regaining convalescence with difficulty, his heart on serious things, he turned for occupation to reading some of Dr Burnet's *History of the Reformation*; the manuscript of his revision of Fletcher's *Valentinian* was laid aside.

The contrast was not an extreme one. He had chosen *Valentinian* for its subject's sake, a lustful sovereign, the corruption of a court. He turned in the weariness of sickness from acting the reformer to reading of past reformers. Into *Valentinian* he had put not only his hatred of Whitehall, in which he had for long, by his own confession, played the pander for the King's pleasures, but some of his despairing search for a religion. He had depended on the world and the world had lamentably failed him. He faced the eternal problem of those who cannot reconcile the idea of an omnipotent God with the horrors of war and want.

The Solemn Mock P

> Supreme first causes! you, whence all things flow,
> Whose infiniteness does each little fill,
> You, who decree each seeming chance below,
> (So great in power) were you as good in will,
> How could you ever have produc'd such ill?
>
> Had your eternal mind been bent to good,
> Could human happiness have prov'd so lame?
> Rapine, revenge, injustice, thirst of blood,
> Grief, anguish, horror, want, despair and shame,
> Had never found a being nor a name.
>
> 'Tis therefore less impiety to say,
> Evil with you has coeternity,
> Than blindly taking it the other way,
> That merciful and of election free,
> You did create the mischiefs you foresee.

It is a very different attitude from the straightforward atheism of his translation of a Seneca chorus:

> Since Death on all lays his impartial hand,
> And all resign at his command;
> The Stoic too, as well as I,
> With all his gravity must die;
> Let's wisely manage this last span,
> The momentary life of man;
> And still in pleasure's circle move,
> Giving our days to friends, and all our nights to love.

The earlier attitude had been derived from Hobbes. It is difficult to exaggerate the philosopher's popularity, even among those who had not read his works. His dogmas were accepted generally, much as the dogmas of Freud were later accepted. In *The Character of a Town Gallant* published in 1675 we read:

His religion (for now and then he will be prattling of that too) is pretendedly Hobbian, and he swears *The Leviathan* may supply all the lost leaves of Solomon, yet he never saw it in his life, and for ought he knows it may be a treatise about catching of sprats, or new regulating the Greenland fishing trade. However the rattle of it at coffee-houses has taught him to laugh at spirits, and maintain that there are no angels but those in petticoats.

For Hobbes the soul was a function of the body. Sensation and desire were the first causes. His argument, progressing with a dry reasonableness from stage to stage, had put motion and matter in the place of God. It was adopted with pleasure by the Restoration Court, for it denied the possibility of any supernatural punishment for vice or reward for virtue. That it banished joy as well was not at first evident, though admirers of Hobbes must have felt some disquiet at the example of a man who sang songs in his bed of a night not for pleasure but for the good of his health.

Yet Hobbes and his followers, who did not believe in any final judgment, were afraid of the vast nullity of death. And in 1679 he died. Mulgrave might mourn him in grandiloquent terms:

LEVIATHAN,

OR,

The Matter, Form, and Power

OF A

COMMON-WEALTH
ECCLESIASTICAL
AND
CIVIL.

By THOMAS HOBBES *of* Malmesbury.

LONDON,

Printed for ANDREW CROOKE, at the Green Dragon
in St. *Pauls* Church-yard, 1651.

> While in dark ignorance we lay afraid
> Of fancies, ghosts, and every empty shade,
> Great Hobbes appeared, and by plain reason's light
> Put such fantastic forms to shameful flight,

but the common people, the ballad mongers, the broadsheet vendors of the town, took a different view:

> Is Atheist Hobbes then dead? Forbear to cry,
> For whilst he liv'd, he thought he could not die,
> Or was at least most filthy loath to try . . .

> In fine, after a thousand shams and fobs,
> Ninety years' eating, and immortal jobs,
> Here Matter lies – and there's an end of Hobbes.

> Here lies Tom Hobbes, the bug-bear of the nation,
> Whose death hath frighted atheism out of fashion.

Hobbes's doctrines had ceased to appeal to Rochester before he began to read Dr Burnet's history. They had appealed less to his intellect (he told Burnet that he had never known a complete atheist) than to his emotion. The idea that 'dead, we become the lumber of the world', pleased his cynicism; it was from his emotion that he wrote the invocation to Nothing and the

206

'Satire on Man'. But sickness damps emotion, even the emotion of cynicism. Sickness left his intellect free to question the nature of 'first causes', which he soon considered to be not, according to Hobbes's belief finite, but infinite and eternal, though sharing their eternity with evil. He had reached this position when he opened Burnet's *History of the Reformation*.

What he read there seems to have disquieted him. He became uneasy, uncertain of his own beliefs. Here was a man of his own intellectual standing, a man of the world (for Burnet had never been the cloistered ecclesiastic), who seemed to share the beliefs on which he had been brought up as a child, but which later he had learnt at Oxford and Whitehall were impositions on the credulity of mankind. If Burnet was right and there was a God who took enough interest in mankind to judge and condemn, what punishments might await him for the life he had led? His life was precarious; he had to face the future. Mrs Roberts, whose favours he had shared with the King, had died the summer before, a few weeks after he had heard news of her from Savile at Mrs Fourcard's and had jested of her presence in 'the palaces in Leather-lane'. The daughter, as she always declared, of a clergyman, she had been attended at the last by Burnet and had repented of her past life; she had faced the eternal future.

'Here lies Tom Hobbes, the bug-bear of the nation, Whose death hath frighted atheism out of fashion.'

So, in October 1679 Rochester sent a friend to Burnet to ask for his company, and in Burnet's words, 'after I had waited on him once or twice, he grew into that freedom with me, as to open to me all his thoughts, both of religion and morality, and to give me a full view of his past life, and seemed not uneasy at my frequent visits. So till he went from London, which was in the beginning of April, I waited on him often.'

The accuracy of Burnet's account of these conversations and the later repentance was impugned when it was first published in 1680. Rochester's friends refused to believe Burnet's story. Burnet was a fashionable confessor; he was making capital out of those on whom he forced his attention; first there had been Mrs Roberts, now there was Rochester. Otway's lines on the fellow who 'crept upon my troubled hours' was the opinion of Burnet held by the wits. His logical support of the Government after the Revolution, a course of conduct followed by Dorset and Sedley, raised the feeling against Burnet to the pitch of hysteria, so that an anonymous wit could write:

> 'Mongst all the hard names that denotes reproach
> The worst in the whole catalogue is Scotch,
> For rascal, rakehell, vagabond, vile sot,
> Are only faint synonyms to Scot.
> To what a height then mounts that mighty *He*
> Who is whole Scotland in epitome!

But with the lapse of more than 250 years, with the knowledge we possess of Rochester's life and parentage, Burnet's book becomes more than credible, it becomes convincing. The greater part is in the form of dialogue; Rochester offers his objections to the Christian religion, and Burnet answers him. It is an intensely dramatic scene, this of the autumn of 1679. Rochester was still arguing with wit and brevity for a universe, if not without a God, at least without a judge. He was formulating for the first time ideas which had been felt rather than reasoned, and he was confronted by a skilled dialectician. The part allotted to Rochester in the dialogue amounts to 302 lines, to Burnet's 1,671. Rochester was overborne by the weight of his opponent; the objections which he tossed out so briefly were caught, turned this way and that way, pulled in pieces. And what was the result?

> The issue of all our discourses was this, he told me, he saw vice and impiety were as contrary to humane society, as wild beasts let loose would be; and therefore he firmly resolved to change the whole method of his life; to become strictly just and true, to forbear swearing and irreligious discourse, to worship and pray to his Maker: and that though he was not arrived at a full persuasion of Christianity, he would never employ his wit more to run it down, or to corrupt others. Of which I have since a further assurance, from a person of quality, who conversed much with him, the last year of his life, to whom he would often say, that he was happy if he did believe, and that he would never endeavour to draw him from it.

It was only a partial victory for Burnet, and it was reached after a long struggle. Burnet's arguments need not be followed; they are much the same as would be used today by any learned and intelligent member of the Established Church. Rochester's arguments are of greater interest; they cast a clear light into those dark places which in most men lie secret.

Gilbert Burnet
'Captain, I would hereafter
This fellow write no lies
    of my conversion,
Because he has crept upon
    my troubled hours.'
        (Thomas Otway)

> For morality, he confessed he saw the necessity of it, both for the government of the world, and for the preservation of health, life and friendship, and was very much ashamed of his former practices, rather because he had made himself a beast, and had brought pain and sickness on his body, and had suffered much in his reputation, than from any deep sense of a supreme being or another state. . . . He told me the two maxims of his morality then were, that he should do nothing to the hurt of any other, or that might prejudice his own health, and he thought that all pleasure, when it did not interfere with these, was to be indulged as the gratification of our natural appetites. It seemed unreasonable to imagine those were put into a man only to be restrained, or curbed to such a narrowness: This he applied to the free use of wine and women.

It was his first challenge, the first attempt to justify the course of his life, and it received a voluminous answer. If his maxims were in-

208

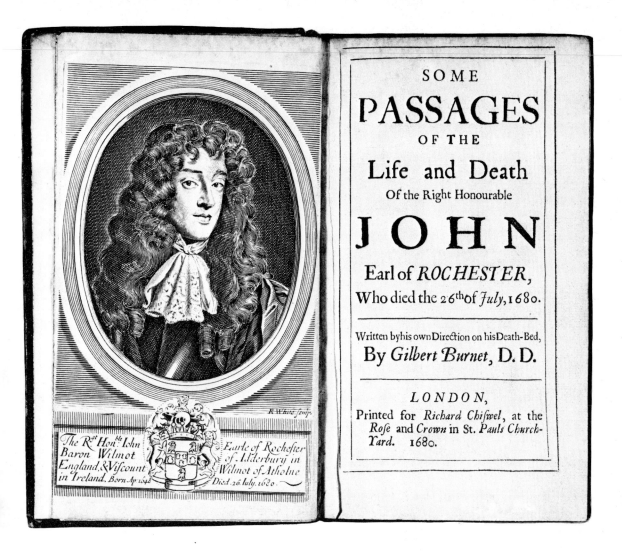

SOME

PASSAGES
OF THE
Life and Death
Of the Right Honourable

JOHN

Earl of *ROCHESTER*,
Who died the 26th of *July*, 1680.

Written by his own Direction on his Death-Bed,
By *Gilbert Burnet*, D.D.

LONDON,
Printed for *Richard Chiswel*, at the
Rose and *Crown* in St. *Pauls Church-
Yard*. 1680.

R White sculp.

The Rgt Honble Iohn   Earle of Rochester
Baron Wilmot   of Adderbury in
England, & Viscount   Wilmot of Atholne
in Ireland, Born Ap 1648   Died 26 Iuly 1680

tended to shock the divine, they signally failed. The judicious bull tossed them and mangled them with great coolness and moderation for six pages. A man could not resist gratifying the appetite with the mere aid of a personal philosophy; man's nature must be internally regenerated and changed by a higher principle. Rochester to this argument showed his only sign of impatience, remarking that it sounded to him like enthusiasm or canting. If the thoughts were to be diverted from the appetite, a problem in Euclid or writing a copy of verses would serve, but his flippancy was weightily answered by arguments which take up as many pages as his objections had taken lines. Burnet could not convince him; he only gained the grudging admission that those men were happy who had somewhat on which their thoughts rested and centred.

The discussion then passed from morality to God and Rochester described his idea of the Deity.

He said, he looked on it as a vast Power that wrought every thing by the necessity of its nature: and thought that God had none of those affections of love or hatred, which breed perturbation in us, and by consequence he could not see that there was to be either reward or punishment. He thought our conceptions of God were so low, that we had better not think much of him, and to love God seemed to him a presumptuous thing and the heat of fanciful men. Therefore he believed there should be no other religious worship, but a general celebration of that Being, in some short hymn. All the other parts of worship he esteemed the inventions of priests, to make the world believe they had a secret of incensing and appeasing God as they pleased. . . . And for the state after death, though he thought the soul did not dissolve at death, yet he doubted much of rewards or punishments: the one he thought too high for us to attain by our slight services, and the other was too extreme to be inflicted for sin.

Once he interrupted Burnet to enlarge on his idea of the future: 'He thought it more likely that the soul began anew, and that her sense of what she had done in this body, lying in the figures that are made in the brain, as soon as she dislodged, all these perished, and that soul went into some other state to begin a new course.'

A little later Burnet won his first victory by forcing Rochester to an admission, which is of importance to a biographer: 'He did not deny but that after the doing of some things he felt great and severe challenges within himself.' The second stage of the discussion ended in the pathetic acknowledgment that 'the whole system of religion, if believed, was a greater foundation of quiet than any other thing whatsoever: for all the quiet he had in his mind was, that he could not think so good a Being as the Deity would make him miserable'.

He was already confused and had forgotten that his idea of God had not included goodness. There was a note of weariness and despair in his statement: 'They were happy that believed, for it was not in every man's power.'

But Burnet had not finished with him. He had tested his ideas of morality and of God and had found them faulty and confused. He drove the sick man on to talk of revealed religion. Rochester said (and the phrases are so characteristic, have so much the tone of the spoken voice that one feels Burnet must have taken note of the conversation immediately he left the house),

He did not understand that business of inspiration; he believed the pen-men of the Scriptures had heats and honesty and so writ. . . . God's communicating his mind to one man was the putting it in his power to cheat the world. . . . The world had been always full of strange stories; for the boldness and cunning of contrivers, meeting with the simplicity and credulity of the people, things were easily received.

Here spoke the man who had been an astrologer on Tower Hill, an innkeeper at Newmarket, who had made love as a porter and gone about the streets as a beggar. And the man who had stood on the deck of the *Revenge* while Teddeman's fleet retired broken from Bergen, who was now watching the innocent sent to the scaffold for their creed, protested that the cruelties enjoined the Israelites were unsuited to the Divine nature. 'Rapine, revenge, injustice, thirst of blood.' It was the question he had asked himself in *Valentinian*, and it was answered for him by Burnet with cold reason.

His contempt for reason he had already shown in 'A Satire against Mankind'. It was an *ignis fatuus* of the mind, he had declared.

> The senses are too gross; and he'll contrive
> A sixth, to contradict the other five:
> And before certain instinct will prefer
> Reason, which fifty times for one does err . . .

To a saint who could have communicated the sensation of faith, he might have capitulated, but to the clever, cunning churchman's arguments he could only repeat: 'If a man says he cannot believe, what help is there? for he was not master of his own belief.'

He had begun to recognize the inability of Burnet to resolve his questions, and as he grew weary he grew flippant. Burnet pointed to miracles as a divine credential to warrant certain persons in the message they delivered to the world. 'But why, said he, could not this be rectified by some plain rules given; but men must come and show a trick to persuade the world they speak to them in the name of God?'

Burnet rebuked him. 'I told him, I saw the ill use he made of his wit, by which he slurred the gravest things with a slight dash of his fancy: and the pleasure he found in such wanton expressions, as calling the doing of miracles, the showing of a trick, did really keep him from examining them, with that care which such things required.'

Next Rochester objected to the Christian belief in mysteries:

> which he thought no man could do, since it is not in a man's power to believe that which he cannot comprehend and of which he can have no notion. The believing mysteries, he said, made way for all the jugglings of priests, for they getting the people under them in that point, set out to them what they pleased, and giving it a hard name, and calling it a mystery, the people were tamed and easily believed it. The restraining a man from the use of women, except one in the way of marriage, and denying the remedy of divorce, he thought unreasonable impositions on the freedom of mankind.

To Burnet's comment on his last objection that 'all that propose high rewards have thereby a right to exact difficult performances', he made the bitter reply, 'We are sure the terms are difficult, but are not so sure of the rewards.'

Finally he told Burnet plainly,

> There was nothing that gave him and many others a more secret encouragement in their ill ways than that those who pretended to believe lived so that they could not be thought to be in earnest, when they said it; for he was sure religion was either a mere contrivance, or the most important thing that could be: so that if he once believed, he would set himself in great earnest to live suitably to it.

Burnet had advanced him reasons for belief, but he had been unable to transmit belief. A kind of repentance there had been, that he had broken laws which were for the good of the human race, but such cold virtue could not endure for long. There would have been nothing in this to save Dryden from the bravos in Rose Alley.

Rochester left London in April 1680 for Woodstock, in a mood of fury and not of repentance. His health had so improved that he rode post from Woodstock to Enmore in Somerset, with all the old desires rioting in his body. He was in the violent mood of his poem 'The Wish'.

> O that I now cou'd, by some chymic art,
> To sperm convert my vitals and my heart,
> That at one thrust I might my soul translate,
> And in the womb myself regenerate:
> There steep'd in lust, nine months I wou'd remain;
> Then boldly —— my passage out again.

He later told Parsons, his mother's chaplain, how during the journey, 'he had been arguing with greater vigour against God and religion than ever he had done in his life before and that he was resolved to run them down with all the arguments and spite in the world'. And the man who to the relief of many had been reported dead a year ago was again writing. To this last and shortest spell of convalescence belonged 'An Imitation of the First Satire of Juvenal'. The poem opens with the old arrogance:

> Must I with patience ever silent sit,
> Perplex'd with fools, who still believe they've wit?
> Must I find ev'ry place by coxcombs seiz'd,
> Hear their affected nonsense, and seem pleas'd?
> Must I meet Henningham where'er I go,
> Arp, Arran, villain Franck, nay, Poult'ney too?

Even friends were not safe. In March Rochester had nearly fought a duel in Arran's cause. He had written to Savile that now he lived chiefly out of spite, and there were few who escaped him in what must have been nearly his last poem ('Rochester's Farewell' is almost certainly spurious). Certainly neither the King nor his mistresses, 'mean prostrate bitches', avoided those roving satirical eyes, now burning with a vain passion to live:

> Who'd be a monarch to endure the prating
> Of Nell and saucy Oglethorp in waiting?
> Who would Southampton's driv'ling cuckold be?
> Who would be York and bear his infamy?
> What wretch would be Green's base-begotten son?
> Who would be James, out-witted and undone?
> Who'd be like Sunderland, a cringing knave?
> Like Halifax wise, like boorish Pembroke brave? . . .
> Who'd be a wit, in Dryden's cudgell'd skin?
> Or who'd be safe, and senseless, like Tom Thynne?

It is difficult to recognize in these lines the sick man who for a short season had listened with humility to Burnet's rebukes and arguments.

His recovery was brief. The journey to Somerset, the hard riding on rough country roads, had been an act of folly. 'This heat and violent motion did so inflame an ulcer, that was in his bladder, that it raised a very great pain in those parts. Yet he with much difficulty came back by coach to the Lodge at Woodstock Park.'

There was to be no more satire, no more rebellion. He had studied medicine and knew the nature of his illness well enough to recognize the unlikelihood of again escaping death. His mind was flung back to its former condition, with the added fear of knowing how soon his virtuous resolutions had been abandoned. He began to look on death as a deliverance from the perjury of his body. 'It was not only a general dark melancholy over his mind, such as he had formerly felt, but a most penetrating cutting sorrow. So that though in his body he suffered extreme pain for some weeks, yet the agonies of his mind sometimes swallowed up the sense of what he felt in his body.'

'The hand of God touched him', Burnet wrote, but it did not touch him through the rational arguments of a cleric. If God appeared at the end, it was the sudden secret appearance of a thief, not a State entrance heralded by the trumpets of an Anglican divine's reason. The occasion was the reading by his mother's chaplain of the fifty-third chapter of Isaiah. The chaplain, imagining like Burnet that the best appeal to Rochester was through his reason, pointed out carefully the passages which were prophetical of Christ's Passion. But even before the arguments were unfolded, conversion had come, suddenly, without reason, an act of grace. 'As he heard it read, he felt an inward force upon him, which did so enlighten his mind, and convince him, that he could resist it no longer: for the words had an authority which did shoot like rays or beams in his mind.' 'He hath no form or comeliness, and when we shall see him there is no beauty that we should desire him.'

The chaplain's comment there struck home: 'The meanness of his appearance and person has made vain and foolish people disparage him, because he came not in such a fools-coat as they delight in.' And there were words that may have touched his emotion because of his own case: 'Despised and the most abject of men'; 'we have thought him as it were a leper, and as one struck by God and afflicted'. So, whatever the charm he held for Savile and Buckhurst and Buckingham, he had appeared to those who had not been corrupted by Courts; to them, as to Lady Warwick, it seemed that he had used his wit only 'as a torch to light himself to Hell thereby'. Now, God's fumble was heard at the latch, and he was escaping.

Such a last-minute evasion was not watched without resentment. The ecclesiastics had begun to assemble. Parsons was constantly at his side; the Bishop of Oxford visited him every week, while Dr Marshall, the Rector of Lincoln College and the parson of the parish, was frequently with him. Between them they took care 'that he might not on terms more easy than safe be at peace with himself'. To these were soon to be added Dr Burnet and Dr Price of Magdalen.

His chief medical attendant was Dr Radcliffe, to whom Tom Brown dedicated *Familiar Letters*, a witty, hard-drinking man: 'I need not, and I am sure I cannot, make you a better panegyric than to acquaint the world, that you were happy in my Lord Rochester's friendship, that he took pleasure in your conversation, of which even his enemies must allow him to have been the best judge.' But if Tom Brown is to be believed the claims of Radcliffe's most distinguished patients were sometimes waived for the bottle. In a poem on the death of the Duke of Gloucester Brown wrote:

> All our complaints we must on Radcliffe spend,
> Who, for his pleasure, can neglect his friend;
> By whose delays more patients sure have died,
> Than by the drugs of others misapplied.
> Three bottles keep him, and for their dear sake,
> Three Kingdoms unregarded lie at stake.

But Rochester had not only Dr Radcliffe to fight for his bodily survival. There was a Dr Short and a Dr Lower, of London, and Dr Edward Browne, the son of Sir Thomas Browne.

That old writer waited with interest for news of his son's patient, not averse from taking advantage of the occasion. On 7 July he wrote:

> My Dear Son, . . . I conceive that in some part of the next week you
> must be thinking again of your visit at Woodstock. And because you

must be then in a park I will set down some particulars 'De Cervis' out of Aristotle and Scaliger, whereof you may inquire and inform yourself. . . . We hear of the great penitence and retraction of my Lord Rochester, and hereupon he hath many good wishes and prayers from good men, both for his recovery here and happy state hereafter: you may write a few lines and certify the truth thereof, for my cousin Witherley, who liveth with J. Witherley, writ something of it to her mother in Norwich.

So the characters gather about the bed in High Lodge: the mother, sixty-six years old by now, who had outlived already two husbands and two sons; the wife, who had in her memory the stopped coach and armed men and a midnight ride and afterwards the long lonely life at Adderbury; the children; old Cary, who had nursed the estate through the evil days; the doctors; the still more numerous clerics; and on one ill occasion, a patient from Mrs Fourcard's 'Baths' and Leather Lane, troubling the penitent in the four-poster with his incredulity, Will Fanshawe, lame and lean, with mouth awry from the pox.

Some time at the end of May or the beginning of June Rochester officially repented and took the Sacraments. Parsons had arrived at Woodstock on 26 May, and at the beginning of June Rochester persuaded his wife to leave the Catholic religion and take the Sacraments with him. John Cary wrote to Sir Ralph Verney, who had been the guardian of the young Earl in the Ditchley days:

I much fear my Lord Rochester hath not long to live; he is here at his Lodge and his mother, my lady dowager, and his lady are with him, and Doctor Short of London and Doctor Radcliff of Oxon. Himself is now very weak. God Almighty restore him if it be his will, for he is grown to be the most altered person, the most devout and pious person as I generally ever knew, and certainly would make a most worthy brave man, if it would please God to spare his life, but I fear the worst; at present he is very weak and ill. But what gives us much comfort is we hope he will be happy in another world, if it please God to take him hence, and further what is much comfort to my lady dowager and us all in the midst of this sorrow is, his lady is returned to her first love the Protestant religion, and on Sunday last received the sacrament with her lord, and hath been at prayer with us, so as if it might please God to spare and restore him, it would altogether make up very great joy to my lady his mother and us all that love him.

About the same time his mother was writing to Lady St John at Battersea:

O sister, I am sure, had you heard the heavenly prayers he has made, since this sickness, the extraordinary things he has said, to the wonder of all that has heard him, you would wonder, and think that

God alone must teach him; for no man could put into him such things as he says. He has, I must tell you too, converted his wife to be a Protestant again. Pray, pray for his perseverance, dear sister.

For the second time the report that he was dead reached London. On 5 June Burnet wrote to Lord Halifax, Savile's brother:

Will Fanshawe just now tells me, letters are come from the Earl of Rochester, by which it seems he must be dead by this time. Dr Lower is sent for, but they think he cannot live till he comes to him, an ulcer in his bladder is broken, and he pisses matter, he is in extreme pain. He has expressed great remorse for his past ill life, and has persuaded his lady to receive the sacrament with him, and hereafter to go to church and declare herself a Protestant, and dies a serious penitent, and professes himself a Christian. Since Mr Fanshawe told me this I hear he is dead. I add no reflections on all this, for I know your Lordship will make them much better.

But the reflection which Halifax made can hardly have been what Burnet was expecting: '. . . the world is grown so foolish a thing, that a witty man may very well be ashamed of staying in it.'

On 7 June Rochester's condition was still critical, and it seemed that time would not be able to test the quality of his sudden conversion. 'He is like to die,' Sir Ralph Verney wrote, 'his mother watched with him last night.' But again he fought himself free from that crisis and London learnt that rumour had been premature.

Burnet, writing to Halifax on 12 June, showed a certain suspicion that penitence would not survive the sickness that caused it; he had had experience of how little argument could weigh with Rochester.

The Earl of Rochester lives still, and is in a probable way of recovery, for it is thought all that ulcerous matter is cast out. All the town is full of his great penitence, which, by your Lordship's good leave, I hope flows from a better principle than the height of his fancy, and indeed that which depends so much on the disposition of the body cannot be supposed very high when a man's spirits were so spent as his were.

Three days later Cary still saw recovery as possible. 'My lord we hope is on the mending hand, but many changes he meets withal, pretty good days succeed ill nights, which help to keep up his spirits, but he is very weak, and expresses himself very good.'

Already in town they were questioning his repentance in less careful terms than Burnet's, and suggesting that he was out of his mind. His mother defended him, but she had not the same fierce heart in defence as in attack, and her spirits were worn with anxiety and watching.

Truly, sister, I think I may say, without partiality, that he has never been heard say, when he speaks of religion, an insensible word, nor of anything else; but one night, of which I writ you word, he was disordered in his head; but then he said no hurt; only some little ribble-rabble, which had no hurt in it. . . . This last night, if you had heard him pray, I am sure you would not have took his words for the words of a mad man, but such as came from a better spirit than the mind of mere man. But let the wicked of the world say what they please of him, the reproaches of them are an honour to him, and I take comfort that the devil rages against my son; it shows his power over him is subdued in him, and that he has no share in him. Many messages and compliments his old acquaintance send him, but he is so far from receiving of them, that still his answer is . . . 'Let me see none of them, and I would to God, I had never conversed with some of them.' One of his physicians, thinking to please him, told him the King drank his health the other day; he looked earnestly upon him and said never a word, but turned his face from him. I thank God, his thoughts are wholly taken off from the world, and I hope, whether he lives or dies, will ever be so. But they are a fine people at Windsor, God forgive them! Sure there never was so great a malice performed, as to entitle my poor son to a lampoon, at this time, when, for aught they know, he lies upon his deathbed. . . .[1] I do believe, if any has reported, that he should speak ridiculous, it has been the popish physician,[2] who one day listened at the door, whilst my son was conversing with a divine: but my son spoke so low, that he could hear but half words; and so he might take it for nonsense, because he had a mind so to do.

It was during the improvement in his sickness that 'the fine people at Windsor' sent down a spy to report, and Will Fanshawe arrived at Woodstock. On 19 June Lady Rochester wrote to her sister:

Mr Fanshawe, his great friend, has been here to see him, and as he was standing by my son's bedside, he looked earnestly upon him, and said . . . 'Fanshawe, think of a God, let me advise you, and repent you of your former life, and amend your ways. Believe what I say to you; there is a God, and a powerful God, and he is a terrible God to unrepenting sinners; the time draws near, that he will come to judgment, with great terror to the wicked; therefore, delay not your repentance: his displeasure will thunder against you, if you do. You and I have been long time acquainted, done ill together. I love the man, and speak to him out of conscience, for the good of his soul.' Fanshawe stood, and said never a word to him, but stole away out of the room. When my son saw him go, 'Is a gone?' says he, 'poor wretch! I fear his heart is hardened.' After that Fanshawe said to some in the house, that my son should be kept out of melancholy fancies. This was told my son again: upon which says he, 'I know why he said that; it was because I gave him my advice; but I could say no less to him than I did, let him take it as he pleases.'

How Fanshawe took it is plain from a letter dated 26 June.

I hear Mr Fanshawe reports my son is mad, but I thank God, he is far from that. I confess for a night, and part of a day, for want of rest,

[1] Perhaps 'Rochester's Farewell' was the lampoon they were ascribing to him.

[2] Was this Dr Short or Dr Lower? It was certainly not Dr Radcliffe who was still Lady Rochester's friend and attendant five years later.

he was a little disordered; but it was long since Mr Fanshawe saw him. When he reproved him for his sinful life, he was as well in his head, as ever he was in his life, and so he is now, I thank God. I am sure, if you heard him pray, you would think God had inspired him with true wisdom indeed, and that neither folly or madness comes near him. I wish that wretch Fanshawe had so great a sense of sin, as my poor child has: that so, he might be brought to repentance, before it is too late. But he is an ungrateful man to such a friend.

And on 2 July she wrote:

I told my son that I heard Mr Fanshawe said, that he hoped he would recover, and leave those principles he now professed. He answered, 'Wretch! I wish I had conversed all my life-time with link-boys rather than with him, and that crew, such, I mean, as Fanshawe is. Indeed, I would not live, to return to what I was, for all the world.'

On 19 June, soon after Fanshawe's visit, Rochester dictated what was to become known as his dying remonstrance, and signed it in the presence of his mother and the chaplain. Written 'for the benefit of all those whom I may have drawn into sin by my example and encouragement', it declared 'that from the bottom of my soul I detest and abhor the whole course of my former wicked life'. It was as though he feared to leave on record only the memory of his spoken words; the signed and witnessed paper could not be explained away. According to Aubrey he sent for all the servants to hear the declaration read, 'even the piggard boy'. On 25 June he dictated a letter to Burnet in reply to one he had received: 'My spirits and body decay so equally together, that I shall write you a letter as weak as I am in person. I begin to value Churchmen above all men in the world, and you above all Churchmen I know in it.' He asked for the doctor's prayers, but gave no sign that he wished his company. The letter impressed Burnet, who read into it a great deal, and wrote what he read to Lord Halifax.

By 2 July the hopes which had been felt for his recovery were again being abandoned.

He gathers no strength at all, but his flesh wastes much, and we fear a consumption, tho' his lungs are very good. He sleeps much; his head, for the most part, is very well. He was this day taken up and set up in a chair, for an hour, and was not very faint, when he went to bed. He does not care to talk much; but, when he does, speaks, for the most part, well. His expressions are so suddenly spoken, that many of them are lost, and cannot be taken; yet, I believe, some part of what he has said will be remembered.

On 8 July Lady Sunderland was writing with confidence to Lord Halifax that he could not live: 'He has ulcers in two places. He sees nobody but his mother, wife, divines and physicians.' One would have thought those to have been sufficient, but some time in early July he was supplicating the prayers of Dr Thomas Pierce. 'Take Heaven by force, and let me enter with you, as it were in disguise.' 'In disguise'. Was he thinking of Alexander Bendo and his father's yellow periwig?

On 20 July Burnet arrived at Woodstock. He found Rochester's spirits very low; the fervour of his conversion had left him, though he spoke of it as 'a thing now grown up in him to a settled and calm serenity'. Some uneasiness he seemed to feel as to the value of a deathbed repentance; in that respect Dr Marshall and the Bishop of Oxford had succeeded. But on the worldly side he had drawn up his account. 'He had overcome all his resentments to all the world; so that he bore ill-will to no person.' In spite of the clause in his will, which he had allowed to stand, giving his wife over finally to the domination of his mother, he seemed to meet death in the quality of the lover and not of the faulty husband. 'He expressed so much tenderness and true kindness to his lady, that as it easily defaced the remembrance of every thing wherein he had been in fault formerly, so it drew from her the most passionate care and concern for him that was possible.' Of his children he had always been fond. Now he asked often for them. 'He called me once', Burnet wrote, 'to look on them all, and said, See how good God has been to me, in giving me so many blessings, and I have carried myself to him like an

To the Right Honourable

ANNE, and ELIZABETH,

DOWAGER-COUNTESSES

OF

ROCHESTER.

Right Honorable,

*Y*Our Ladiſhips, or any elſe, cannot think meaner of this Performance than I my ſelf do; for beſides the great hurry and diſorder that I was in upon the loſs of ſuch a Patron as my Lord, I am ſufficiently conſcious how unfit I am to appear in public, eſpecially upon ſuch a nice and great Subjeɛt. As his Lordſhips particular Commands brought me to the Pulpit, ſo Yours only have brought me to the Preß. And therefore I hope, whatever uſage the following Diſcourſe may meet with abroad; I ſhall always find a ſhelter in your Ladiſhips Favours: and the rather, becauſe you can, both of you, largely atteſt the truth of moſt of the remarkable Occurrences that I have taken notice of during his Lordſhips Penitential ſickneſs.

A 2

A

SERMON

PREACHED

At the Funeral of the

Rᵗ *HONORABLE*

JOHN Earl of ROCHESTER,

Who died at *Woodſtock-Park*, July 26.1680, and was buried at *Spilsbury* in *Oxford-ſhire*, Aug. 9.

By *Robert Parſons* M. A. Chaplain to the Right Honorable ANNE *Counteſs-Dowager* of ROCHESTER.

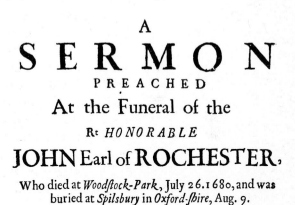

OXFORD,

Printed at the THEATER for *Richard Davis* and *Tho: Bowman*, In the Year, 1680.

I

ungracious and unthankful dog.' And once, before Parsons, he expressed the wish that his son might never be a wit.

He had only a week more to live when Burnet saw him. Though once, after a night's sleep procured by laudanum, he thought himself on the road to recovery, he showed no passion for life. He was often in pain, his body was drained by ulcers leaving little but skin and bone, and his back was covered with sores.

> He professed he was contented either to die or live, as should please God, and though it was a foolish thing for a man to pretend to choose, whether he would die or live, yet he wished rather to die. He knew he could never be so well that life should be comfortable to him. He was confident he should be happy if he died, but he feared if he lived he might relapse.

On Friday, 23 July, Burnet understanding from the doctors that there was no reason to expect an immediate end, thought to go, but Rochester implored him with some passion to stay one day more. At four o'clock in the morning of the 24th, Burnet slipped away without taking leave for fear of disturbing him.

> Some hours after he asked for me, and when it was told him, I was gone, he seemed to be troubled, and said, Has my friend left me, then I shall die shortly. After that he spake but once or twice till he died. He lay much silent. Once they heard him praying very devoutly. And on Monday about two of the clock in the morning, he died, without any convulsion, or so much as a groan.

On 9 August 'this noble and beautiful count' (the expression is Anthony Wood's) was buried in the vaults of Spelsbury Church, whither his wife and his only son were to follow him the next year. The funeral sermon was preached by Robert Parsons, and his description of 'so great a man and so great a sinner', published a little later in the year at the same time as Burnet's account of Rochester's life, opened a chorus of adulation. Only Mulgrave held aloof with his reference to 'the nauseous songs which the late convert made'.

On the stage the death of Count Rosidore was described by Lee; in a prologue to Rochester's own unfinished version of *Valentinian* Mrs Behn put into the mouth of his mistress, Elizabeth Barry, lines comparing his genius with that of Fletcher, while women who had loved him listened in the galleries.

> Some beauties here I see,
> Though now demure, have felt his powerful charms,
> And languish'd in the circle of his arms.

To Aphra Behn he was 'the great, the godlike Rochester'; to Sir Francis Fane 'Seraphic Lord'; to Thomas Flatman

> Strephon, the wonder of the plains,
> The noblest of th' Arcadian swains,
> Strephon, the bold, the witty, and the gay;

to his kinswoman, Mrs Wharton,

> He civilized the rude and taught the young,
> Made fools grow wise, such artful music hung,
> Upon his useful, kind, instructing tongue.

If his past life was mentioned it was curiously transformed. According to Samuel Woodforde who had preceded him at Wadham:

> Now glorify'd again is the Eternal Name,
> Rochester in the Lamb's fresh blood new dy'd
> All robed in white sings Lauds to Him whom he deny'd.

Sir Francis Fane, comparing him to General Monck who 'brought three kingdoms to his master's laws', suggested that Rochester had sinned only to lull Satan into a false security, while he obtained the allegiance of mankind.

> Satan rejoic'd to see thee take his part,
> His malice not so prosperous as thy art.
> He took thee for his pilot, to convey
> Those easy souls whom he had led astray:
> But to his great confusion saw thee shift
> Thy swelling sails and take another drift,
> With an illustrious train reputed his,
> To the bright regions of eternal bliss.

Fanshawe and many at Court laughed away his repentance, declaring that he had gone out of his mind, but the voices of old companions from Leather Lane and Whetstone Park could not compete with 'thousands of harangues, Urg'd with grimaces, fortify'd with bangs, On dreadful pulpits' which brought word of his conversion into the City, where he had once acted the sober merchant and the fantastic astrologer, and into small country parishes where his name had stood for the infamies of Whitehall. Some of his poems remained to attest to the darkness and confusion of unregenerate days, but many more were lost for ever in the final victory of Puritan over Cavalier. A greater loss still, a history of the Restoration Court in the form of letters to Savile, went to the bonfire. For Rochester had asked his mother to burn his papers, lest the example of his works should lead others to sin, and she obeyed with alacrity. 'Apropos,' wrote Horace Walpole, 'did I ever tell you a most admired *bon mot* of Mr Bentley? He was talking to me of an old devout Lady St John, who burnt a whole trunk of letters of the famous Lord Rochester, "for which," said Mr Bentley, "her soul is now burning in heaven".'

Mr Elliston as Lord Rochester in a 'new comic historical burletta', *Rochester or King Charles the Second's Merry Days*, performed at the Olympic Theatre in November 1818

221

Bibliography

Rochester's correspondence with Mrs Barry is printed in the Nonesuch Rochester, and I have not troubled to go back to Gildon's original edition. The MSS have never been found. Rochester's letters to his wife and family are printed both by Professor Prinz and John Hayward from the MSS Harleian 7003. There are certain differences between the two, and I have used my discretion in choosing between them and my own reading of the MS.

The letters written from Rochester's deathbed by his mother are printed by John Hayward from *Lives, Characters and an Address to Posterity by Gilbert Burnet* (Ed. John Jebb 1833).

One of the prime authorities is inevitably the *Diary* of Samuel Pepys. I have brought my quotations as far as possible up to date to accord with the new transcription of Mr R. C. Latham and Mr W. Matthews, but the last volumes of their edition have still to appear, so after 1666 I have had to leave the quotations as they appear in the Wheatley edition of the *Diary*.

Mention must be made of *The Complete Poems of John Wilmot, Earl of Rochester* edited by David M. Vieth for the Yale University Press, 1968. We disagree in some particulars (including an incorrect attribution to me in his bibliography!). As Mr Vieth admits the attribution to a great many poems depends on subjective judgment, and our ears often differ. To me it is almost inconceivable that 'The History of Insipids' is by another hand, just as 'To the Postboy', which he attributes to Rochester, seems to me an obvious attack on the poet after the affray at Epsom. Rochester's poems from his death on became more indecent with every year, and I have the impression that M. Vieth is inclined to prefer the hotter versions.

Anon. *The Character of a Town Gallant* 1675.
  An Elegie upon Mr Thomas Hobbes of Malmesbury, lately deceased 1679.
  Satire on both Whigs and Tories 1683.
Aubrey, John. *Brief Lives*. 2 vols. Ed. A. Clark 1898.
Brown, Tom. *Familiar Letters* 1697.
  Works 1719.
Browne, Sir Thomas. *Works*. Ed. Simon Wilkin 1836.
Bulstrode, Sir Richard. *Memoirs* 1721.
Burnet, Gilbert. *Bishop Burnet's History of His Own Time* 1723–34.
  Some Passages of the Life and Death of the Right Honourable John Earl of Rochester, who died the 26th of July, 1680.
  Unpublished Letters. Camden Society 1847.

Calendar of State Papers Domestic Series of the Reign of Charles II. Ed. M. A. Green.
Calendar of Treasury Books 1660–80. Ed. W. A. Shaw.
Camden Miscellany vol. 5 1847.
Carte MSS, Bodleian Library, Oxford.
Cartwright, Julia. *Madame: Memoirs of Henrietta, Duchess of Orleans* 1894.
Cibber, Colley. *An Apology for the Life of Mr Colley Cibber Written by Himself* 1740.
Cibber, Theophilus. *The Lives of the Poets of Great Britain and Ireland* 1753.
College, Stephen. *Trial of Stephen College* 1681.
Corbett, Elsie. *A History of Spelsbury* 1931.
Davies, Tom. *Dramatic Miscellanies* 1783.
Delaune, Thomas. *The Present State of London* 1681.
Dennis, John. *A Defence of Sir Fopling Flutter* 1722.
  Original Letters 1721.
Downes, John. *Roscius Anglicanus* 1708.
Dryden, John. *Critical and Miscellaneous Prose Works*. Ed. E. Malone 1800.
  Original Letters 1721.
Essex, Arthur Capel, Earl of. *Correspondence*. Camden Society 1890.
Etherege, Sir George. *The Dramatic Works*. 2 vols. Ed. H. F. B. Brett Smith 1927.
Fane, Sir Francis. *Commonplace Book*, preserved at Shakespeare Birthplace.
  Love in the Dark or the Man of Business 1675.
Fell-Smith, Charlotte. *Mary Rich, Countess of Warwick* 1901.
Firth, C. H. Article on Henry Wilmot, First Earl of Rochester, in *Dictionary of National Biography*. Ed. Sir Leslie Stephen and Sir Sidney Lee 1885–1900.
  Articles in *English Historical Review* 1888–9.
Forneron, H. *The Court of Charles II* 1897.
Fox, George. *Journal* 1694.
Gadbury, John. *Ephemeris or a Diary* 1698.
Gepp, Rev. H. J. *Adderbury* 1924.
Gosse, Sir Edmund. *Leaves and Fruit* 1927.
Granger, J. A. *A Biographical History of England from Egbert the Great to the Revolution* 1779.
Ham, Roswell. *Otway and Lee* 1931.
Hamilton, Anthony. *Memoir of the Comte de Gramont*. Ed. C. H. Hartmann 1930.
Harleian MSS 6913, 7003, 7312, 7316, 7317, 7319, British Museum.
Hatton, *Correspondence of the Family of*. Camden Society 1878.

Hearne, Thomas. *Remarks and Collections*. Ed. C. E. Doble 1885–9.

Hearnianae Reliquiae. Ed. P. Bliss 1869.

Hill, Birkbeck. *Notes to Dr Johnson's Lives of the Poets* 1887.

Hinchingbrooke MSS.

Historical Manuscripts Commission: Anglesey Diary; S. H. le Fleming MSS; R. R. Hastings of Ashby-de-la-Zouch MSS; Longleat MSS; Marquess of Ormond MSS; Duke of Portland MSS; Duke of Rutland MSS; Sir H. Verney MSS; Report No. 7; Appendix to Fifth Report Appendix to Seventh Report; Appendix to Eleventh Report; Appendix to Twelfth Report.

Hore, J. P. *History of Newmarket* 1886.

Hutchinson, Life of Colonel. By his wife 1806.

Hyde, Edward, First Earl of Clarendon. *The True Historical Narrative of the Rebellion and Civil Wars* 1702–4.

Jaffray, Alexander. *Diary* 1833.

Langbaine, Gerard. *An Account of the English Dramatic Poets* 1691.

Longe, Julia C. *Martha, Lady Giffard: her Life and Correspondence* 1911.

Macky, John. *Memoirs of the Secret Service* 1733.

Marshall, Edward. *A Supplement to the History of Woodstock Manor and its Environs* 1874.

Misson, H. de V. *Memoirs and Observations made during a journey in England* 1698.

Mulgrave, John Sheffield, Earl of. *Works* 1726.

Nicholl, Allardyce. *A History of English Drama 1660–1900* vol. 1, *Restoration Drama 1660–1700*. 1923.

Oldham, John. *Compositions in Prose and Verse to which are added Memoirs of Life*. E. Thompson 1770.

Oldys, William. MS notes to Langbaine. British Museum C.28, g.1.

Otway, Thomas. *Collected Works*. 3 vols. Ed. Montague Summers 1926.

Parsons, Rev. Robert. *Sermon Preached at the Funeral of the Rt. Honourable John Earl of Rochester* 1680.

Pepys, Samuel. *Diary*. Ed. H. B. Wheatley 1928. Ed. R. C. Latham and W. Matthews 1970.

Perwich, William. *Despatches from Paris*. Ed. M. B. Curran. Camden Society 1903.

Pinkethman. *Book of Jests*. 2nd edition 1721.

Pinto, Professor V. de S. *Sir Charles Sedley* 1927.

Prideaux, William. *Letters*. Camden Society 1875.

Prinz, Johannes. *John Wilmot Earl of Rochester. His Life and Writings* 1927.

Rawlinson MSS, Part 25. Bodleian Library, Oxford.

Reresby, Sir John. *Memoirs 1634–89*. Ed. J. J. Cartright 1875.

Rochester, Anne Lady. Letters. Ditchley Park.

Rochester, John Wilmot, Earl of. *Collected Works*. Ed. John Hayward 1926.

'St Evremond'. *Letter to the Duchess of Mazarine prefixed to Rochester's Works* 1707.

Sandwich, Earl of. *Journal*. Ed. R. C. Anderson. Navy Records Society vol. 64 1929.

Savile, Henry. *Letters to and from 1661–89*. Ed. W. D. Cooper. Camden Society 1858.

MS letter in author's possession.

Scott, Sir Walter. *Life of Dryden*. Ed. George Saintsbury 1882.

Shadwell, Thomas. *Works*. Ed. George Saintsbury 1903.

Smith, 'Captain' Alexander. *The School of Venus* 1716.

Spence, Joseph. *Anecdotes, Observations, and Characters of Books and Men*. Ed. S. W. Singer 1820.

Stowe MSS 969, British Museum.

Tate, Nahum. *Poems by Several Hands and on Several Occasions* 1685.

Thomas Tobias. *Life of the Famous Comedian Jo Hayns* 1701.

Verney Memoirs 1925.

Wadham College, Register of. Ed. Rev. R. B. Gardiner 1889.

Waller, Edmund. *Letters to M. St. Evremond* 1769.

Walpole, Horace. *Letters*. Ed. Mrs Paget Toynbee 1903–25.

Wills from Doctors' Commons 1495–1695. Ed. J. G. Nicols and J. Bruce. Camden Society 1863.

Wolseley, Robert. *Preface to Valentinian* 1685.

Wood, Anthony. *Athenae Oxoniensis* 1691–2.

Life and Times. Ed. A. Clarke 1891–1900.

Notes on Spelsbury in the Rawlinson MSS. Bodleian Library, Oxford.

Woodcock, Thomas. *Papers of, 1695*. Ed. G. C. M. Smith. Camden Society 1907.

Illustrations and Acknowledgments

Page numbers in **bold** type denote colour illustrations

endpapers The ceiling of Charles II's Dressing Room at Hampton Court Palace by Antonio Verrio. By gracious permission of Her Majesty the Queen.

reverse of frontispiece Painting by John Michael Wright for the ceiling of Charles II's bedroom at Whitehall *c*. 1665. Nottingham Castle Museum. Photo: John Webb.

frontispiece Portrait attributed to Jacob Huysmans *c*. 1675. By kind permission of Lord Brooke, Warwick Castle. Photo: Derrick Witty.

12 Drawing by W. N. Gardiner from the Devonshire Clarendon. Ashmolean Museum, Oxford.

(inset) Watercolour on vellum by Samuel Cooper 1647. The Earl Spencer.

14 Engraving by M. Van der Gucht after P. La Vergue. National Portrait Gallery, London.

15 From a painting on panel *c*. 1674. The Ditchley Foundation. Photo: T. A. Titherington.

19 Photo: Christina Gascoigne.

20 By courtesy of Wadham College, Oxford. Photo: Derrick Witty.

22 Engraving by A. Bosse. Radio Times Hulton Picture Library.

25–30 From D. Loggan's *Oxonia Illustrata* 1665 (from a copy in the London Library). Photos: Derrick Witty.

31 From a drawing in the Bodleian Library, Oxford.

32 Portrait by Sir Peter Lely. National Maritime Museum, Greenwich Hospital Collection.

33 From D. Loggan's *Oxonia Illustrata* 1665 (from a copy in the London Library). Photo: Derrick Witty.

34 Frontispiece by Hollar to John Ogilby's *Britannia* 1675. British Museum.

37 (left) Present owner unknown. Photo: National Portrait Gallery, London.

(right) Portrait by Sir Peter Lely *c*. 1666–7. Victoria and Albert Museum, London.

38 One of a series of woodcuts entitled 'Cries of London' from *London and Westminster*. By permission of the Master and Fellows of Magdalene College, Cambridge.

39 Portrait by Sir Peter Lely *c*. 1675. By kind permission of the Earl of Bradford.

41 Portrait by Sir Peter Lely. From Goodwood House, by courtesy of the Trustees.

42 'Coaches in St James's Park.' The Crace Collection, British Museum.

43 Portrait by Sir Godfrey Kneller 1689. National Maritime Museum.

44 (above) Sutherland Collection, Ashmolean Museum, Oxford.

(below) Engraving. By courtesy of the Society of Antiquaries of London.

46 Painted by Antonio Verrio for Charles II and placed in the Second Privy Lodging Room at Whitehall. By gracious permission of Her Majesty the Queen.

48 Battle by H. van Minderhout. National Maritime Museum. Portrait by Sir Peter Lely. National Maritime Museum, Greenwich Hospital Collection.

49 Painting by William van de Velde I *c*. 1680. National Maritime Museum.

50 Portrait by Sir Peter Lely. National Maritime Museum, Greenwich Hospital Collection.

51 MS Harleian 7003, f. 193. British Museum.

52–3 Gold medallion by Christopher Adolfszoon 1666. British Museum.

54–5 By permission of the Master and Fellows of Magdalene College, Cambridge.

55 Portrait attributed to Charles Wauttier. By gracious permission of Her Majesty the Queen.

56 Engraving by Hollar. British Museum.

59 Painting by A. Storck. National Maritime Museum.

61 Portrait by Sir Peter Lely. Collection Colonel Sir Edward Malet. Photo: Douglas Allen.

62–3 Painting by William van de Velde II. National Maritime Museum. Photo: Derrick Witty.

64 (above) Painting by Hendrick Danckerts. Berkeley Castle.

(below) From *Le Mois de Janvier* (detail) designed by Charles le Brun, Tapisserie des Gobelins 1665–80. Mobilier National. Allo Photo, Paris.

66–7 Engraving by Hollar (detail). Radio Times Hulton Picture Library.

68 Engraving by Hollar from *Political and Personal Satires* 1681. British Museum.

71 Portland MS PWV, 31. Nottingham University Manuscripts Department, by permission of the Duke of Portland and the University Council.

73 'Winter', one of a set of four etchings by Hollar depicting the seasons 1643. British Museum.

74 Portrait after A. Hanneman. National Portrait Gallery, London.

75 Portrait after W. Wissing *c*. 1683. National Portrait Gallery, London.

79 Portrait after Philippe Mignard c. 1665–70. National Portrait Gallery, London.
80 Engraving from *The Almanack* 1667. Mansell Collection.
83 Portrait by Sir Godfrey Kneller. National Maritime Museum.
84 Portland MS PWV, 506. Nottingham University Manuscripts Department, by permission of the Duke of Portland and the University Council.
86 By courtesy of the Society of Antiquaries of London.
87 Engraving by J. Boydell. Photo: Rumens Antiques, Woodstock.
89 Engraving by Hollar from *London and Westminster*. By permission of the Master and Fellows of Magdalene College, Cambridge.
91 (left) British Museum.
(right) Portrait by Sir Peter Lely c. 1675. National Portrait Gallery, London.
93 The Reindeer Inn, Banbury. Bodleian Library, Oxford.
94 Broadside. By courtesy of the Society of Antiquaries of London.
95 Woodcut from *The Works of the Earls of Rochester, Roscomon, and Dorset, the Dukes of Devonshire, Buckinghamshire, etc.* 1766. Author's collection. Photo: Derrick Witty.
97 Portrait by Sir Godfrey Kneller. Walker Art Gallery, Liverpool.
98–9 Painting by Thomas Danckerts. By courtesy of Lady Cholmondeley. Photo: Derrick Witty.
100 Portrait by Philippe Mignard 1682. National Portrait Gallery, London.
102 Portrait by Sir Peter Lely c. 1665. By gracious permission of Her Majesty the Queen.
103 Portrait from the studio of Sir Peter Lely c. 1675. National Portrait Gallery, London.
104 Woodcut from *The Works of the Earls of Rochester, Roscomon, and Dorset, the Dukes of Devonshire, Buckinghamshire, etc.* 1766. Author's collection. Photo: Derrick Witty.
107 Miscellaneous MS 1489. Nottingham University Manuscripts Department, by permission of the University Council. Photo: Library Photographic Unit.
109 Coleraine Collection. By kind permission of the Society of Antiquaries of London.
110–11 Silver-mounted shagreen case, bearing the arms of the Barber-Surgeons' Company. The Wellcome Institute of the History of Medicine, by courtesy of the Trustees.
111 'London Curtezan', engraving by Tempest after M. Lauron. Guildhall Library.
112 By courtesy of the Society of Antiquaries of London.
118 Enthoven Collection, Victoria and Albert Museum, London.
120 Raymond Mander and Joe Mitchenson Theatre Collection.
122 By courtesy of the Society of Antiquaries of London.
125 Enthoven Collection, Victoria and Albert Museum, London.
128 Portland MS PWV, 31. Nottingham University Manuscripts Department, by permission of the Duke of Portland and the University Council.

129 By courtesy of the Society of Antiquaries of London.
133 Portrait after Sir Godfrey Kneller. Garrick Club, London. Photo: Derrick Witty.
134–5 Portrait by Sir Peter Lely. D. E. Bower Collection. Chiddingstone Castle, Kent.
136 By permission of the Duke of Marlborough. Photo: Christina Gascoigne.
140 Portrait by Sir Godfrey Kneller. By gracious permission of Her Majesty the Queen.
141 St Mary's Parish Church, Acton. Photo: Derrick Witty.
142 Engraving by Francis Barlow from *The Gentleman's Recreation* 1686. British Museum.
144 From the Roxburghe Ballads. Bodleian Library, Oxford.
145 Etching by Edmond Marmion from *London and Westminster*. By permission of the Master and Fellows of Magdalene College, Cambridge.
146–7 MS Gough, Maps 26, fol. 50v. Bodleian Library, Oxford.
148 Etchings by Edmond Marmion from *London and Westminster*. By permission of the Master and Fellows of Magdalene College, Cambridge.
149 Portrait by William Wissing c. 1678. Collection of the Earl of Lisburne. Photo: Derrick Witty.
150 Photo: Christina Gascoigne.
151 MS Harleian 7003, f. 214. British Museum.
152 From a letter. Author's collection.
153 Pastel portrait by Sir Godfrey Kneller. Collection of the Earl of Lisburne. Photo: Derrick Witty.
154 Portrait by William Wissing c. 1678. Collection of the Earl of Lisburne. Photo: Derrick Witty.
155 Painting by Sir Peter Lely c. 1668. National Library of Wales, Aberystwyth. By permission of the Earl of Lisburne. Photo: Christina Gascoigne.
156 By courtesy of Oxfordshire County Council. Photo: Christina Gascoigne.
158 From *Political and Personal Satires* 1681. British Museum.
163 (above) From a portrait by Sir Peter Lely. Collection Major Ralph B. Verney.
(below) Author's collection. Photos: Derrick Witty.
167 Sutherland Collection, Ashmolean Museum, Oxford.
169 Engraving by R. White 1679. National Portrait Gallery, London.
171 From *London and Westminster*. By permission of the Master and Fellows of Magdalene College, Cambridge.
172 Engraving by M. Beal. Enthoven Collection, Victoria and Albert Museum, London.
175 Woodcut from *The Works of the Earls of Rochester, Roscomon, and Dorset, the Dukes of Devonshire, Buckinghamshire, etc.* 1766. Author's collection. Photo: Derrick Witty.
179 Enthoven Collection, Victoria and Albert Museum, London.
181 Portrait by Jacques Maubert. National Portrait Gallery, London.
182 Portrait by Sir Peter Lely. Collection Colonel Sir Edward Malet. Photo: Douglas Allen.
184 Engraving by Dobson. Enthoven Collection, Victoria and Albert Museum, London.

186 (left) Enthoven Collection, Victoria and Albert Museum, London.
(right) MS Add. 28692. British Museum.
189 Portrait by an unknown artist. By kind permission of Lord Sackville of Knole.
190 From a broadsheet of 1674. Radio Times Hulton Picture Library.
192 Engraving by Peters. Enthoven Collection, Victoria and Albert Museum, London.
196 By permission of the Duke of Marlborough. Photo: Christina Gascoigne.
199–200 Photos: Christina Gascoigne.

203 Author's collection. Photos: Derrick Witty.
204–5 Caricature of 1679. The Mansell Collection.
206 Frontispiece and title-page to Hobbes's *Leviathan* 1651 (from a copy in the London Library). Photo: Derrick Witty.
207 Portrait (detail) by J. M. Wright *c*. 1669–70. National Portrait Gallery, London.
208 Portrait (detail) attributed to Riley. By courtesy of the Earl of Haddington. Photo: Tom Scott.
209–19 Author's collection. Photos: Derrick Witty.
221 Engraving by John Robinson. Raymond Mander and Joe Mitchenson Theatre Collection.

Index